THE ICONS OF MAN 1

THE ICONS OF MAN: BOOK ONE
BY ROBERT H. LANGAN

UNIVOCITY BOOKS

This is a work of fiction. Names, characters, places, and incidents either are the products of the author's imagination or are used fictitiously. Any resemblance to actual persons, living or dead, businesses, companies, events, or locales is entirely coincidental.

Copyright © 2017 by Robert H. Langan

All Rights Reserved. This book or parts thereof may not be reproduced in any form, stored in any retrieval system, or transmitted in any form by any means—electronic, mechanical, photocopy, recording, or otherwise—without prior written permission of the publisher, except as provided by United States of America copyright law. For permission requests, write to the publisher, at "Attention: Permissions Coordinator," at the address below.

Univocity Books - univocitybooks@gmail.com

The Icons of Man: Book One

First Edition

Paperback ISBN: 978-0-9995669-2-3

Ebook ISBN: 978-0-9995669-0-9

Visit the author's website: www.iconsofman.com

Copy editing by Sarah Kolb-Williams www.kolbwilliams.com

Book/ebook formatting by Mike Littrell

Cover illustration by Chris Puglise www.instagram.com/cpuglise9

Chapter headings are set in the Farmhand typeface, designed by Adam Ladd. Copyright © 2017 by Adam Ladd. All rights reserved.

Cover copyright @ 2017 Robert H. Langan

Map copyright @ 2017 Robert H. Langan

To the Third
To Anne
To NJL
To Firecheetah
To MJL
To the Cun
And to Karl Hans

You made me what I am.

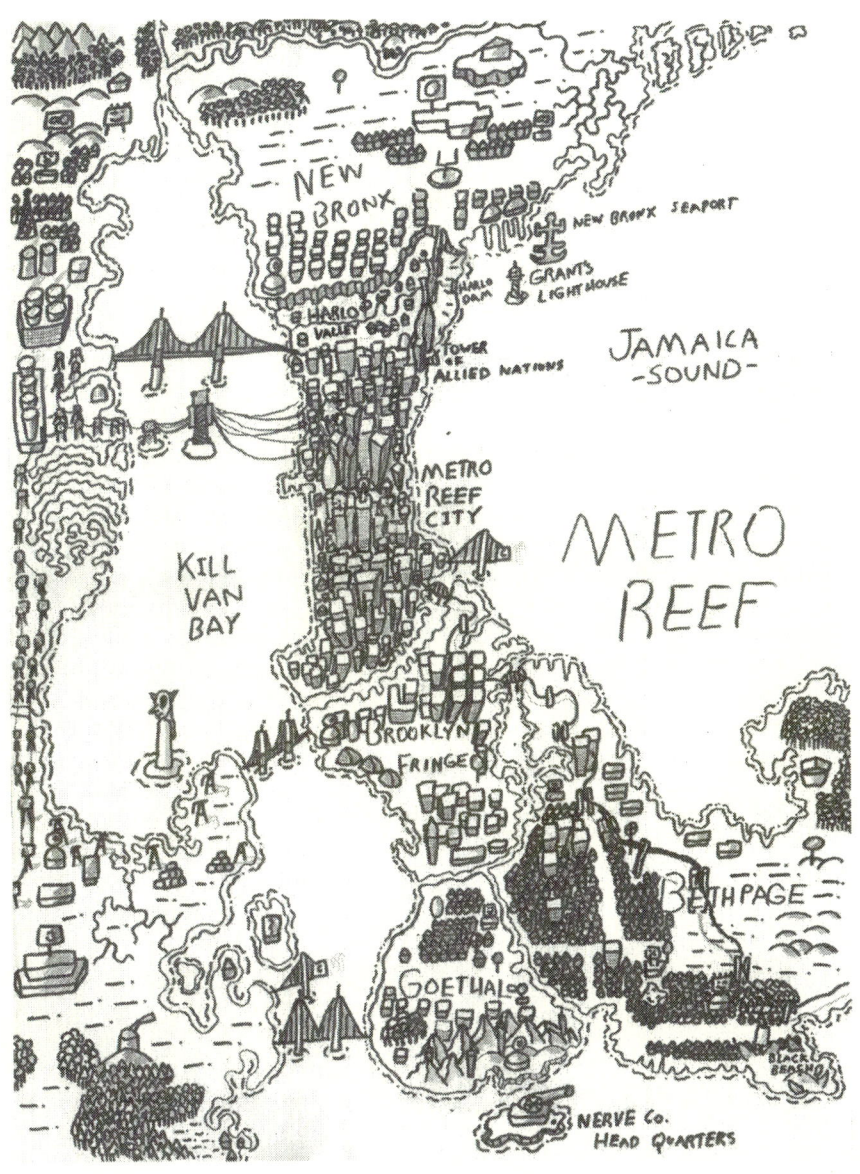

PROLOGUE

—*I* CAN STILL HELP *you, you know.*
She ignored the thought that was not her own. But the thought persisted.

—*I've never told you this before, but . . . I have many regrets.*

—Get out of my head, Old Ghost.

—*If I had only acted sooner. Then the Blood Poachers might never have—*

—I said out.

—*Hmm. Fine. Then I guess this is really goodbye.*

—I've heard that before. I'll try not to get my hopes up.

—*Can you blame me for being persistent? You were the best, Sophia. I have admired your career from afar, hoping that one day you would come back to me. For guidance.*

—I don't need you.

—*Really? Only I know what you went through.*

—Oh, fuck off. You can't hold that over me. Go to the Barra for all I care. Just leave me alone.

—*I don't want to do that. I still believe in you. I know how great you could be.*

—*Dammit, Courier. Are you trying to threaten me or flatter me?*
—*Neither. I'm trying to help you, Sophia. No one has to know. We can go back to the chapel together. Run more tests. It might not be too late.*
—*I. Don't. Need. Help.*
—*Are you sure?*

A pause as doubt crept in.

—*Yes. I'm sure.*
—*So why are you doing all this?*

She held her breath. *Because,* she thought to herself. *Because . . . I need to beat you. To beat the Barra. To beat . . . dammit, I don't know.*

She answered with the only thing she knew to be true.

—*Free. Because I want to be free, that's why.*
—*I doubt that. And you may find that freedom isn't for you. But I won't lecture you any further. Goodbye, Sophia.*
—*Wait. Before you go, I think you owe me an answer for once.*
—*Oh?*
—*Tell me about Lucas from Slag Falls.*
—*Now why would I know anything about Lucas?*
—*I thought he seemed like your kind of player. A real crackpot. A loser.*
—*Why, my dear Sophia, you know I never divulge the identity of any Durationists I keep counsel with. It is a policy I always do my best to uphold, even with you . . . unless you give me some reason to turn you in for the sake of my country.*
—*And what country would that be, Courier?*
—*Roslyn, obviously. What other country did you have in mind?*

She didn't answer. She did not want to play these games with the Courier. It was so pointless. Always pointless.

She expected a farewell, but he had already left her. There was only silence.

She shook her head.

You're wrong about me, Old Ghost. I can do this. I'll prove it.

1. Storm Killer

THERE WAS NO INDICATION of any foul weather the next day, not until late that afternoon. The sun sank deep into the western sky, mottled by harmless wisps of waning smog that chugged up from the Smokestack Grotto across the bay. Golden rays of light reached across the five islands, only to be blotted out by the shelf of green darkness rolling in from the East Sea. The thunderhead grew near, draping long shadows across the boroughs. The glint of sky-ads that floated over the coral towers in Barrier Village grew dim, and the vibrant streets and colorful row homes of the Brooklyn Fringe turned to shades of gray and black. The trees in Metro Park billowed nervously, and paper trash tumbled across Sixth Avenue. The wind was restless. Thunder murmured in the distance.

The thoughts of a million people mingled with one another, skittish as the stirring leaves.

—*The wind is really starting to blow,* someone at Mohawk Beach thought.

—*No storm is scheduled,* a resident of Brooklyn Fringe observed. —*What the hell's going on?*

—*Everyone relax,* someone in the Glare-Glam scoffed. —*It's just a little shower. It'll break up before it hits land.*

Just then, sirens groaned across the five boroughs. For every citizen in the Metro Reef, all other thoughts froze, and a mandatory dispatch jammed itself into their heads. What followed quashed any hope that this was simply an unusually strong but regularly scheduled storm brewed by Weather Control.

—*Storm Watch has issued a Poacher Storm warning for the Metro Reef... Spotters confirm a Poacher Storm approaching the city... This is a dangerous situation... Follow protocol and take shelter immediately.*

Panic.

All at once throughout the five boroughs, everyone frantically scrambled for shelter. People scattered into oval buildings that looked like they were carved out of ice. Red exclamation points flashed in the air over each of these buildings, marking them as storm shelters. Other people too fearful to even journey outside simply hid in shops or their homes. The bridges that knitted the Metro Reef and the mainland were gridlocked.

—*Riots breaking out on the Goethals Bridge,* warned one hapless driver. —*Drivers getting out of cars, demanding to be allowed in the warp lanes. Waves are really high. Bridge is rocking. Please help!*

For anyone who lived out on the Metro Reef, time was of the essence, especially for those unfortunate enough to live on the outermost island of Bethpage, for the storm would hit them first. The sea surged across the beaches, gnawing away dunes that protected seaside amusement parks and coastal villages. The gales came, scouring reeds along the shore and rocking streetlights further inland. Those who tarried too long started to hear the strange, hoarse whispers that those winds carried; they likely would become too gripped by fear to ever reach safety. The rain began to pour, and through the deluge yet to carry a foul stench or tear through people's skin, it lashed at them in a way that seemed personal. Vindictive. The clouds roiled over the island, and the sky cracked with crimson lightning, as if the clouds were bleeding.

—*Seawall already breached!*

—*Waves crashing onto M Beltway, just saw man swept off road. Please let us use the warp lanes!*

—*Help!*

The thunder cracked like a whip over Sam's head, urging her to run faster. She scampered up the dunes, stumbling as the tar-colored sand gave way. She cursed her small legs, her little body. The gale stung her face with dirt and rain, and it filled her nose with the smells of ocean and ozone. She scrambled up the last of the dunes, not daring to look back, terrified that the East Sea would catch up with her legs, pull her down, and wash her away. Sam had been out on the pier when she got the warning. The skies had looked mean, way meaner than they did during any scheduled rainfall. She had been working with her hands at the time, cutting up freshly caught fish for the daily deliveries, and so she clearly saw the pulse run through her halo-hand when the dispatch arrived. Her and her coworkers' eyes had widened as they heard the same howling siren, minded the same blaring warning that interrupted their idle thoughts at the exact same moment.

Then the dispatch faded, and they all noticed the black skies rolling towards them . . . and then everyone ran. Sam had tried to run with the throng up to the boardwalk, but the mob was so big, so chaotic, and thus of course she had been pushed off the pier without thought, effort, or care, and so she had been forced to crawl up the beach like some runaway crab.

She threw herself over the dune. The sky flared blue as she tumbled down the slope, and she landed against the dune fence. Groaning, her eyes grew wide as she saw the sand around her become dotted with water, and she felt the rain pelt her neck and back. She pushed herself up and hurried down a gravel path that led to the street. The wind lashed at her hair, and the rain was drumming atop the shipwrecked houses around her. But she hurried on, not even stopping as she minded thoughts from people she knew. They occurred to her like memories from a present she had never been in, desperate messages from coworkers and friends at the edge of her own awareness . . .

—*Help! I'm stu—*

—*No power in . . .*

—*Blighters everywhere . . .*

She started up the slope, wind pushing against her, big people shoving past her, the water lapping at her heels. Black Beach was founded atop a round hill that straddled the northern shore of the island. It was built out of old tankers that had shipwrecked against the outcropping over the ages, piling atop one another, presently fixed up to make a variety of houses, shops, and lodges that were stitched together by winding back alleys and twisting catwalks. Normally at this hour the whole town would be bustling with activity, with customers loitering outside pizza parlors or bantering at the trendy taverns. But now only crumpled trash was left on the lower streets. Hundreds of people had taken sanctuary at the piazza at the town's summit, the highest point for many miles. There, they could escape the storm surge and gape at the Poacher Storm as it arrived. The sunset was fighting through the haze, still visible. Then a bolt of lightning split the horizon, and the sun vanished behind gray curtains. The clouds seemed to be consuming themselves.

Sam continued up the street, water splashing with every step. She heard a roaring crash somewhere behind her, but she did not dare look back. Everyone else had beaten Sam up the hill. The whole town had abandoned her. She wished she could keep up, but she just couldn't.

Too slow, she told herself. *I'm too slow.*

The rainfall was relentless. The only reprieve she ever got was wherever bows of ships kissed one another over her head, and she would feel fleeting relief before she kept moving and the lashing resumed. Everything was becoming hard to see in the downpour. She passed an old truck, thought about breaking into it. But she didn't know how to drive a vehicle, much less jump one, and it wasn't like her feet could reach the pedals anyways! She was sure she would drown before she ever found a solution.

Too slow. I'm too slow . . .

About halfway up, the hill became very steep. An uneven stairway along the road would be the quickest way to reach the summit. Sam began the climb, only to trip on the first step.

She broke her fall so that her head landed against her halo-hand, hard. Blinking through stars, she gazed at the shining, shamrock-colored circles etched into the back of her wrist, one nestled crookedly inside the other, scribbles of evergreen light revolving between them. Her halo wavered nervously, warped by either the rain slicking her wrist or the pain dancing across her forehead. Her eyes widened. Was she so weak that such a little fall had shaken her life force that badly? Or was this something else entirely, maybe an omen of her own impending doom?

Too slow. Just give up. Too slow.

Water lapped at her legs, jolting her to her feet. She looked over her shoulder and saw that the street was already flooding with storm surge.

Back down by the beach, huge foaming breakers were crushing the dunes, submerging parked cars, and creeping up the hill. Sam forced herself to turn and keep climbing.

Again she cursed the puny form she had been granted for this life. Sam could not recall a time in the past three hundred years where big, 'normal' people had not mocked her for her impish body, looked down upon for her diminutive features. She also could not remember a day in that span where she had not yearned to have the power of those who wielded the gauntlets. What she would give right now to be a Durationist—to have the ability to simply *will* the rain and winds to a halt!—and what she would give to be able to even *slightly* defend herself against the Blood Poachers, if their madness arrived . . .

But instead, she was just Sam from Black Beach, the puny urchin girl running for her life.

Finally, after slipping once more and scraping her knee, she reached the summit. But when she started towards the plaza, a pair of redcoats crossed their muskets and blocked the way.

"What's your affiliate?" one of the cops asked.

"Blood Works Society," Sam said breathlessly, wincing as she rubbed her knee. "I work down on the—" She paused and stared at the halo on her wrist in bewilderment as the lime-green circles flickered twice.

"You're *charging* me for sanctuary?"

"Gotta make sure you're not a blighter, kid. If you don't like it, you can turn around."

She shoved past them angrily. What choice did she have? *No, I'm not a blighter. Are Commonwealth Services so clueless about who's infected by dark thought and who isn't that they're just guessing now? Maybe just going after little runts like me? It's not like my halo went dark, or my eyes rotted out. And my thoughts are clean!* She shuddered, imagining what it was like to be a blighter . . . to be alive, but only just, and through madness . . .

There were so many people crammed together on the summit of the village that she was almost shoved back down the steps. Determined, she slipped between trembling legs, weaved under waving arms, and covered her ears against all the yelling and shouting. The wind was much worse up here, and every few feet someone staggered into her. Sam did not stop, nor did she dare look at the great thunderhead looming over her: impossibly tall, pulsing with crackling light, about to rear down on all the Metro Reef. For if she stared at the Poacher Storm, she was terrified at what might stare back.

She kept burrowing forward until at last she reached the obelisk fountain at the center of the square. Sam stumbled against the basin, gasping for air.

"There must be a warp point we can use just to crib across the bay," someone was yelling over her head. "They have to save us!"

"They don't care about us," a woman's grave voice responded. "They'll get the big shots out of the city first. They'll leave us for the Kappos, you watch!"

"Where the hell're the Durationists?"

They're coming, Sam thought confidently. *They'll save us.*

The gales were howling, and the pattering of rain over the fountain turned to the clatter of hailstones. Most of them were small pellets, stinging arms and head; but then a larger one smacked a man in the skull. He slumped forward, out cold, blood running from his head. People started screaming. Fights broke out on the perimeter of the square as everyone tried to climb past one another to squeeze into the shops or hide under the canopy of a café. Sam knew she would never make it over there, so she just covered her head with her arms and shut her eyes.

Thunk. Thunk. Thunk. The hail landed around her with loud slaps.

Sam took a deep breath. If this was the end, she liked to think she had done okay. Her New Life hadn't been an easy one, being stuck in the Cellar and all, but she had done her best. She had some of the better gigs of the Cellar over the past three hundred years, or at least she *thought* she had. Sam's halo-hand wasn't exactly bursting with color and light; she didn't have enough cogs to remember everything. But she had always dutifully followed the thought-feed that her affiliate sent out every Monday. She had been a loyal member of her machifare—much more, she felt, than most people in Roslyn ever were.

Many friends told Sam over the years that her devotion to the Blood Works Society was all for naught, that she was being silly, that as an urchin, her prospects of getting steady work were slim to none. Sam had never allowed herself to buy any of that. This was Roslyn! The New Life, where anything was possible. One day she'd have enough blood money to do more than just survive. It could still happen, Sam knew it. Roslyn was still her New Life to go out and get.

At least, it would be—if she survived the night.

Thunk. Thunk. Thunk. Lightning flashed.

"They're not going to take me," a grim-looking fisherman declared to no one in particular. "I'd rather die before the leatherheads take me. Y'understand?"

No one responded, but everyone felt the same way. Sam sure did. Normally on a Friday night she'd head to the pizza parlor after work, maybe take a train into the city, revel in having the weekend off. Now she wasn't sure if she'd see the next sunrise. Poacher Storms were rare these days, but whenever they did occur everyone knew what to expect: teams of Durationists would swoop in, repel the storm, and save the day. But even Sam found herself wondering what *would* happen if no Durationists came, if the Kappos got to them first . . .

She took a deep breath. They said thoughts themselves, whether someone else's or one's own, became a hazard during a Poacher Storm. It was another reason Sam was largely ignoring the constant stream of scoops from strangers and friends. Commonwealth Services had taught time and time again to be wary of minding desperate messages during a Poacher Storm, for they could be from someone who had already been broken by the Blood Poachers. And though Sam desperately hoped her friends were all right, she did not want to risk succumbing to dark thought, to become one of the blighters. Or worse. . .

She began to do what she knew everyone else was doing: she shut her eyes and imagined her mind floating among the hundreds of other minds stranded with her on the summit, all of them nestled amid millions more minds scattered across the country, each of those millions of minds mustering a million thoughts about a million things, all those billions of ideas intermingling at each and every moment to weave together the interpsychic network that Roslynians called the codex. One could get lost minding the codex's endless web of thoughts, spend dozens of seasons chasing an avalanche of random nonsense—but if you had a specific question to ask, it would present to you the thoughts of people who might have answers.

In this case, Sam minded the codex to simply find out what the hell was going on. She let her attention drift through the sea of mental panic that arrested the city, until she settled upon the ramblings of a local thought-talkie. His broadcast could provide news, and he might give Sam a reason to hold out hope.

— ... *Kappo mobs are spreading through all five boroughs ... Thought-cascades are imminent, and Commonwealth Services are urging everyone to disregard all scooped thoughts not from approved media or commonwealth sources. Those of you who are Sponsored or higher can see the images citizens in New Bronx scooped with us. Kappos butchering people in the streets ...*

Sam frowned. She couldn't imagine the pictures, but others around her who were also minding the thought-feed had lustier halo-hands than she did. They gasped, their faces blanching. It told her all that she needed to know.

—All right, if you are just joining us now, we are looking at what is now confirmed to be a Poacher Storm, the first to hit any of Roslyn's major cities since the infamous Geaga Bay event nearly a century and a half ago. We are still trying to learn details of how the Poachers were able to organize this deep into Roslyn. I'm told the Durationist League was caught off guard by this attack and is scrambling to get as many clubs out to Metro Reef as quickly as possible to try and rescue the city...

"Great," someone nearby muttered. "We're fucked."

—However, I am told that Tremont United have gotten out ahead of the other Durationist teams, and right now they are punching the core of the storm at New Bronx Seaport. Our country's highest-ranked club will engage the Blood Poacher head-on. They will try to kill the Poacher before things get any worse ...

Nervous cheers started to break out across the square. Gasps of relief filled the air.

A woman in the distance openly wept. "Save us, please!"

"Best team there is," a man next to Sam murmured. He smoked a cigarette that spat blue smoke between his quivering fingers. Tears were in his eyes. "They've killed a Blood Poacher before. They'll beat this storm, too."

"Wish it was *my* team," a freckled half-urchin—a head taller than Sam but still much shorter than the big people—laughed in a shaky voice. "But shit, I'll wear red and blue the rest of my New Life if they get us out of this."

"Agreed," said a bald man dressed in the cloth of the Last Church. He kissed a colorful mandala hanging from his neck. "Beggars can't be choosers, not in times like this. Even a follower of Red Tide like myself must be grateful for . . . any help . . . *please* . . ."

The half-urchin guffawed loudly. "You guys always shit the bed, anyways!" His voice still cracked from nerves. "Trebolio chokes! Everyone knows it. What about you, kid? You must be happy, huh? You're gonna make a score off tonight!"

Sam realized he was talking to her. She reflexively put a hand over the maroon flag pin on her jacket, the token of the Blood Works Society. "W-well," she stammered nervously, "I—"

"Nah, her favorite team isn't Tremont United," the smoking man said. The blue puffs from his cigarette formed a miniature cloud over Sam's head. "She's wearing blue and maroon. Old Atlantic's colors, yeah?"

The half-urchin laughed. "Old Atlantic, eh? Hell of a second-ranked club! Big Sophia fan I bet, right? Who isn't these days? Man, she's *great*, but I can't fucking stand her . . . hey buddy, you mind if I get a hit off of that?"

Sam let them talk over her, eager to be left alone. The half-urchin hadn't been wrong: Sophia from Belmont Chapel was definitely her favorite player. Old Atlantic's star closer, she was widely considered the best player in the game today. Sam wondered if Old Atlantic would enter the field tonight. She clutched her halo-hand eagerly. Despite how horrible things were now, *her* team might show up and help get the victory! She could practically feel the extra jolt of cogs inside her. Maybe she would even get to see Sophia in action! That was an exciting, distracting thought. *Thump. Thunk. Thump. Thunk.*

—A fan rally is gathering at Black Beach! If you're up here, help us! Help us help our team!

Everyone stampeded towards the north end of the plaza, and Sam realized—after everyone had left her in their dust, of course—that they might be able to see some of the battle from there. Once again her tiny form had left her behind everyone else. She began to despair, until an idea struck her. She climbed into the fountain and swam up to the obelisk. Then she climbed using the notches etched into it until she was about ten feet off the ground, well above the rest of the crowd and with a clear view to the north.

To the northeast, she could see the rainbow skyline of Metro Reef just as it vanished beneath a burst of rain. Straight ahead was the Jamaica Sound, where the whirring light of a stone lighthouse faded away in a ghastly haze, which was already gnawing away at the seaport across the channel, dozens of miles away. That was where the Durationists were taking on the Blood Poacher.

The crowd gasped, and Sam thought she saw flashing red lights along the miniature catwalks and cruise ships just before it was all consumed by a curtain of rain; whether it was lightning or the valor of the players fighting off the storm, she had no idea. Her eyes were wide, her mouth agape. Nobody was talking now. No one could believe they were witnessing an actual Durationist team in action, against a Blood Poacher. Even if they couldn't really see anything, everyone knew they were a witness to history. Sam tried to imagine what the battle was like, but she could only see a lot of lightning. *Thunk. Thump. Thunk. Thump. Thunk. Thump.*

In the foreground, a group of fans had assembled at the edge of the square. They had bravely decided to perform an old tradition, in hope of turning the tides. Many were fans of other clubs and simply cheering on for survival's sake; others were true Tremont diehards, clad in red-and-purple sweaters and holding up signs that read *Glory to Tremont United!*; they waved flags that bore their favorite club's letters; they cried out in support of their favorite players: *"Glory to Ahmed from Pilgrim's Bay!"* and *"Bleed for Elizabeth!"*

The storm, as if eager to quell the spectators' enthusiasm, responded to their chants and applause with bursts of harsh wind and snaps of thunder. Up in the throng, Sam saw the man of the Last Church who had been standing next to her holding the mandala to his lips and murmuring a prayer to the Barra. Next to him, the half-urchin was puffing away on a blue cigarette he had nicked from the man who had been smoking earlier. Sam wished she still had some of her seasonal fix that was proffered by the Blood Works Society every year, but she was all out. Instead she found another way to stay calm: she minded the thoughts of other fans from afar, people who were rooting for their favorite Durationist club or player to show up and save the day. Scoops ranged from a simple show of support, like —*May Golden Bridge win the night!*, to an entire verse of "Goethal Towers Stand Tall," as well as pledges to specific players, such as: —*All hail Trebolio from Red Tide, beloved left-winger of Red*

Tide Cathedral. Retorts from rival fans often ensued: —*Fuck off, Red Tide. Go Toledo U!*

Sam felt how each slogan, each rallying cry scooped towards the Durationists was laden with them the love and devotion each fan had for their team—their hope and worry for their club's chances of success that night—and their affection flickered across the codex to land on the halo-hands of players, perhaps giving them just the slightest extra glimmer of cogs that they would need in the heat of battle. To feel that kinship between team and player across the codex reassured Sam too, and she felt compelled to offer a scoop of her own.

She shut her eyes and scooped: —*Go Old Atlantic. And go Sophia.*

The fans of Tremont United were not so easily deterred. In the next lull a local band hastily assembled at the piazza's edge, and Sam watched as they played a defiant blast of trumpets and drums, while the spectators all sang in concert:

Glory to Tremont's golden team
Victory shall be achieved
Strong in blood with hearts o' fire
No storm nor demon is too dire

With fists of silver raised up high
Roslyn shall hear our battle cry:
Glory to Tremont United!
Shake down evil from the sky!
Glory to Tremont United!
Restore the sunny skies.

With each lyric the crowd sang, the glowing circles on their wrists beamed brightly, as if the people had already gleaned power just from trying to bolster their club's strength from afar. Claps of thunder drowned out the chorus, and a swell of stinging rain and salty wind scoured the square. But the band kept on playing.

It soon became too foggy to see across the sound, and for a while nothing happened. Then the mists parted.

At first, the storm clouds didn't look so impressive. They resembled a routed navy sinking into the sea. The lightning began to flicker weakly, and the thunder became a small murmur. The wind died, and the rain tapered to a mere drizzle. The beam of the old lighthouse, freed from the gloomy ether, whirred past again.

The crowd roared in excitement; strangers who had come together that night exchanged high-fives and hugged each other, certain they had witnessed another victory for Tremont United. Only the most knowledgeable of fans continued to stare uncertainly at the sky, hiding their concerns with nervous smiles. There was seemingly no reason to doubt their team's win: to even the most seasoned of forecasters, it would look as if whatever disturbance had occurred offshore was dying.

Sam didn't know enough to make anything of it. She just thought the sky still looked mean.

The thought-talkie continued his report.

—*August of Tremont, Owner of Londinium, has just scooped a statement. He condemns this attack as a 'despicable act of aggression' by the Shadow Powers and a flagrant violation of the Treaty of Camulodunum, the h-historic document signed by our country to . . . the Echomar . . . 459 CE, which . . . c-ceasefire within . . . r-respective . . . b-borders . . . promises . . . s-swift d-decisive r-response . . . Meanwhile . . . n-no n-news . . . T-Tremont U-United . . . s-seems t-to b-be a-a—*

The thought-feed died. There was a sharp whining noise, and then a deep pain shot through Sam's forehead. She shouted and covered her ears, but she didn't know if it was a real sound or all in her head. Her fingernails dug into her head as she tried to block it out, tried to think of something else, but it was like she had no other thoughts, like her entire head was ringing with that terrible screech. Her heart pounded. She tried to mind the codex, desperate for a thought, *anyone's* thought, but it was gone, out of her reach. She heard a chorus of cries and groans and thought maybe it was the source of the terrible noise. But as she winced through her nausea, scanning the plaza, she gradually realized it was the whole crowd cowering and cringing, rooted on the spot, stricken by the same awful sound, a hundred minds cut off from the rest of the codex, from the rest of the world.

Sam slowly peered upward between her fingers. Her stomach dropped. She feared she knew what was happening.

Thump. Thump. Thud.

Oh, no.

Lightning struck nearby, and the sky flared crimson and burst with deafening thunder. Power lines snapped, transformers burst, and everything turned pitch-black. The downpour wiped away the world, and a burst of screaming wind riddled people with twigs and trash as forked thunderbolts frayed the inky night. The citizens in Black Beach Square began to flail and shout, dropping their banners and instruments as they clambered over one another in the dark.

Sam had just begun to climb down the obelisk when a streak of lightning ripped across the sooty sky and smashed into the fountain. She had no chance to react; she never even heard the boom of thunder. Everything went up in a scarlet flash. She felt herself tumbling through the air, and in a blur she saw the entire crowd thrown off their feet, and stone burst into fire and water burned away, and the steam wrapped around a jagged stalk of glass now jutting out of the broken obelisk.

The last thing Sam saw before she hit the ground were people cowering and covering their ears, even though there was no thunder, just a shrill whining noise, so high and terrible that the entire mob cried out in pain, collapsing onto the pavement and clutching at their heads.

She was on her back. She couldn't feel anything. Her head was spinning. White-hot stars filled her vision. She raised her hand in vain, as if to reach out for someone, anyone, and saw the lime-green light dissolving from her halo like a forest at sunset. The sight frightened her. Then her arm fell at her side, and she couldn't move again.

A dark melody, mindless and pervasive, bored into the entire mob at once:

—*Death to Tremont's Golden Team!*

—*Eat their brains and let them bleed!*

—*Death to all of Roslyn!*

—*Eat. Kill. Have fun!*

Sam tried to ignore the song—she had to ignore the song, any chance of living through this depended on her ignoring the song—but the more she tried, the louder she heard it, until her head split with so much pain that a thousand more thoughts, random and unbidden, burst into her.—*I can't touch the sky,* someone randomly scooped.

—*Do we sing songs in the rain?* another person wept.

—*Death to all of Roslyn! Eat their brains and let them bleed!*

—*How about . . .*

—*Why am I . . .*
—*That wasn't mine. Hello?*
—*Eat. Kill. Have fun!*
—*Heh.*

Sam felt everyone around her writhing on the ground, heard them howl wordlessly and claw at the floor, heard them gag and start to fall silent. Everyone was seized by madness. Sam's mind spun, fast and violent, overwhelmed by the flood of pointless, perverse ideas battering her from within and without. The thunder kept roaring, the rain kept falling. She vaguely sensed her whole body shaking, convulsing; she retched and imagined dark, oily smoke pouring out of her mouth. Twin white suns floated over her . . .

—*Mind the void!* an icy voice shrieked.

A cold chill went down her shattered spine. Dimly, she realized the white-hot stars *weren't* stars. Something else was in the jet-black sky, something that filled Sam's limp body with dread: a pair of baleful eyes, each larger than a falling moon, whiter than lightning itself, peering out of the thunderhead. No lightning bolt, no flood nor twister could match the dread Sam felt from glimpsing those White Eyes of Thunder as they scoured the Metro Reef from their lofty perch within an anvil of slate and smoke.

The storm's penetrating gaze fixed upon its prey like rats in a maze. Anyone somehow still conscious under the siege of these vicious thoughts instantly succumbed to the glare of those pitiless eyes. Unbidden, Sam imagined more dark, wispy smoke leaking out of her nose and mouth and eyes and from unseen wounds riddling her body. She no longer could see a thing—just the White Eyes, floating in the abyss.

The shrieking blared on without end. If the sound alone did not kill them all, then the dark thoughts shredding their minds would. The stricken could no longer move, could no longer think. The insane scoops neared a crescendo from which Sam knew no one would survive. Sam no longer had any sense of her body, of herself. She felt herself drifting—no, *pieces* of herself drifting, as if she *was* the smoky ether leaving her body—mixing and mingling with the vapor from others broken around her, dissipating across the entire square. Whatever was left of her knew she ought to be horrified, ought to do something, fight back, because what was going to happen to her now was much, much worse than if the lightning had simply killed her. But she had no strength left. She went numb, no longer feeling pain from the thunderbolts clanging in her head. The only thing she still knew was cold despair.

Sam saw herself as if she was peering into a distant, foggy mirror. She saw herself close her eyes, saw herself accepting the worst.

Then, when it seemed certain that everyone's minds and bodies would crumble, everything stopped. The whining noise dropped to a low pitch. The wind and rain slackened. There was a low murmur, swift and repetitive, like an incantation being uttered. Then silence. Sam, or some remnant of Sam, thought she heard someone scoop them.

—*People of Black Beach. This is Lucas from Slag Falls, Captain of Bedlam Athletic. If you can hear me, you're going to be all right. We'll be there soon. Hang on.*

Some of the people sprawled around the plaza heard the thought, or perhaps they imagined hearing the calming incantation that was being murmured somewhere over the square, and their dim halo-hands flickered in response like hopeful whispers.

And just like that, Sam was back inside herself, coughing uncontrollably, still unable to move her limbs, her body still in a painful position, a small plume of smoke still hovering a few feet over her heart. But she was awake. Ever so slightly, she turned her head to her right.

Her neck instantly protested with a jolt of raw pain. In the foreground was her own halo-hand, dim and colorless. Beyond she saw a handful of fans in red and purple, the ones who had been singing so boisterously just a few minutes ago, now coughing in fits, wincing from pain but brought back to life. Intermittent rain stippled over them, and thunder grumbled somewhere far off. The awakening victims raised their heads, struggling to sit upright, eager to see whoever had managed to stave off the attack.

Instead, they saw a nightmare.

No, Sam thought. *Please, no.*

A thick blanket of fog had fallen around the storm-swept hill. Four roads, one from each cardinal direction, led up to the town square. Climbing up those streets, emerging from the mists, were dozens of hunched, scarecrow-looking figures. They were dressed in long grungy coats the color of mud, and their heads were adorned with grubby leather helmets, the flaps to either side rocking to their staggered, bouncing gait; they moved as if tugged along by strings. Their faces looked like a patchwork of old dinosaur hide, the kind anyone might buy from a cheap thrift store in the deserts of Jumano: colors of tan, brick, and myrtle, all sown together with stitched lines that cut across their faces, contorting their mouths into permanent grins or scowls. Their heads were held together with bolts where ears should have been. The flattened, crooked nose could only breathe the listless air of a Poacher Storm, while the eyes, void of detail, glowed a lifeless brown.

The White Eyes of Thunder leered down at its loyal infantry.

—Kill. Eat. Have fun!

The Kappos growled and giggled as they surrounded the stricken crowd. Some held long, crooked knives; others carried crude, rusted pistols; a few simply carried brown sacks over their shoulders, from which wispy shadows seemed to leak. More and more people awoke as the Kappos approached: shouting in fright, they scuttled and crawled towards the scorched fountain, as if it could somehow protect them.

One woman tripped as she tried to crawl away, and a pair of Kappos hopped onto her, daggers drawn. Sam shut her eyes. The screams were horrible . . . but only for a few seconds. Then they faded away, like a radio being turned down, and out of morbid curiosity Sam couldn't help but open her eyes. The woman was still writhing, screaming; one Kappo was still stabbing at her, but it was all happening in slow motion, in black and white; there was no blood, just plumes of black shadow. The second Kappo speared the plumes with its knife, catching wisps on the edge of the blade like cloudy strings. It giggled as it tossed each clump of smoke into the sack over its shoulder.

No, Sam again pleaded. *Please, no.*

A shadow fell over her. Sam wanted to scurry away; she urged her body to flee, bit her lip till it bled, but she could not move. She whimpered as the shadow of a Kappo drew over her. Her halo-hand blackened and waned, as if merely coming within arm's length of the twisted creature was too high a cost to bear. The Kappo let out a stilted cackle and raised its knife high. Its lifeless eyes blotted out the rest of the world.

A decisive crack echoed across the plaza. The Kappo's entire body snapped back, the flaps of its leather helmet flailing wildly as the bolts and stitches that kept its head sewn together blew apart. The impish monster staggered and swayed like a puppet whose wires had become tangled. Then, as if its puppeteer were fed up, the Kappo flung itself onto its back and lay still, sparks spraying from its shattered face.

The other Kappos froze, gawking at the body of their fallen comrade. Then, one by one, they started to yelp and point towards the tallest of the landlocked ships overlooking the square. Standing on the bow was a tall, skeletal figure holding a rifle. His face was shrouded by a hood, but his stark eyes had a sickly green and gold glow, and Sam found their odd lack of detail unsettling. His outstretched halo-hand, encased in a silver-and-black glove, coruscated with a cobalt hue.

At the sight of the silver-and-black gauntlet, the entire Kappo horde barked and raised their weapons. The storm rumbled. The White Eyes narrowed into menacing slits. Wind howled across the village.

The Durationist slung the grudge shot back over his shoulder, smoke still rising from the barrel. With a spindly arm, he drew a long, basalt-colored sword in his gauntlet hand, then pointed it over the mob, right at the storm, as if to cast judgment. Lightning crashed nearby, and in one effulgent moment the Durationist's grim, pallid face was revealed for the entire square to see.

Sam's eyes widened in shock. It obviously wasn't Sophia—but it was the *last* player she expected to see.

Without preamble, the Durationist vaulted himself high over the square.

The Kappos opened fire as he soared past, the scrap guns making jangling thuds with each blast. But a winged shadow swept over the square, and jets of icy mists plumed down into the creatures' faces, causing them to growl and shoot wildly off the mark. A second figure riding a hang glider landed on the rooftops: short and stocky, he too wore a glove of silver and black. With a running start he again flew over the plaza, twirling a metal rod out in front of him to catch rain on the staff's bladed end. He moved too fast for Sam to really see, but she thought she saw the raindrops freeze as they dripped off the weapon, and there was a crackling sound as the water rapidly condensed into icicles that he flung down at the Kappo horde, again and again. The hail shattered with screeching bursts, coating the pavement with black ice and filling the air with glacial murk, so that soon the Kappos were slipping off their feet and engulfed in tendrils of freezing fog.

At that point, Sam was no longer aware of her broken body, no longer aware that her mind was still leaking from her. Whether she observed the fight from above or from her own eyes, she did not know. But she knew that she was witness to a Durationist team in action.

This was something she had wanted to see all of her New Life.

The hooded Durationist descended towards the far end of the square. Scores of Kappos squealed and leaped out of rank, desperate to escape the painful, blinding haze, hoping to make a few quick kills before the Durationist cut them down. But a series of deep cracks echoed across the plaza, and before the hooded figure with the black sword had even hit the ground, six Kappos slumped over, twitching, sparks and smoke bursting from their chests and faces. A third Durationist stood on a parapet opposite of where his teammate batted ice: one foot on the railing, he lazily brushed a lock of hair out of his eye, lined up another round of targets with his rifle, and fired with blinding speed. Though the cold fog smothered the square, Sam got the distinct sense that the gunman could *see* through the brume, as if the tattered outline of each Kappo gleamed brightly in his sight. She heard a swift succession of gunshots, and she saw Kappos fall so fast that one of them could only gawp as others fell to its left and right before it too burst with smoke and cinder.

The tall man with the black sword landed in mid swing, cutting through the dirk and head of a Kappo feebly trying to defend itself. A leather helmet tumbled between the feet of the other Kappos, who squealed and yelped as the hooded Durationist overtook them, his blade whirling and arcing at a pace so furious that few living beings, much less Kappos, could match it, a blur of translucent slashes and swings that in mere seconds rendered a quarter of the enemy horde into a smoking, sparking heap.

A few of the Kappos hid beneath the bow of a ship to escape the striker's fire. They aimed their pistols at the swordsman's back. But before they could fire, a streaking flash of silver and gold tore across them, and they howled as their limbs erupted with fire. A flying sickle cut through the horde, sending arms and leather helmets flying high. Then the sickle rebounded as if on a string, taking out what Kappos it had missed on its initial flight. It returned to the hand of a fourth Durationist sitting atop a moped in an alleyway. She was a half-urchin with dark hair, clad in a yellow moto jacket. With a grin she revved her engine and charged into the fray, her sickle sizzling with sunlight as she hacked and sliced through the leather and smoke.

The fog became so dense that the Kappos were running into one another; one by one they were cut down by the sword now thrumming with indigo light, the crackling sickle as it bounded through the gloom, or the resounding blasts from the striker's scope shot. As if to try to bolster its minions, the storm intensified: rain and wind swept away the mists, and lightning bolts raced over the village. The Durationist wielding ice was forced to let go of his glider as the gales tore it from his grip. He dropped down into the horde, while the long-haired sniper ducked beneath forks of electricity and lunged down to the street to stand back to back with him. Kappos rushed at the pair from all sides, but the burly Durationist conjured discs of fire at his feet and slapped them with his metal club, causing them to rip right through the Kappo's chests and legs; the long-haired striker switched to a pair of pistols, and he proved as adept with them as he had with the scope shot, gunning down Kappos from all sides, never turning his head or moving from where he stood.

The flurry of slices and shots went on, unyielding, until the rain tapered and the winds died. Just one Kappo was left standing. Caught between the four Durationists, it scampered about, desperate to make a stand. It ambled over to the urchin girl in a blue-and-maroon sweater and grabbed her roughly by the hair. It held a dirk to her throat, and Sam realized it was *her*, and once again she was back inside her head. She winced from the touch of the sharp, jagged knife.

The Kappo growled at the tall swordsman. The hooded Durationist raised a hand to his peers, signaling them to do nothing. He held his sword calmly at his side. The Kappo giggled, twitching its head excitedly. Sam waited—waited to die.

The Durationist's free hand shot over his shoulder; in a blur he brought his rifle forward. A final boom cracked across the plaza. The urchin girl fell onto her side, gasping and shuddering. The Kappo stumbled forward, a shower of sparks emitting from its broken mouth, before it pitched onto its face and lay still.

Then the rain broke, save for a calm drizzle. For the moment, the only white in the sky over Metro Reef was a sliver of the pale moon.

Sam didn't know much after that. She was dully aware of the rain falling on her face. It felt nice and cool. There were flashing red lights somewhere nearby and a lot of people running around. At some point a man in a white uniform was standing over her, shaking his head. Sam felt sorry for him. At least the rain felt good. Even the thunder sounded distant, peaceful. She couldn't see that well anymore, but she didn't see any dark smoke filling the air, nor any trace of Thunder's Eyes.

There were two people above her now, the hooded Durationist and his teammate in the yellow jacket. They were talking about her. The girl in the jacket looked upset. Sam didn't understand why. Didn't they know they had saved her?

The man was kneeling next to her. He was close enough that Sam could make out his features beneath the cowl. The heavy hood shrouded a ruin: He had a dark face, a gaunt, bleak wedge framed by a scraggly, black beard. His face and forehead were deeply creased, as if the company of his own thoughts was too much to bear, and his eyes—it was his eyes that really got to Sam. Fathomless and solemn, they lacked any detail whatsoever, but they emitted a vivid, eerie glow, swirls of sun and earth, two lambent rocks of green and gold embedded in a crumbling cliff. They were just like the eyes of Kappos and people enthralled to the Echomar. Except he couldn't have been a blighter, because the man wore the silver gauntlet over his halo-hand, the glove that only Durationists wore, and he was holding Sam's own little hand, and Sam could feel him carefully scooping her his cogs, sharing his strength with her, willing her to stay alive just a little longer.

The hooded Durationist said something to the girl, and the girl left. Sam felt strong enough, not to talk, but to at least scoop this man.

—Am I . . . am I going to die?

—Yes. I'm sorry. Considering your injuries, it's amazing that you're still here. You have a strong heart.

The man's eyes, though unfathomable, were warm, Sam thought. Friendly. He wasn't so bad.

—Please tell me . . . they didn't . . . take any part of me, did they?

—No, they didn't.

Sam let out a rattling sigh. —Thank you. I didn't . . . I didn't want a part of me to be . . . to be stuck—

She couldn't finish the thought. To no longer be living, but to still have fleeting, meaningless experiences, from the parts of her soul that might have been used to build new Kappos . . . to simply die, or even driven mad by the Blood Poachers, would be better.

The man gave Sam's hand a firm squeeze. —*I know.*

Again Sam felt her halo-hand pulse as the man shared the glow of his own halo . . . it was intense. Vivid. He couldn't save her, couldn't fix her, but just an ounce of his power made her calm.

—*Can I ask you one last thing, Captain?*

—*Of course.*

—*Do you have any idea what happens if you die? In Roslyn?*

He laughed. She was happy to see that.

—*If I knew the answer to that, I could retire! No, I don't know for sure what will happen to you. I only know that the Blood Poachers can't hurt you anymore. Your soul will be safe. Hold onto that feeling, Sam. It'll last beyond all this. So will you.*

He gave her hand a final squeeze. Sam smiled dreamily. Rain pattered against her face. If she closed her eyes or if the Durationist did it for her, she never knew.

2. League Stewards

—*IT'S ILLEGAL FOR YOU to be out there, Captain.*
 —*If we didn't go out tonight, every person in this village would have been harvested. No one else recognized that Bethpage was at risk.*
 —*Lionel is right, Lucas. You know the law: only county league teams or above may take the initiative out in the field.*
 —*In other words, your 'experiment' has no business out there.*
 —*I'm sorry, Stewards, but I don't really care what the law says when a severe Poacher Storm is about to hit the biggest city on the eastern seaboard.*

Gemini from Bedlam Ghettos listened to her captain's conversation with League Command while she walked through the town square. Squads of cops and medics were rushing across the plaza to tend to the wounded, lifting them onto stretchers and carrying them to a triage set up nearby. She stepped around a pile of mangled Kappos, little flurries of sparks still shooting out of their hides, and she suppressed a shiver as she glimpsed one of their frozen, grinning faces. Gemini had nothing to fear from a mere Kappo anymore, not since she had donned a silver-and-black glove; but in the silence after a battle, she could still admit that they were unnerving. League Command liked to call them Rook Kappos, or just Rooks: a perfectly sterile term that was an apt way to describe how the Blood Poachers used them like disposable puppets. But Gemini would always know the Kappos by what they were called on the streets of Bedlam: leatherheads, and the stuff of every Roslynian's nightmares. Before she ever became a Durationist, it had always been her greatest fear to get caught in a storm like how these poor people had been, and to be jumped by a horde of Kappos, knives drawn and with a bag for her soul, which the Blood Poachers used to stitch together more of the demented little monsters.

She suppressed another shudder and kept moving. She saw a body bag being taken away, and she replayed the battle in her mind.

Too slow, she thought, frowning. *I was too slow.*

The death of the urchin girl and five other victims caught in the lightning storm had quashed whatever enthusiasm she might have otherwise had about her team's performance. Gemini had been a fan of Duration long before she ever dared to wear a gauntlet. She knew that her team had done a good job, but it wasn't good enough. Lucas was aiming for more than just being some county-caliber club, and Gemini had come to be a true believer in one of his favorite sayings: *The day you become content is the day you're no longer a Durationist.*

The rain had tapered to a drizzle, and the thunder was weak and distant. To the untrained eye it might seem that the storm had passed. But Gemini knew better. Lightning streaked across the skyline, and she glimpsed a fresh row of cumulonimbus clouds firing up over the north. The local radar was linked to the codex, so she had no trouble envisioning a weather map of the city out of the corner of her eye, and it confirmed her sight. Heavy bands were reorganizing over the Jamaica Sound, deep with rain and charged with lightning. The codex was flooded with the cries of people going mad from lightning strikes across all five boroughs of the Metro Reef, and reports of insurgent Kappos were now surfacing from the slums uptown. There was still a lot of cleaning up to do. It was going to be a long night.

She walked under the awning of a café, where Lucas stood with his hands clasped behind his back and his head bowed, so that his face and beard were shadowed by his cowl. The light rain pattered against the canopy. She exchanged glances with her captain as she stood level with him. He was at least two full heads taller than her; his double-breasted navy coat hugged his rail-thin frame down to his knees, and his denim pants were tucked into shin-high boots. His musket and sword hilt jutted over either shoulder to form a cross at his back. Other than the tiny interlocking *B* and *A* on the breast of his hooded coat, he displayed none of his current allegiances. It was a far cry from Gemini, whose jacket was adorned with various badges from their victories in exhibition games and out in the field, and her lace-up jersey was embroidered with the club logo in huge collegiate letters for all to see.

She wore those letters with pride. It was something her friends she used to train with on the amateur circuit back home found baffling. Bedlam Athletic was the flagship team of Lucas from Slag Falls' fledgling new affiliate, the Meta-School, and while many pundits considered them a bunch of castoffs, led by a Durationist who should never have been allowed back in the league, Gemini had come to believe that they were really building something new and different. She was proud of that, and she wanted everyone, especially other Durationists, to know it.

But for their expansion claim to be taken seriously by officials in Londinium, they needed a big victory. And to get a big victory, they needed to be out in the field on a night like tonight, when one of Roslyn's greatest cities was under attack.

Lucas offered her a weary smile. She did not need to mind with him to know it was not going well.

—*That bad?*

He laughed.

—*You're about to find out.*

Suddenly Gemini pictured the wavering, translucent forms of Lionel and Bion, the senior Stewards of the Durationist League of Roslyn, sitting at the table before them: their arms sinking through the counter, their bodies floating over the chairs they weren't really sitting in. Gemini supposed she and Lucas appeared just as awkwardly to them, at the league headquarters in Londinium.

Lionel from Londinium Level Four was tall and sinewy, his stern face shadowed by a neat, cropped beard. A small purple-and-red helix was pinned to his tan jacket to acknowledge his proud legacy with the Blood

Works Society's Durationist corps. He regarded Gemini with an annoyed frown before turning his attention back to Lucas. Gemini could now hear his voice in full.

"Until your machifare is ratified by Londinium and the Stratushold, your team *cannot* be out chasing. That's the end of it."

"Clearly we are capable," Lucas said with a negligent wave to the heap of Kappo corpses behind him. He had a cool, quiet voice that cut a steady path between thoughtful and amused. "You know how long it's been since a storm of this magnitude has hit us."

Lionel sighed and rolled his eyes, as if he was talking to a belligerent fan. He smoked on a pipe, strange puffs of orange fumes rising around his head. "This is a squall line, Lucas, nothing more. I grant you, it's a reckless move by the Blood Poachers to attack one of our biggest cities. It's an outrageous violation, and it won't go unpunished. But if you bothered to mind the radar, you would have noticed that the first front broke up the moment it reached the city limits. Metro Reef is too vivid a city; the total sum of cogs that its population affirms is too great for the Blood Poachers to penetrate. The Echomar has grown desperate, as such a cowardly attack clearly demonstrates. Our teams will dispatch these pockets of showers without any trouble."

Lucas folded his arms and shook his head. "You know commonwealth radar can't detect everything. The system is culling warm air off the sea. Pressure is still dropping. I believe there's going to be an escalation that our models can't predict."

"Why don't you consider a new career with Weather Control, Lucas? Since you know so much more than our experts . . ." The Senior Steward of the Blood Works Society paused for a moment, as if, Gemini feared, to all but scoop the unspoken conclusion: *And that way . . . for good.*

Lionel continued: "The Echomar could send a typhoon tonight, and it would collapse against our prosperity. What difference does it make?"

Gemini looked to her captain, hoping to catch any indication that he was growing impatient with the Steward's derision; yet his smile remained calm, his ghastly eyes unflinching. Either he was demonstrating unparalleled control of his emotions—which, of course, a Durationist as powerful as he was would have achieved long ago—or he was simply so used to the Alumni Circle's brusque treatment, from Lionel in particular, that he simply no longer cared.

"The Poachers would brew a potent storm *only* if they sensed weakness," Lucas said. "The city's affordance may be more vulnerable than we realize. Remember Geaga Bay or the Dixie Outbreak; many of the cities leveled by those storms were not nearly as prosperous, their citizens not remotely as happy nor their wrists brimming as brightly, as we fancied beforehand. In retrospect, we were forced to admit that there were not nearly as many cogs in those towns as we wanted to believe, and the glow of the people's halo-hands went dark alarmingly fast when the storm clouds rolled in. The same may be true with Metro Reef."

"All conjecture. You have no proof."

"I witnessed a volley of red bolts overtake Tremont United in mere *seconds*; it was unlike anything I have ever seen. The Echomar has not been as dormant as the almanac led us to believe. They have taken us by surprise."

A loud peal of thunder quaked overhead. Grimly, Gemini wondered if Captain Ahmed's team had been killed outright or if their souls had been harvested first. She guessed the Blood Poachers didn't really give you a say in the matter.

Lionel's stony eyes narrowed. "Even if what you said had an ounce of truth to it—and that would be a first for you—why would I want a rogue party like yours out there tonight?"

"Many of our best clubs are still en route. Red Tide Cathedral is still down south, and as I understand it no clubs from the Bellatrist have yet to even acknowledge our requests for help. There are scores of people trapped uptown with a Kappo horde bearing down on them. The storm beacons at Harlo Valley and Grant's Lighthouse must be activated—"

Lionel groaned. "There is no need to waste *their* power against a storm like this!"

"If not now, Steward, when? Even if you are right, and this storm cannot sustain itself over the inner boroughs, the beacons would immediately destroy the Kappo horde uptown. It might even incapacitate the Blood Poacher. Wasn't Tremont United supposed to activate them? Why not finish the job?"

"The situation has changed," Lionel said. "Every expert at our disposal—except *you*, of course—has judged this storm to be a controlled disturbance, not worth the exhaustion of tens of thousand tons of blue ore."

Lucas nodded. "Fine. But if we're not activating the storm shields, you clearly need as many able players out here as possible. And if you doubt our strength, I remind you that Bedlam Athletic is comprised of two Duke's Class players, a veteran of the county circuit, and"—he nodded to Gemini—"one of the nation's top-ranked amateurs. That matches the rank of many of our Duke's League clubs. Common sense says you should disregard league protocol. Let us intercept this thing head-on."

"You think very highly of yourself, Lucas, don't you?"

Lucas spread his hands out in front of him. "Believe me, Steward: I've yet to meet anyone in three hundred years who is harder on myself than I. And I've had some pretty unforgiving company in my time. I do, however, have complete faith in my teammates. We can handle this."

Bion shook his rumpled head, the technicolor mandala he wore on a chain over his neck jangling back and forth. "We don't deny your sincerity, Lucas"—Lionel snorted with disdain—"but your assistance is not required tonight. Our *best* teams are leading the offensive: a company led by Toledo U is advancing from New Bronx, while Old Atlantic is coming across the Kill Van Bay."

"Old Atlantic?" For the first time, Lucas's voice emitted surprise. "I thought they were on patrol in the Lakes and Bay Territory."

"They were," Bion said carefully. One stubby finger tapped on the center of the huge mandala. It weighed so heavily around his neck that Gemini feared he might topple over. "However, they were recalled shortly after the storm broke out over Metro Reef. The league office, ah, provided Captain Fernando with the location of a secret warp point in the Forest of Erie so that they could make it down here as quickly as possible. Londinium feels that Old Atlantic's ... recognition with the public, not to mention their *vetted* field experience ... are appropriate for a situation this traumatic." He added quickly: "To reassure the people, you know."

—Sophia!

The thought left Gemini's mind before she even knew she was venting to Lucas. Of *course* the league wanted Sophia's team out on the hunt! *Everyone* loved Sophia. How couldn't they? Once just a fringe codex activist; now the ace closer of Old Atlantic, the biggest star in the whole league. Roslyn's love affair with Sophia had begun long before she had ever laced up a gauntlet. That an old thorn in Londinium's side turned out to be a transcendent Durationist made her a national legend. Yes, *everyone* loved Sophia: the people loved her because she stuck it to the Ownership; the Ownership loved her because she had sway over the people. Now, rumors were rife that Sophia from Belmont Chapel was tabbed to become captain of her own team. Or, perhaps, even more . . .

—*I told you this was gonna happen! They're trying to upstage us! Not again*—

Lucas silenced Gemini with a slight lift of his index finger, his arms still crossed.

—*It doesn't matter. Sophia may be popular, but she has no claim for expansion.*

The claim. Lucas was right, of course. Everyone could talk all they want; Sophia had no claim for the expansion bid. Lucas did. Nothing the league said or did could change that.

So the hell with her, Gemini thought to herself. *Just let us play.*

"It's odd that you're insisting on a more established team to be out here tonight," Lucas said. "If this storm really is defeated, as you insist, then why the concern?"

"We're not fools," Lionel spat, an orange overcast spouting furiously from his pipe. "We're taking necessary precautions. You just said yourself, it's important we beef up the city's affordance. Having a team with the most popular player in the country might be better for morale than you, frankly."

Bion cleared his throat, his finger tapping the center of his necklace quite nervously. "Old Atlantic and Toledo U will rendezvous at the Tower of Allied Nations," he explained, taking a tremulous breath before adding: ". . . along with Tremont United." He coughed and adjusted his thick-rimmed glasses. "Yes, Captain, they're alive."

Gemini felt her heart flood with relief. While Tremont United was in a sense their competition, and while their captain, Ahmed from Pilgrim's Bay, had never given Lucas the time of day, they were still peers, and to hear that the country's number-one team had survived the Blood Poacher's attack was fantastic to hear. She looked to Lucas, eager to enjoy at least one bit of good news with him. But she was surprised to see him simply raise his eyebrow and say nothing.

"Ahmed has just contacted us," Bion continued. "His team had to fall back from the seaport, but they halted the storm's advance and are awaiting reinforcements. Together, they will fend off the storm from hitting the heart of the city."

"*And* they've provided direct observation of the storm's faltering at the city limits," Lionel added with a puff of his pipe, his chin raised. "Ahmed thinks it would be overly aggressive to try to activate either coastal beacon at this point; they're close enough to the storm that leading a mission out to either might give the Blood Poacher the confrontation it wants; it might not be able to take the city, but it still could kill a reckless team that gets too close. Ahmed's decided to let the storm bleed itself out before our affordance while our teams pick off any insurgent Kappos. A wise, measured strategy."

Gemini was surprised at her captain's reaction. He did not seem surprised or happy, nor did he ask how the Reigning Premiere team had managed to escape the Poacher's grasp. Instead he murmured: "Are you sure it was really him?"

"You think we can't recognize his thoughts?" Lionel snapped. "Enough of this. The combined power of our three top clubs, not to mention the other *legitimate* teams defending the outlying boroughs, will drive off this storm. Proper teams, from proper affiliates . . . they have the right to such missions. Not an expansion team from a *false* machifare. If you really are so eager to help out tonight, Captain, why not help defend the fan rally across the bay?"

Lucas raised an eyebrow. "A *fan rally?*" He enunciated his words deliberately; Gemini knew it as a sign that he was restraining his contempt. "Sounds like a nice way to fatten our wrists, but I think I'd rather sit out."

Bion frowned. "Fandom inspires our players in the field, Lucas. You know that."

"Maybe he doesn't know that," Lionel said through gritted teeth, "seeing that he has no fans to speak of."

Lucas laughed. "I do have fans, Steward! Peculiar folk, I admit, who often send me illiterate scoops in the middle of the night, and who show many signs of crashing on stiff fixes . . . but fans nonetheless. I certainly appreciate them enough to *not* put them in harm's way, not even for a cheap cog boost."

Lionel's jaw bulged. The Steward of the Blood Works Society leaned forward in his chair, his image half submerged in the table. The orange smoke erupted from his pipe. It was so thick that Gemini could practically smell it; it was tangy and bitter.

"Don't talk to us like you're so virtuous, Lucas. You think it's selfish for the machifare, for *us*, to put established talent out in front of the Blood Poachers? To place Roslyn's security in the hands of people we know we can trust?" He pointed a finger at him. "As a Steward of the league *you* allegedly serve, do you know what I deem to be selfish? *Your* actions. The Durationist League of Roslyn does not let dropouts back in so easily. Nor do we broker a waste of cogs. Especially from someone who embraces such a *disturbed* view of our nation. You belong on the sidelines while the *real* Durationists do their jobs."

The rain drummed overhead. Gemini's heart was beating fast, faster than it had during the battle just a few minutes ago. She knew the Alumni Circle and Lucas had their differences, but never had she witnessed them openly tear him apart like this before or tersely bring up controversies from his past. She glanced nervously up at her captain, but again he seemed untroubled. A friendly smile cleaved his creased face, his eyes inscrutable, the indigo of his halo-hand hummed crisp as ever.

"Then I suppose your attitude will change, once the Barra acknowledge the Meta-School as a machifare." He clasped his hands in front of him, as if to act graciously. "Is that right?"

Lionel's eyes seemed to focus upon the center of Lucas's gauntlet hand. Like all Durationist gauntlets, it ran the length of his forearm: tight, black mail encased by coils of silver plating, which grew deep and jagged right below the wrist. Over the wrist was his halo: two nonconcentric circles of deep, humming indigo that shone through the metal. What stood out, though, was the coil of metal that bordered the bottom of his halo: it was not silver or black but rather gold, with twin rivets on either side, each decorated with the miniature carving of a ringing bell.

Such a decoration of one's gauntlet—called a token—imbued a person's halo with special cogs that granted that individual abilities far beyond the normal capacities of their halo. The kind of token that Lucas wore was rare, with only a handful known to exist. It carried a deep reservoir of cogs, but it did not brighten his own halo; it did not bolster his abilities, nor did it offer him personal fortune of any sort. Instead, the token amplified his presence on the codex, so that when Gemini closed her eyes, she felt his presence tower over the other souls on the hilltop like a spotlight, and she could see many smaller, teeming lights representing people in the city and across the nation, turning towards him with growing curiosity. A handful of other such beams of light sat across the country, and in their case, tens of thousands of people tightly surrounded them, transfixed by their glow; these bundles represented the machifare. Gemini knew that someday, Lucas too might garner such a following. Such a presence on the codex tethered him to the halos of all those who followed him, so that all their cogs were bound to the success of whatever cause he chaperoned. It was the kind of token that only the Owners of Roslyn's great machifare wore.

Gemini was often impressed by the intensity that token bore; she could practically feel the history of all the great leaders in Roslyn's history who wore it before Lucas. But for just a moment, Lionel seemed at a loss for words, his mouth slightly agape, and Gemini was stunned to see that even the obdurate leader of the Alumni Circle was taken aback by the very sight of a rare Token of Power.

"That's right," he muttered, his eyes still transfixed on the token, his lip curling as if he was disgusted by the sight of Lucas wearing it. "*If* and when that happens, then I will *have* to condone your delusion."

"Then I eagerly await the Stratushold's verdict."

"So do I. Until then, get off the field."

Bion, who had been listening to the exchange with his head bowed uneasily and his mandala pressed against his heart, said in a sad voice, "This is a wasteful argument. We are content with the active teams tonight, Lucas. Your rescue of Black Beach will not go unnoticed, I promise you."

If Lucas was frustrated with their rejection, he was keeping it to himself. He closed his eyes and nodded placidly. Perhaps, Gemini thought, he simply conceded that this night wasn't theirs. She stared hard at the ground and frowned.

"Well," Lionel said gruffly. "If that will be all . . . *we* have work to do."

"Wait a second," Gemini blurted out before she knew what she was doing. "This—this isn't right. We've already helped win the battle. I . . . I . . ."

She froze before Lionel's cold glare.

"Your captain *must* have many valuable things to teach you, amateur," he said in a stony voice. "His impudence is not one of them."

Lucas held his hand out in front of Gemini. "She is just passionate about our cause, Stewards. As am I."

"That is not a sin," Bion said, before Lionel could retort. "That said, our word is final. Return to Bedlam, Lucas. We will speak again after the storm has passed."

Bion and Lionel started to fade away. Gemini wished nothing more than to proclaim how unfair this all was, how they weren't just some conceited experiment, that she and everyone else involved in the Meta-School really believed in Lucas, that Bedlam Athletic would prove them all wrong. But it was not her place to defy the game's all-time greats, and she feared she had already said too much.

Then the two Stewards vanished, and it was just her and Lucas under the awning.

"Captain, I'm sorry I spoke out of turn. I just—"

"It's all right, Gemini." Lucas eyed the northern sky, hands clasped behind his back. He looked pensive. "Why don't you go check on Peppy and Griffin? I'll be over in a bit."

Gemini was about to argue, but she only nodded and said, "Yes, Captain."

She sighed and walked out into the square. Twice she kicked the sparking carcass of a leatherhead to express her frustration.

3. SLEEPER AWAKES

GEMINI SPENT THE next hour running around the deck of an old tanker that was the town's recreation center. A triage had been set up on the deck, and all around her medics were frantically treating patients who had suffered during the cascade, massaging freshly ground ore over their waxing halo-hands and forcing them to swallow vials of potent, bubbling fixes. Gemini did what she could to help out, eager to get her mind off the night's disappointment. She went from table to table, using her abilities with the Icon of *Energy* to try to cauterize scrapes and cuts, searing patients' wounds shut with the gentle heat of her hands. Some victims had gashes far too severe for her to fully heal, so instead while the medics worked she would grab the patient's hand and try to share calming thoughts, for whatever they were worth.

This worked for everyone except a skinny man dressed in a white shirt and jeans, who was screaming and writhing on his table. Medics had to hold him down just to force the fix down his throat. The man seemed particularly enraged when Gemini tried to help, yelling angry, incoherent words at her. The whitecoats suggested she let them take it from there, and so Gemini trudged out onto the ship's stern to commiserate with her teammates.

The northern sky continued to shutter with red light. If Tremont United really had staved off the attack, they certainly hadn't destroyed the Blood Poacher that controlled it. The storm was not over.

Not that her team would help finish the job.

Her wingmates had just finished helping take medical supplies off a truck and were now leaning against the parapet. Peppy and Griffin each wore the same black sweater that Gemini wore under her jacket, replete with the interlocking letters of their squad. Griffin from Mettleburg, their starter at left wing, shook his head as she approached. His wing glider was propped up next to him, freshly stitched from the tears it had incurred during the fight.

"This stinks," he said by way of greeting.

"I know."

"The captain's been in some of the biggest battles in league history. We just saved this town. We earned the right to keep going. They should at least let us hold the damn line."

"I know."

"I figured they'd at least let us stay here," said their striker, Peppy from Toledo Flats. Peppy was sitting atop the parapet with the sleeve of his sweater rolled back, wrapping a bandage over the cut left by a Kappo's knife. His scope shot was propped up next to him. "What exactly did they say, Gem?"

"That we, um, don't deserve to be out here. Sounds like Tremont United is all right and still fighting. Toledo U and Old Atlantic are gonna meet them at Harlo Valley and help finish the storm off. So . . . they don't need us."

"Such bullshit," Griffin muttered.

"Tell me about it," Gemini agreed, plopping down against the railing. She sighed and looked up at Peppy. "How's the arm?"

"Just a scratch," he said, chuckling as he winced. Peppy wore a patch over his left eye, which he had lost in an incident during a scrimmage early on in his career. The accident had impelled him to take up the Icon of *Shapes* as his dedication so that the proximity of things became an instinct for him, making his impaired vision irrelevant. He carried himself with a careless grace, his mouth always edging to a smile. He slapped his fellow winger on the back and said in a self-assured lilt: "Will take more than a couple blighters to beat us, ain't that right, Griff?"

"Such bullshit," Griffin grunted again, shrugging him off.

"Aw, come on, Griff. Don't be so bummed out. We made a nice haul here, didn't we?"

"Who gives a shit about beating leatherheads?" Griffin leered out at the storm with discontent. Jagged bronze armor covered his broad shoulders, what he claimed to be the husk of a Slasher Kappo that he killed in his first field mission. *Tense* was the word that came to mind whenever Gemini thought of Griffin. He was as short as she was but bound with muscle. His square face was so rigid, his jaw tightly clenched so often, that when he first joined the team Gemini was convinced he was unhappy to be there, until he explained to her that his appearance was a lingering side effect from years of taking go-fixes back when he played in the Blood Works Society.

"We should be punching the core. Not Old fucking Atlantic. Us. What would cap off the night better than killing an actual Blood Poacher?" He chuckled humorlessly, and Gemini was certain he was playing out a tired fantasy in his head. "Shit, man. I'd love to knock off one of those fuckers."

Peppy yawned. "I don't think the captain's gonna hand either of us a silver bullet, Griff. You know our motto: cover and defend."

"You *would* say that, Pep. Just cause the captain made me left wing doesn't mean I have no idea how to lead an attack, yeah? I have more experience fighting Kappos than you. Or Gem. Or both of you combined."

"You've never fought a Blood Poacher."

"None of us have besides the captain. Besides, you think you have what it takes, Pep? If you came face-to-face with a Poacher you'd fucking shit yourself."

"Knock it off," Gemini said tiredly. She was in no mood to brook their banter. She took a deep breath. "It doesn't matter now. League Command wants us off the field. That's that."

No one spoke for a few minutes. They listened to the whitecoats scrambling from patient to patient, barking orders and grinding up ore. Someone was still screaming. Gemini thought it might have been the same patient who couldn't stand her. She was too dejected to even lift her head and see.

Griffin shook his head. "I bet you half my halo that this is all about fucking Sophia. The league is trying to give her a damn Theomark moment."

"I think so too," Gemini said. "They basically bent over backwards to make sure Old Atlantic got out here."

Peppy whistled. "You gotta admit, it *would* be pretty awesome to see Sophia take on a storm like this."

"Fuck Sophia," Griffin said. "She's a bitch. My friend from Tremont says Fernando can't stand her. When amateurs ask her for advice she blows them off. A total poser."

"Yeah, but do you know she's so strong with *Light* that she can make the sky go dark? During the Maritimes Derecho, they say she made the sun dance."

"Good for her," Gemini said glumly. Normally Peppy's everlasting cheer lifted her spirits, but not tonight. She rested her head in her hands. "I was just really hoping we could prove everyone wrong tonight . . ."

Purring engines resounded up the hillside. Gemini glanced over her shoulder, through a hole in the parapet. A squad of Durationists dressed in silver-and-white jerseys were riding up the street on mopeds. Gemini recognized them as Metro Reef Watch, county team for the NERVE Company. She supposed they were here to take over the defense of the borough—and to make sure Bedlam Athletic went home.

"Is that Dale's team?" Peppy asked.

"Ah, shit," Griffin said. Growling engines echoing down the street preceded the arrival of their rival peers. The road wound around the shipwrecked hill, cutting between the triage and the bow of the ship where Gemini, Peppy, and Griffin sat. Metro Reef Watch stopped in front of them, kicking up mud and water from the cobblestone street. The splash forced Gemini to her feet.

"Hey, Gem!" shouted Dale from Goethal Heights. The pudgy captain of Metro Reef Watch had a big harp strapped to his back—Gemini had read that using music was the latest fad for Durationists who practiced the Icon of *Word*. Dale was straddling his motorbike alongside his teammates, who were all dressed in white jerseys with silver berets. They were laughing at some unheard joke, undoubtedly made at Bedlam Athletic's expense.

"Where's your captain?" Dale raised his gauntlet hand over his brow and scanned the terrace as if he would find Lucas hiding in plain sight. Gemini knew full well what he was really doing: making sure that she, Peppy, and Griffin noticed the three golden rings that bordered his turquoise halo, a sign of his recent promotion to Duke's Class player.

"You think he's fleeing the country again? Already?"

His teammates sniggered.

"I don't know where he is," Gemini said coldly. She held her gauntlet hand at her hip so Dale could plainly see that she had just one ring around her sunbeam-splashed wrist.

You see? she thought to herself, hoping the defiant stare on her face told him everything he needed to know. *I don't give a shit about what Circle you're in, so why don't you go brag to someone else?*

"Just tell us what you want," she said.

"Before we get onto *real* Durationist stuff, we're supposed to escort you back to the Goethals Bridge."

"We can find our way out, thanks."

"Suit yourself . . . anyway, nice job up here. Since no one else is gonna give you credit, my 'mates and I thought it'd be nice to chip in and give you a reward. Should be enough cogs to pay the tolls back down to that shit hole you call a gym."

Their rival peers started to clap. Gemini, Peppy, and Griffin's halos all shimmered, ever so slightly, in concert with the mocking applause. Gemini's fingers curled as an unpleasant tingle shot up her arm. The scant cogs that Dale and his team had sent their way were cheap and phony, but even if their gratitude had been sincere, she had little interest in accepting them. Impulsively she wagged her hand to shake off the tingling, as if to dislodge unwanted cogs from her halo, and she swatted away their sarcasm with an imaginary flick. The members of Metro Reef Watch jeered and guffawed as Peppy and Griffin also shook their wrists.

"You sure you want to waste those, Gem?" Dale snickered. "That's probably more cogs than you ever saw on the amateur circuit. *Over-Soul* only knows why the Cowl took a liking to you. Guess he wanted the only player he could find worse than him . . ."

Griffin started forward, but Gemini held her arm out in front of him. "Why don't you just get moving?" she said in a testy voice. Her face turned deep red, and she was so pissed off just then that she was somehow not immediately chilled by the bloodcurdling scream from back in the triage. Out of the corner of her eye, she saw a man sit upright as whitecoats struggled to hold him down. It was the same victim she had seen earlier. For some reason, that unsettled her.

"Well," Dale chuckled, "we *do* have an island to defend. But hey! Maybe once your captain splits for Kairos you can join a real squad."

"I wouldn't play with you if you were captain of the last team on earth," Griffin growled.

"I think you'll be begging to join *any* team soon enough. Just a matter of time before that washed-up dropout gets his glove revoked—"

"Watch your mouth," Gemini warned.

"—for good. I'm amazed the Barra let him stay Top Star! Shoulda been bumped down to the Cellar, if you ask me. There's gotta be some justice—"

"I said watch your mouth. Don't talk shit on Lucas. None of us would even be here if it wasn't for Lucas, you got that?"

"Yeah, okay, Gem. Real *hero*, that Lucas. Everyone knows we were better off without that fucking blighter. But shit, if you guys are that desperate—"

Gemini wasn't even aware of getting in Dale's face, but the county captain practically fell off his moped as both she and Griffin started towards him. His harp fell off his back and clattered on the pavement.

"Fuck!" Dale cried. "*Fuck!*"

The other players of Metro Reef Watch got off their bikes, reached for weapons.

At the same time, a pair of redcoats ran into the triage, and for a wild moment Gemini thought they were all about to get thrown out for causing such a ruckus. But instead the cops were moving towards the shouting man's table to try to help the medics restrain him.

Dale was sobbing over his harp. "Look at the strings! Fuck! This was the last Soundwar ever produced! You fuckers! Your blighter captain better pay—"

"Call him that again and you'll be playing a Soundwar out the ass," Griffin growled.

Gemini was no longer paying attention. She saw that the mad patient sat up again, and now his eyes were rolling over. Dark veins ran up his face and arms, except they weren't veins; they were jagged lines, and they etched themselves into his skin like tattoos forming out of nowhere. The bands seemed to converge around his halo, which seemed to be shrinking like a whirlpool of collapsing light.

His eyes clouded, and when Gemini met their gaze, she shivered. It was the same expression she saw in Kappos and any other creature bound to the Echomar . . .

"We can crush you guys," said Metro Reef Watch's closer, Shane from Londinium. "*Both* Dale and I are Duke's Class."

"It's not the amount of cogs," Peppy said. "It's how you use them."

"Maybe, but there's four of us and three of you, so—"

"Watch out!" Gemini cried.

The screaming patient had wrestled himself free of the table. The cops tried to fall on him, but he threw them aside with inexplicable strength. One of the redcoats landed at his feet, and the patient grabbed his gun. His eyes bulged and rolled over white, and his arms went taut with dark winding bands.

"He's a Thrall!" Griffin shouted.

The pistol, transformed by dark thought, shook with steam and sparks as the patient raised it at the Durationists. His body started to recoil as he squeezed the trigger, as if his own life force was about to be sucked through the barrel of the gun—

He howled as the tin shot was knocked out of his hands. Gemini caught her flying sickle on the rebound. The Durationists swiftly worked in tandem. Peppy and Lucy from New Bronx kept their rifles pointed at the patient, who snarled and collapsed to his knees as Karla from Judas Beach stretched out his hands, willing every nerve and fiber in the man's legs to weaken through the Icon of *Blood*. Griffin spiked the floor with his zero-iron and webs of thick frost conjured around the patient's feet and ankles. Gemini and Shane from Londinium cautiously approached, sickle and sword drawn. Meanwhile Dale blinked in confusion, as if grieving over his broken harp had made him oblivious to the events of the past few seconds.

The Thrall had no chance against *seven* Durationists, and even he seemed to realize this. His inroad lines were ablaze, shrinking and constricting his skin till it turned hot red. Ghastly smoke rose out of his mouth. Gemini walked up to him, kreisflyer held over her shoulder, but she halted as the patient clutched at his head and started to scream.

"*Vlaz Echomar!*" the man howled. "*Vlaz Echomar! Vlaz Echomar!*"

His whole body quavered with scarlet smoke, and the ground beneath his knees started to crack.

"*Vlaz Echomar! Vlaz Echomar! Death to Roslyn!*"

His shirt tore open, and Gemini's eyes widened in realization as she saw throbbing, translucent red rock protruding out of his chest, right over his heart, searing inroad lines dispersing from it like rivers of lava, and she felt a rush of horror as she realized what was about to happen . . .

"Move!" she cried desperately, waving at the other players, the whitecoats, and the patients. "Everybody, mo—"

The man froze, rooted on the spot. The smoke rushed back into his body. The pulsing rock at his chest darkened. He gasped, then fell to the floor in spasms.

"*Get back.*"

Everyone obeyed Lucas's command. His gauntlet hand was raised as he knelt over the would-be shooter. A whitecoat holding a vial of ground ore took a tepid step forward, but Lucas raised his hand.

"That will not help."

He placed his hand over the man's forehead and minded with him. The stricken twitched and gasped, but he did not try to get free. Nobody moved. The medics, redcoats, and other Durationists watched breathlessly. The sky rumbled.

Gemini felt a chill go down her spine, and she turned to see that the White Eyes of the Blood Poacher had reappeared over the sound. Shane from Londinium pointed and exclaimed, "*Oh, shit!*" His teammates turned and gasped.

Lucas lifted his head and met the Poacher's gaze. The White Eyes leered at him until they receded behind clouds. Thunder echoed across the island.

The minding with Lucas seemed to have given the man a surcease. His muscles slackened. The inroad lines on his arms faded away, and the growth on his chest fizzled into steam and vanished. His eyes were closed. It looked like he had fallen asleep.

"His mind is severely broken," Lucas told the stunned medics. "But he could still be saved if he's taken to asylum immediately. Do you have a warp point set up?"

"We tried setting it up across the square," one of the whitecoats said uncertainly. "But the storm's screwing with our mind box's power. It's not strong enough to get him across the bay."

"Contact the Courier. He'll know how to boost the signal. Have him cribbed directly to Hoboken Medical. Get him out of here, now."

The whitecoats hastily placed the stricken onto a stretcher and carried him away.

Metro Reef Watch gave Lucas an exceptionally wide berth as he approached.

"Well, uh, Captain," Dale stammered. "I guess we owe—"

"Move on to whatever task the league has assigned you," Lucas said pleasantly. His hands were clasped behind his back, boundless eyes trained on his own teammates. Or perhaps, Gemini thought, the skies beyond.

"I want to speak to my team alone."

4. Captain's Plan

"I'VE NEVER SEEN SOMEBODY snap like that...."

"Tonight's cascade certainly broke him. But his soul had probably been poisoned for a long time. Sometimes people who have become susceptible to the gradual pull of dark thought don't crack until they hear the thunder."

Lucas tugged at his beard as he paced back and forth. Behind him, the beacon of the distant lighthouse had broken through the storm, intermittently bathing the captain's spare frame in buttery light. The haze parted to the north, where the lurid skyline of Metro Reef stabbed furiously at the halting clouds, a cavalry of thick yellow spotlights, neon glare and jutting skyscrapers that crashed through the graphite swirls.

"When I glimpsed into the poor fellow's despair, I saw the madness of those who had infected him, and in turn others he had infected. I glimpsed the shadow of other Thrall out there, who are bound to this storm."

"What do you mean?" Griffin asked. "That there's more blighters we gotta worry about?"

Red-and-blue lights whirled through the streets of Black Beach, sirens shrieking in the mists.

"There are no doubt thousands of Sleeper Thrall living in Roslyn. Even in its heyday, the Sky Watch could not possibly keep track of them all. In the past fifty seasons, our abilities to keep tabs on Bounders who live furtively among us have waned considerably. That costs us dearly on a night like tonight. For those with forged halos on their wrists, and false cogs in their hearts, their true faces only show during a Poacher Storm. Heretofore they do all they can to underwrite the spread of dark thought in the hearts and minds of their friends and coworkers, or strangers on the codex, in order to rot Roslyn from within, so that the Echomar can gnaw away at us from without."

"If there's more blighters causing trouble, let's stop them," Griffin said.

"Low-level, middling Thrall like the one we just subdued will simply try to harm whoever they can through violence and dark thought—even if it means annihilating themselves and everyone in their wake. Groups of Thrall will attempt more sophisticated forms of tribute to the Blood Poachers, such as sadistic games or ritual killings.

"However. I am not talking about a low-level Thrall. The Bounder I glimpsed cast a big shadow under tonight's storm. In other words, it was someone embedded high within the machifare, and whoever it is, they are now here in Metro Reef."

The sirens danced around the hill. Lucas stood still as his teammates slowly comprehended what he was saying, the golden halo of light periodically engulfing him. Gemini, sitting against the parapet, shook her head in disbelief.

"A Sleeper *high up?* Like some affordaire, an exec or something?"

"Maybe. It is ... difficult ... to peer very far into the Void. Even someone versed in the ways of Sky Watch like myself can handle only so much. As you navigate the dark thoughts that stain the codex, you must be quick to jump from one tainted soul to the next, never lingering on one mind for too long, for if you do, you too may *feel* the bonds that enthrall them, that tether them to the heart of the Echomar in Vlaz Gal. But I did see one clue."

"What was it?"

"... A silver-and-black glove."

The northern sky flickered, and the spotlights over the city crisscrossed one another, as if to parry a blow.

Gemini, Griffin, and Peppy were equally incredulous.

"No way," Peppy said.

"That's insane," Griffin agreed. "A Durationist can't become a blighter. It's impossible."

"It has happened before, though rarely, and the league seldom speaks of such cases. But I am certain that is what I saw."

"I could see if it was an amateur," Gemini said hesitantly. *Like me.* "But you think it was, ah, a high-profile player?"

"Yes. I have no doubt."

Gemini did not respond, because suddenly, out of nowhere, she remembered the dream she had last night, the one that had awoken her, breathless and in a cold sweat.

She was wearing a silver-and-black glove . . .

A sudden gust brought the pungent odor of the bitter, salty sea.

"I don't believe it," Griffin was saying.

"There are other reasons to suspect it *is* a Durationist," Lucas said. Gemini realized she must have looked distressed, because he was staring right at her, so she hastily tried to compose herself.

I'll tell him later, she thought. *Maybe. If there's time.*

"But for the moment, let's assume it isn't one of us," Lucas continued, still watching her curiously. "The point remains: someone here in Metro Reef with *a lot* of cogs to their name is a Thrall, and whoever it is, they are affecting the city in a way that someone like the Sleeper we encountered here never could."

Thunder murmured across the sound.

"If our suspect is an affordaire, for instance, he or she won't be merely spreading dark thought around their colleagues. No, those bonds will seep down into the lower rings, into tens of thousands of people. It has a devastating effect. One which League Command cannot account for, and which confirms my fear that they have completely underestimated this storm."

The crumpled peelings of a billboard started to tremble.

"What do you mean?" Gemini asked.

Lucas resumed pacing. He started talking fast, the way he always spoke when an idea arrested him. It reminded Gemini of the frantic ruffling of old parchment paper.

"Tremont United did *not* delay the attack. The Blood Poachers are dividing their forces to confuse us: a front of weak bands are assaulting the outer boroughs, like the storm we just disrupted."

"Weak?" Griffin laughed. "You call what just happened here weak?"

"Compared to what the rest of this system is capable of, yes. What we saw here was nothing but shock and awe, and unfortunately, it has completely fooled the league. These outlying bands are a ruse, a distraction to keep us occupied from the brunt of the Poacher's wrath."

Gemini frowned. "Lionel *was* right, though: all the cells look the same on radar. It's a big disturbance, but I don't see anything that looks peculiar . . ."

"Ignore the radar. The signs are in the sky. There is a wickedness to those thunderheads. You can feel how restless the air is, like the wind itself is retreating from the city. The temperature is dropping, the pressure is crashing: a dark precursor of something to come. Thanks to what I saw in the Thrall, I am able to project what those portents might be."

He raised his gauntlet hand before him, and he and his team imagined a map of Metro Reef floating over his palm. The crescent of five islands was stained by green and yellow blotches that seemed to be spreading out from one another in slow motion, as if they had once been whole but had broken apart; buried within the flurry of diminishing storms was an ugly, crimson whorl that looked like a flaming buzz saw. The coral metropolis at the heart of the five islands, as well as the slums uptown, disappeared beneath swirling, burgundy stains.

"Are you sure about this, Captain?" Peppy squinted at the northern sky. "I don't see anything that well organized."

"The precipitation from the weaker cells is enough to obstruct even your unparalleled vision, Peppy. Trust me: that anvil is glowering over the sound. It will escape Commonwealth Services' detection until it is too late. The supercell will cut Toledo U off from its rendezvous with Old Atlantic. Without the help of Toledo U, Old Atlantic will be overwhelmed, and the Poacher will cleave through what it has judged to be a fault line in the heart of the city."

As he spoke, the miniature he had imagined before them became riddled with wounds: a lone, needle-shaped skyscraper at the northeast end of the city, which Gemini recognized to be the Tower of Allied Nations, flashed red, as did the scores of apartment towers and shipwrecked slums that filled the strath separating the northern boroughs.

The thunder clapped louder now, and the spotlights over the skyline started to blink. Neon signs went dark.

"The Courier has tipped us off. The ambassadors to the AN were meeting with several of the NERVE Company's wealthiest affordaires at the TAN building uptown. The storm has trapped them there and knocked out their warp point. Old Atlantic is charged with rescuing them, but I fear the severity of the storm will prevent them from doing so . . ."

"One of those high-necks might be our Sleeper," Griffin said.

"Possibly. Which would make a bad situation even worse. Those affordaire affirm much of Metro Reef's total cogs. Their deaths would shatter the city's affordance."

"Not only would a ton of people here be at risk," Gemini thought aloud, "but so would *anyone* across the country who belong to NERVE Co."

"Correct. And just as important for the fate of Metro Reef is preventing wanton destruction of Harlo Valley. I'm betting a lot of Cellar Folk are trapped there. Two hundred thousand, perhaps more. The Blood Poachers must see that as an easy harvest. Their overall plan is obvious: they are trying to deal as much damage to us as possible, first by suckering our three best teams—assuming Tremont United *is* still going, that is—into a trap. Then their forces will try to overwhelm our peers before finishing off the trapped affordaires and plunging the Cellar dwellers of Harlo Valley into floods and fire."

Lightning flashed over the skyline. One by one, lights disappeared. The lighthouse beacon seemed to shudder as it revolved past.

Griffin furrowed his brow. "I don't get it, though. Tremont United has taken down Poacher Storms before. Same for Toledo U. Even if this storm is stronger than we thought, it's not exactly like we're going up against the Dixie Typhoon. Why are the Poachers so confident they can handle *both* Premiere teams *and* Old Atlantic?"

"Well," Lucas said calmly, "for starters, I am certain that Tremont United *did* lose at the seaport."

A tense silence ensued, broken by someone downhill, who was shouting either in relief or anguish.

"But . . . Bion and Lionel said they survived," Gemini said. "They said they spoke to Ahmed, remember?"

"I know," Lucas said. "But from the start, I was skeptical that Tremont United could have survived punching the core; the attack on their position seemed so savage. It was one of the most violent displays of red lightning I have ever seen! I do not see how anyone, even a Durationist, could have survived.

"Still, let's assume they somehow made it. I have talked shop with Ahmed before. The man is no fool; he understands the nuance of storm hunting. I am confident he would agree that league command is wrong on this, that this storm is just beginning to coalesce. He would be emboldened to activate the storm shields uptown, not just withdraw and wait. So why make such a bad mistake? Meanwhile, we know there may be a Sleeper among our ranks . . ."

The fraught pause froze out the cries below and thunder beyond. Gemini, Peppy, and Griffin stared at their captain in astonishment. What Lucas was suggesting was borderline insane, even to them. And yet . . .

"Are you *actually* saying"—the outrage in Griffin's voice perfectly expressed what his teammates felt—"are you actually saying the Sleeper is someone on *Tremont United*?"

Lucas shrugged. "It could be. It could also be a player from one of the other high-ranked teams out here tonight, though that would not explain Tremont United's curious survival. I can only tell you what I see *now*: a storm we are underestimating, a team that should be dead, and a Sleeper whose presence opened the gates of the city to the storm. But there's more . . ."

He suddenly looked very distant. "I must confess, I have some hard evidence too. While analyzing the storm a few minutes ago, not a moment before I sensed the presence of a Sleeper up here, I was minded by Elizabeth from Ogunquit."

Gemini gasped. Elizabeth from Ogunquit was the closer for Tremont United. A league Steward, she was one of the few members of the Alumni Circle who was friendly with Lucas. Gemini had met her once, when she visited the Meta-School just after it opened. Gemini had been intimidated to meet a Premiere League player face-to-face, but Elizabeth had turned out to be really nice, and she was kind enough to give Gemini a whole gym session just to help hone her techniques.

"What did she say?" Gemini asked. "Did she say anything about the Sleeper?"

Lucas sighed, the weak light from the sound briefly illuminating his face. For the first time that night, he looked genuinely worried.

"No. It was a very weak scoop, but I am certain I know what she was thinking: *We've fallen. It's making landfall.*"

Gemini was aghast. "No one else heard her?"

"The Blood Poacher is swallowing up all our thoughts; the storm itself is completely disabling the codex here. All of our minds are caught in the fog. I only heard Liz because of our friendship, and—not to congratulate myself for my grim prognosis, but—also because I was the only one bothering to look for these kinds of omens. The codex will show you only what you're willing to see, as the Courier so often reminds us. But again, even if I hadn't heard from Liz, the volley of red bolts that we witnessed assail Tremont United were of such devastating magnitude I'm not sure even our most advanced meditation techniques would protect us."

Thunder crackled eagerly.

"How could they have gotten that strong?" Peppy asked.

"I do not know. No one thought the Blood Poachers were powerful enough to attack us here, in one of Roslyn's most vibrant cities. Yet here they are. It stands to reason they have mastered capabilities we cannot even begin to imagine."

"Like what?"

"I'm not sure." Lucas closed his hand, and the map disappeared. "But *that* is why I am not surprised if the traitor is in fact one of us. The signs are in the sky. This is no ordinary storm. And the league is walking right into a trap."

The tense silence resumed. The shouting downhill turned to sobs.

"We have to warn other teams," Peppy finally said. "Get more squads out here."

Lucas shook his head absently. "I already tried to warn Kip and Fernando, but both, unsurprisingly, have ignored me. Ditto for League Command. Or perhaps the storm is so strong that our scoops can't break through. Either way, you are right: our peers will need help. And they must be warned of this Sleeper Thrall. So . . . at least there's good news."

Gemini raised an eyebrow. "There's good news?"

"Of course there is," Lucas laughed. "We have work to do! The Blood Poachers' main thrust is concentrated uptown. They have ignored downtown Metro Reef City; in theory, a team coming from the south could slip behind their assault undetected and catch off guard the Kappo hordes that will soon be dropping from the sky. As luck would have it, *we* are the team best positioned to do this. If we can break up that Poacher's army—if we shake the spider's web, as it were—we can give the poor people trapped uptown more time to evacuate, and us and the other teams more time to fend off the attack."

"Are you sure one club is gonna make a difference?" Peppy asked. "I want to get out there as much as the rest of us, but if the top three teams in the league aren't enough against this thing . . . maybe we should see if Richie's team can get up here to back us up?"

"There is no time to wait for our other squads; in any event, their inclusion in the field would be deemed even more illegal than our own activity. Besides, it will work to our advantage, I think, to travel light in numbers. The Blood Poacher lost track of us the moment we severed its connection to the cell here on Bethpage, like lopping a tentacle off a Maradu squid. Now its Eyes are focused on the high-profile teams headed its way. The lower the amount of cogs, the less likely it is to see our advance."

Gemini got to her feet. "So wait a second. This whole time you suspected the storm was a lot worse than Londinium was making it out to be, right?"

"From the moment I saw the sky."

"So you never *really* planned on leaving the field?"

"Of course not."

"But if this was your plan the whole time, why did you tell Bion and Lionel we'd stand down?"

There were flecks of mischief in Lucas's abyssal eyes, as if he was greatly amused by a joke he thought too complicated to explain. "Zeno once told me to never be a martyr for a worthless cause. Debating with our Alumni Circle tends to be just that. I should add that, in league tradition, there is no greater way of validating an expansion team's worth than turning the tides in a battle. That, my friends, is the opportunity before us tonight. But to do that, we must get to the city quickly."

"Okay . . ." Gemini said. "But how? All the roads are flooded."

"Indeed. Nor will the skies"—he gestured to Griffin's glider—"be safe for anything long-distance."

"So what do we do?"

"Well, the train station is right down the road . . ."

Griffin looked dumbfounded. "Captain, do you really think the trains are running at a time like this?"

"No, Griffin," Lucas laughed. "I do not have that much faith in the local infrastructure. But the sky-class trains work partially out-of-step. They should run just fine in these conditions."

Gemini and the wingers exchanged perplexed looks. While riding a train that warped itself out of existence between stops would certainly protect them from the weather, there was a problem with simply getting on board such a privileged form of transportation. "Captain, even if they're running, none of us can afford to ride sky-class. Can you?"

"Nope," Lucas said cheerfully. "But there are ways around that."

"How?"

"Follow me."

He waved his hand, and a pair of silver mopeds and a black ATV appeared on the street. Another wave and Griffin's glider flickered out of existence, then returned in pristine condition, all the tears gone.

This was nothing unusual: Lucas was their captain, and thus it was his responsibility to hold all their field equipment out-of-step. It was also not unusual for him to hop onto his ATV and immediately drive away, simply assuming they would follow, but this was admittedly a bit more bemusing. Gemini and the two wingers again exchanged puzzled looks before she and Peppy got on their motorbikes and zipped away. She looked in her rearview mirror and saw Griffin sling himself into his glider and start to run after them, right before he jumped into the air, and she felt a rush of wind as he soared over their heads. Together, the three teammates followed their captain down the zigzagging road that led down the hill, passing medics and cops still searching for anyone who had been stricken during the cascade.

As she rode, Gemini looked ahead. Lucas's path took Bedlam Athletic northward towards the shoreline, and from their viewpoint they could still see the entire panorama of Metro Reef. The coral skyline was almost entirely without power so that it resembled a field of colossal tombstones in the shade of the storm; further north, the suspension towers of a freeway wound over gloomy slums that were mottled by trails of smoke from fires that had broken out in the streets. Just off the coast was the rolling beam of Grant's Lighthouse, but the ray from the seaport's ancient beacon was dulled by the towering thunderhead rolling over the water, a coal-colored mountain flickering and pulsing with veins of lightning; a moment later a cloudburst engulfed the beam once more, and its rays no longer reached across the sound. Gemini frowned. Lucas's forecast was playing out before their eyes.

There was a low howl. Plummeting winds descended upon Black Beach, and Gemini found herself squinting through harsh gales. Windows rattled and streetlights wobbled. Griffin hovered unevenly overhead, and Gemini and Peppy struggled to stay straight.

Their captain continued on untroubled. About halfway down the hill, he scooped them.

—*Let's see if our ghost in the codex can help us out . . . Courier, do you think you could do us a favor?*

Something stirred in the darkness above. Blotches of deep mauve smoke and flashes of yellow light spread across the sky over the street. Peppy and Griffin reached for their weapons, but Gemini scooped them, —*It's okay! It's just the Courier.*

All four of them minded the Courier's response.

—*Good to hear from you, Captain. Hope your crew is faring well. What can I do for you?*

—*Courier, I need you to check if there are any sky-class trains at Black Beach station. Think you can do that?*

The amethyst cloud rumbled.

—*Certainly. Hold on one minute.*

Gemini was always impressed by the strength of the Courier's thoughts. Maybe even a little intimidated. But she didn't have time to mull over whatever he and her captain were discussing at present. The wind had grown so strong that she, Peppy, and Griffin found themselves weaving clumsily against it, their arms and legs nicked by hurtling twigs, rocks, and pieces of debris from buildings that had been damaged earlier in the attack.

The smoke rippled. —*Yes, Captain. There is one train in reserve. It's normally reserved for NERVE Company affordaires. I am assuming you want me to lift the restrictions . . .*

—*Please.*

Griffin fluttered close to Gemini as they both struggled to push against the wind.

"Whatever it is they have in mind," he said, "they better hurry up."

A minute later they arrived at Black Beach Station. Gemini and Peppy skidded to a stop, while Griffin was nearly blown off the platform before he managed to touch down. The gales were so fierce that the three of them had to cringe just to stay on their feet.

Lucas waved his hand, and all four vehicles vanished. He stood perfectly straight as he said: "Courier, is our train ready?"

Paper peeled straight off a billboard. Lamps swayed dangerously.

"What train?" Griffin shouted over the wailing gusts. "What the hell are they talking about?"

—*Yes. It's at platform two. You'll have to activate it yourself, but once you get moving, the train's mind box is programmed to take you where you want to go and back out-of-step.*

"Perfect." Lucas took a step towards the tracks, reaching over his shoulder for the hilt of his sword. "How much time do you think we have?"

Lightning flashed. A piece of wood flew past Gemini's face.

—*Toledo U and their company are about to engage the cell on the south side of New Bronx. Old Atlantic is entering the city now; they will reach the Tower of Allied Nations in about seventeen minutes, but I fear the southern cell will cut them off.*

"Have you tried to warn the other teams what they're walking into? I can't reach them . . ."

—*Neither can I. The storm seems to be disrupting the codex entirely.*

Thunder rumbled. Deep, reverberating gunfire resounded somewhere very far off.

"How long is our ride?"

—*Twenty minutes. Unfortunately, the south cell will beat you to the city.*

"We'll manage." Lucas drew his sword, the zeitblatt. He held the bare, black blade in both hands. The coruscating patterns along his gauntlet pulsed with a crisp indigo gleam, and the sword thrummed with the same deep hue.

"Captain?" Gemini said, nearly stumbling over. "What is going—"

Lucas cut at the air with a simple, diagonal swipe.

Even now, Gemini had never gotten used to seeing the folds within reality being exposed, and Lucas's slagging filled her eyes with total disbelief. There was a snipping sound, like the cutting of paper, and it was as if the very space before them began to ripple and peel back, like curtains parting on a stage. First they could only see the glimmer of metal . . . then windows, then an entire cabin.

The wind, as if abashed for daring to interrupt Lucas's performance, abruptly and instantly died.

"I'll be damned," said Griffin, sighing in relief.

Lucas withdrew his sword. A two-car Sky-Line train sat at the platform, lights blinking, engine buzzing.

Thunder murmured again, unimpressed.

The purple clouds pulsed over the station.

—*I've directed the train's mind box to take you directly to Upper East Side Station. If you evoke the radar, you will observe that there are several heavy bands along the route, but since you're on the skyrail, that shouldn't be a problem for you. I recommend making your presence as light as possible. If the Blood Poacher notices you, I cannot guarantee your safe passage . . .*

"We will be careful. Thank you, old friend."

—*My pleasure, Captain. I just hope the league gives you the credit you deserve for once. I would not have blamed you if you did not even try to warn Kip or Fernando what they are walking into . . .*

Lucas smiled. "When cities are in flames and folks are being butchered by Kappos, somehow gamesmanship just doesn't seem all that ethical to me. Saving the city is paramount."

—*You are a more noble man than I, Captain.*

"Only because you aren't a man, Courier."

—*Good luck. Be careful.*

The minding ended. The purple clouds dissolved.

Lucas turned to his three teammates. "I should acknowledge that this is going to be more difficult than anything any of you have ever encountered. I am asking quite a lot of you. Should any of you object—"

"Fuck no," Griffin said.

"We've come too far to turn back now," Peppy agreed.

Gemini smiled, despite feeling more apprehensive than she ever had in her whole career.

"We're with you," she managed to say.

Lucas laughed. "I shouldn't have doubted. Good! You three are the best talent our new machifare has to offer. There is no doubt that tonight's attack is going to start an Open Season. Let's see to it that Bedlam Athletic 750 goes into the new year with a victory."

Open Season. Gemini knew the enormity of those words, the upheaval that they would bring. She could barely remember the last one she lived through, about fifty years ago. She showed up to work one day to find out that she had been laid off, and so had the rest of her coworkers; the minor affiliate they had been part of, the Peoples' Party of Bedlam, had ceased to exist, and the next thing Gemini knew she was scrambling across the country to find work. Eventually she managed to nab an office job within the Cog Mind—miraculously something of a promotion compared to her previous gig, since the Cog Mind was one of the five major machifare—and she held onto that new stint like she was clutching a branch hanging over a raging river. The fact the Cog Mind had their own Durationist corps was also a blessing, since it allowed Gemini to stoke her latent dream of someday donning the silver-and-black glove. Still, it had been a very stressful time, and she relaxed only when the shuffling in Londinium had been complete.

The memory of such chaotic times made her stomach churn. But now Gemini would experience the Open Season in a very different way: as a Durationist. The Open Season was the opportunity Lucas had long been planning for, when he could prove the Meta-School's worth and get them a permanent seat in Londinium. This was their chance, just like tonight was their chance to immediately prove their worth as a team. Her heart beat a little faster.

"Now," Lucas said. "It's better if we don't travel as four; it gives our occupation away too easily, I think. Gemini, you will stay out here with me. Griffin and Peppy, I am going to hold you out-of-step until we get into the field. Peppy, this will help heal your arm faster."

"Sounds all right by me," said Peppy, rubbing his bandaged arm. Griffin nodded without complaint. Gemini was grateful for that. She wouldn't blame him if he felt slighted by Lucas's decision. After all, he was a veteran player, Duke's Class, second only to Lucas himself in terms of experience. But Gemini always performed the best in their gym's scrimmages; more importantly, she was the team closer, and in traditional formations it was the closer who acted as the center's second-in-command. It was a role Gemini took great pride in. She hoped she could live up to it tonight.

"It's possible we may arrive in the midst of battle," Lucas told the wingers. "Stay sharp and wait for my instructions. And stay in formation unless I say otherwise. We can't afford any freelancing on this mission."

He waved his hand, and Peppy and Griffin froze. Their outlines flashed and faded, like traces of light that linger when you close your eyes. Gemini blinked, and her wingmates were gone. It was like they had never been there.

Lucas turned and beckoned. "All right, let's see if we can get this train to be locomotive."

5. Doom Ship

LIZ WAS NOT AFRAID to die.

No true Durationist was. Especially not a Premiere League player, an active member of the Alumni Circle, and the closer for the league's Reigning club, Tremont United. In her six hundred seasons of play, Elizabeth from Ogunquit had taken part in some of the DLR's biggest battles, including *both* sieges on the Theomark and the Dixie Typhoon of 401 CE. She had faced off with more Blood Poachers than any other active Durationist, and outside of Bion and Lionel, no player had vanquished more storms than her. No, it wasn't death that Liz feared. A Durationist accepted long ago that their fold of Duration would someday cease to be. If that end came in the line of duty, all the better. That was an honor.

What Liz feared most was failing to serve her country.

Killer Fives knew that. A Blood Poacher always knew what scared its prey the most. So it did not kill her, did not dismember her piece by piece, thought by thought, like it had done to her teammates, who had also been betrayed. Instead, the Blood Poacher had filled Liz's mind with just enough dark thought, just enough realization of her worst fears, to render her unconscious. She knew only blackness after that, until she became dimly aware of the rough mists stinging her face and a howling wind popping her ears.

She was shackled and bound to a metal pole. Immediately she fought to wriggle free; but these were no ordinary chains, and whatever material they were made out of singed her wrists and ankles with each movement she made.

Slowly, she opened her eyes. She was on a long and lonely highway that stretched out into bloodshot skies between rolling layers of lava-scorched clouds that spanned the world above and below. Her first guess was that she was somewhere along the Harlo Freeway, since the road was high enough for low-hanging clouds to roll beneath its overpass. She thought she could discern the outline of the colossal suspension towers that rose from the very center of the freeway, maybe a mile away. Lightning lashed at the towers, and the whole road seemed to rock from the whistling gusts.

That was when Liz realized she was not alone: dozens of people dashed across the street, taking cover inside stranded cars or hanging onto guardrails on either side of the freeway. A deep buzzing noise reverberated under the road, shaking the column she was bound to. Was it the storm? Was a twister approaching? She had to do something.

"I can help you," she called to the people scurrying about. "Stop and let me—"

No. She had it all wrong. She was seeing what she wanted to see.

Liz blinked and saw that there was no road, just a long, obsidian slate that sliced stealthily through the red sky. The were no streetlights, but instead rows of sleek cannons, pointed upright like jagged teeth. The great suspension towers were in fact tremendous lightning rods, and with each strike of thunder, there was the leaden thrum of a terrible engine, somewhere far below. Liz realized in disbelief that they were not rocking in the wind; instead they were hovering right in the core of the storm! The stranded drivers too had been a hopeful fabrication: instead of cars, rows of flatbed airboats sat with their rear propellers idling, waiting for deployment, while dozens of ragged Kappos, helmets flapping stupidly atop their stitched, grinning faces, gamboled across the deck of the great Echomar warship, the most dangerous of its kind.

A Doom Ship: the class of Thunder Nation vessel commanded by a Blood Poacher.

—*Killing* you *would have been* humane, *Durationist. But* that *is not our way.*

The shrill, icy voice jammed itself into her head, a knife taken to her skull, so harsh and grating that Liz threw her head back and groaned from the pain. At that same moment the skies lit up, and through half-open eyes she saw the specter of monstrous, wicked wings that eclipsed the entire horizon, wings wider than the length of the ship itself—a ship she had mistaken for a highway. A ghastly glow reflected off the sable deck, and just that mere trace of the White Eyes' reflection was enough to make the hairs rise on the back of Liz's neck.

It was right behind her. She could *feel* it.

—*Your teammates were* spares. *We only needed* one *of you.* One *Durationist is worth a* thousand *cheap lives. A Premiere League player, ten thousand lives. Your* fascist psychic masters *will give anything to reclaim you. But first you will become a witness to our power.*

With each thought the Blood Poacher forced into her, her carmine-colored halo flickered and waned. Every word was laden with pain and despair: pain from the thunderbolts clanging in her head, despair from the memories unwittingly dredged from the ether of her mind. She saw some of her worst defeats, vividly bethought the loss of her teammates, how Benjamin and Kim had died in the maw of their enemy. A future occurred to her, the bleakest future possible, where she would die: her *islamor* was widowed, and the league remained ignorant over how dangerous the Echomar had become. Liz tried to shut it out, tried to defy the Poacher's wrath and declare she would not play the hostage game. But a fiery ice was running down her spine, coursing through her veins, numbing her senses and setting her body aflame, so that hopelessness fell over her like a heavy fatigue and urged her to just give up. Her halo grew dim and cool.

Just as her vision darkened and the world seemed to fade, something horrible snapped her back to life. A cold, slimy rope ran down the side of her face and neck, chilly yet electrifying, scaly and pulsing. What felt like a massive scythe grazed her ankles, and a thorny snake seemed to constrict across her back.

One of the Poacher's tails.

—*You cannot* die *yet,* Steward.

So repulsed was Liz that she did not immediately notice the man standing in front of her. The Thrall was in horrible shape, with inroad lines cutting so deep into his skin he looked blanched from all the bleeding. His grizzly hair was missing chunks across his skull; his eyes were sunk so deep into his face that they might have been vacant holes. He wore grimy rags, and chains were shackled to his ankles and arms.

"Commander," the Thrall whimpered. "A Durationist company led by Toledo U is approaching from the north. Just as you predicted, a Duke's League team is also approaching from Bedlam."

—Good. Concentrate starboard fire on the company in the north. Port cannons, attack the Tower of Allied Nations. We will kill the cog-addicted fascists *who live there, as well as* Old Atlantic *when they try to rescue them. Send out the hordes.*

The Thrall nodded meekly, then scurried out of sight.

A terrible, guttural screech resounded over Liz's head. Rook Kappos yelped and barked at one another, jostling up into seats before the upright cannons adorning the deck. They punched a series of buttons and the turrets swiveled downward to face the earth. Dozens of other leatherheads, as well as larger, armored Slasher Kappos, leaped onto the airboats as the huge turbine engines begin to whine.

—Mind the Void, Durationist. Death to your teammates . . . death to Metro Reef *. . . death to* Roslyn*!*

Another earsplitting screech. Lightning struck the dual towers at the ship's center. The sky lit up, and Liz again saw the shadow of spiked wings blot out the world. The Kappos helming the guns yelped and fired.

Endless volleys of crimson flames launched from the cannons on the ship's starboard side, streaking northward like molten comets to pummel the city. Airboats took off, falling beneath the clouds under the Doom Ship to drop infantry on the besieged Durationists below. The clouds above and below roiled faster and faster. Bloody lightning caught between the twin towers, where it seemed to sparkle like scarlet starbursts before it ricocheted down towards the earth with a deafening roar, punctuated only by the mad giggling of the Kappos firing away.

Liz felt the spiked tail drift away from her, and then twilight briefly befell her as the Blood Poacher flew away to circle over the north. She could not see the Poacher through the cloud ceiling, just five barbed tails dangling through the haze like hellish wind chimes. But she saw the shadow on the fog below, saw the outline of horned wings contract, then swing open.

There was a blinding crash, thunder so loud that it might have split her head open. Five bolts of frayed lightning flung towards the earth, and somewhere far below was the muffled crack of an explosion.

Liz closed her eyes. It was madness, pure madness. She had to warn the league about their enemies' powers, about how her team had met its end. Whatever strength she had left, she would dedicate it to that task or die trying.

A small, white capsule materialized between her teeth. Any player raised in the traditions of the Blood Works Society knew what this fix was. The white pill provided a pure rush of cogs so intense it would kill most people who tried to use it. Even a Durationist was advised only to use it in the utmost vital moments of a battle, when they were already pushing their minds and bodies to their very limits, such as when one was battling a Blood Poacher. So valuable and dangerous was the white pill that few Durationists of her machifare had ever been chosen to carry it. Liz always kept hers completely hidden, out-of-step, and only through her own sheer will had she been able to keep it secret during the Blood Poacher's torture, so that it did not discover it. She had focused obsessively on her memory of the pill, trying her best not to forget what it looked like while she had been in agony, or else it would have slipped from her mind and fallen completely out of existence.

Liz wouldn't be using the pill to fight Killer Fives. But she could use it to gain enough strength to escape and warn her friends. That was all that mattered to her.

She bit down on the capsule and swallowed the hot, peppery vapor within it. Immediately, a throbbing pulse like an electric shock rushed through her. She strained forward, struggling to catch her breath. Her heart rammed against her chest, and her arms and legs went rigid. She suddenly saw a dozen colors she never knew existed, heard the angry sea a thousand feet below. Her halo glowed like the ring of a fiery eclipse.

Something poked her roughly in the side. It was a Rook Kappo holding a pike. It gave a stilted laugh.

Liz balled her hands into fists, stretched out her arms. The red shackles still singed her terribly, but she was numb to it now, as if her pain suddenly no longer mattered to her. Her rose-colored halo shone through her gauntlet, matching the hue of the world around her. The Kappo, oblivious, giggled on and jabbed her again.

Fresh cogs flooded her veins. Liz let out a sigh of relief and closed her eyes. She was grateful once again to engage in Duration, to lose herself in the power of the Icons. Like she had done countless times over her career, she felt the ebb and flow of everything around her. She saw the stark, uncompromising hull of the Doom Ship; the fragile, rickety form of the leatherheads hopping about; the accursed, irredeemable blackness of the storm and the Blood Poacher that conjured it; as well as the millions of endangered lives beneath them, which she saw like tiny candles flickering in the wind.

The Icon of *One* was one of the oldest and most difficult dedications for a Durationist to master. One of the "Divine" Icons, it focused not on a single aspect of the world to manipulate, but rather on the very flux of Duration itself. Thus, a *One* practitioner understood how everything was entwined, how everything was part of one substance to be culled and manipulated. It was that thought that allowed Elizabeth from Ogunquit to see the ship, the storm, the Kappos, and the shackles that bound her body as all connected, which is why it was now a simple thing, the simplest of things, to imbue her chains with the luster of the cogs burning inside her. The red rock around her wrists and ankles began to fade and turn white, then hints of blue seeped through like fissures of water.

The Kappo stopped poking her. Looking perplexed, it stared at the trembling Durationist.

Liz shouted and flung her hands forward. There was a loud crack, and the air seemed to hum with vibrant colors. The Kappo plopped onto its back, a rainbow of fire bursting from its chest. The shackles around Liz's limbs fell to the floor.

Two more Kappos ambled towards her. She raised her palm to the sky, and she imagined the shape of her sledgehammer, her prized weapon that she had lost during the fight with the Blood Poacher. She had watched it tumble into the sea, had seen its outline sink into the choppy waters. Yet she knew a way, against all odds, that she might call it back to her . . .

She grunted as the handle of the massive weapon landed in her hands. The Kappos lunged at her, daggers drawn. Liz cried out and heaved the hammer at the misshapen creatures. There was a high-pitched clang; plumes of color burst out of the air, and both Kappos went flying off the ship.

An airboat took off in front of her. Liz leaped aboard, and before a single Kappo could raise a weapon against her, she whammed the sledgehammer down into the center of the deck. Another screaming clang; shards of rainbow rocked the boat, and a dozen Kappos exploded.

Liz advanced upon the controls. Quickly, without even knowing how she knew what she was doing, she pushed the wheel forward and the airboat shot off the port side of the Doom Ship. She heard more Kappos barking, the thumping clap of cannons, and saw red shrapnel fling past her.

There was a shrill cry. A dark cloud zipped overhead, and she ducked from a hanging sickle that swung for her neck. She cried out as the Poacher's tail ripped at her shoulder.

Lightning flashed. Whether it was from the skies, the ship, or the Blood Poacher, Liz had no idea. Her vision blurred; already the surging strength of the silver pill was escaping her. There was another electric flash, a tremendous crash, and then the airboat started to pitch wildly onto its side.

As the skiff plummeted through the clouds and towards the earth, Elizabeth from Ogunquit reminded herself that she was not afraid to die.

6. Gemini's Dream

It did not take Gemini very long to coax the skytrain to movement. She was still a fairly new practitioner of the Icon of *Energy*, and she had yet to completely hone some of the finer techniques. Fortunately, slagging electrical currents was a fairly elementary process, so long as there was existing circuitry for electricity to flow. She had no doubt that Lucas really had no need of her help for this; he probably could have had the train up and running without even glancing at the controls. But, as Gemini had expected, Lucas had made a test of it to make sure her fundamentals hadn't gotten sloppy. After she was finished, he rigged the controls to ensure the train did not stop until they reached the Upper East Side; after all, the last thing they wanted was to stop for any Kappos.

"The Courier said the train should crib back out-of-step," Lucas said.

"So we can show up unseen."

"Well, yes, that too . . . but I also think it will be more pleasant of a ride if we don't have to worry about—"

There was a whining howl. Gemini froze as she was hit by a whirl of color and light. She had heard that the luxury of the skyrail was that the wealthy could enjoy their daily commute while blowing by all the other trains—but if that meant it actually blew right *through* the other trains, she was glad she was too poor to ride it! Her stomach churned as the ghost of silver walls, metal chairs and flickering lights whizzed by and passed in and out of them, blindingly fast. Then the stranded train was behind them, and everything returned to normal. Gemini stared at Lucas, wide-eyed and breathless.

"—other trains," he finished.

They cleared Black Beach. Now they just had to wait out the ride, so they moved from the operating room to the passenger cabin. The winds wailed over the squealing train, rocking the car back and forth as they turned towards the inner boroughs. That was where they were headed, assuming the storm didn't hurl them right off the tracks.

Gemini paced back and forth, then stopped to stare out the window. Rain began to pelt the glass. Below, the crisscrossing bridges over the narrows were washed out and broken, and plumes of smoke rose from tower blocks of the Brooklyn Fringe. Beyond, the Metro Reef City skyline was illuminated by fresh rounds of lightning as the storm clouds arrived from the sound to hover over the skyscrapers. Even with the codex, it was difficult to make sense of the playing field, what outlying boroughs were being penetrated by Kappos, or what neighborhoods were the Durationists were pushing back. Even more impossible was to match the landscape of flooded flats and burning buildings with the tens of thousands of thoughts still flooding the codex, still clamoring for aid, still crying for help.

Gemini wished she could piece the scene together, since it would distract her from all the other things on her mind. The worry had returned the moment she and Lucas had boarded the train.

She wore a silver-and-black glove.

She clenched her own gauntlet hand.

I'm going to have to tell him. But how?

"It's horrible out there," she said.

She had her back to Lucas, who sat against the opposite window, hands propped atop the hilt of his sheathed sword. "This is just the beginning," he said. "If we can't intercept the main cell, the damage to Metro Reef will be tremendous. Worse yet, the Blood Poachers likely see tonight as just an opening salvo, an expo to demonstrate how powerful they've become."

"But why now, Lucas? It's been a hundred fifty years."

"Good question. The past few years, reports from the frontier campaigns were getting pretty odd. The Blood Poachers were inactive, like they were waiting for . . . something. But Londinium was quick to claim instead that this was clear evidence of our victory, that the mere presence of Durationists out in the territories had scared away the Poachers for all time. In defense of Commonwealth Services, I don't think anyone could have forecast a night like this. It's all certainly a puzzle . . . but I suspect we may get some answers soon enough."

"Do you know which Poacher is commanding the storm?"

The train groaned back and forth. "*Killer Fives*," Lucas said. His grim eyes flashed beneath the hood.

Gemini spun around, genuinely taken aback.

"But . . . Killer Fives? Isn't he the one you—"

"Yes. At the Dixie Reach Outbreak. Two-hundred-mile-wide squall line abruptly splintered apart before it reached shore. Red Tide Cathedral was convinced the attack presented no threat to Orleans, so they prematurely called their division off the field. Almost cost their home county dearly. Several of the weakening cells rapidly tightened up—sound familiar?—and converged on Creole Power. Much of the reach was without electricity for months, and had our Cog Mind company not stayed so stubbornly vigilant—may the *Over-Soul* bless Zeno—the Creole Bay dam may have been breached, causing catastrophic flooding. The storm would have inundated the reach's biggest cities without putting a single cloud over them. A Blood Poacher will do anything to obtain a high butcher's bill, and Killer Fives is bloodthirsty even for its kind. Fortunately, my team played very well that day. Deke from Solonboro had the match of his life."

Gemini knew her captain was being modest. Even Lucas's biggest critics admitted that he was almost single-handedly responsible for Nimbus Deep's victory at Latin Key: a twelve-hour brawl between the team he helmed at the time, Nimbus Deep, and the architect of the Dixie Reach Derecho, Killer Fives. Few Durationists had ever actually killed a Blood Poacher, and Lucas's shocking victory had been rewarded with his promotion to Duke's Class, as well his team's overall graduation to the Duke's League. At that point, Lucas seemed like a surefire bet to someday make the Premieres, even though disapproval over his methods was common even back then.

Lucas cast Gemini a knowing smile. "Don't think for a second that a win from ninety seasons ago helps us, Gemini. A resuscitated Blood Poacher is always more dangerous and deranged than before, so long as it has misery to feed off of . . ." He jerked his head towards the window, as if to indicate Killer Fives had no shortage of food tonight. "That, plus this threat of some new kind of weaponry, should urge us to be extra careful. Still, we know its tactics, which gives us an advantage. Moreover, I would not be bringing us this far if I did not have confidence that we can prevail . . . are you all right? You've been marching back and forth since we left Black Beach."

Gemini held her breath. "It's nothing," she lied. "I'm just . . . nervous, is all. Of what's ahead." This was not entirely untrue, considering the gravity of their assignment. But the fact that she used her nerves as an excuse made Gemini's face flush. *Great,* she chided herself. *Now he thinks I'm scared.* She wished she hadn't betrayed her worry so easily.

Lucas nodded at her slowly. "It is perfectly natural to be afraid of what we're about to do," he said, "but you can only master your fear through experience. I should remind you that in Duration there is no intermission; you should seize any opportunity for respite that you come across, however brief. So please, sit down and relax."

Furious with herself, Gemini suppressed a roll of her eyes and sat down across from him. She knew Lucas was still studying her from behind the hilt of his blade, so she stared intently at the tile at her feet. It was grimy and adorned with used, well-trodden gum. Lightning hit in the distance, and in the glow Gemini looked up and caught a glimpse of a Kappo mob, hopping about a railway platform as their train shot by. The leatherheads might have passed as everyday commuters on the way home from work, except that their twisted countenance and dismal eyes, burning so gloomily in the rain, put a quick end to the comparison. Gemini was glad they were taking an express train. Lightning hit in the distance, and in the glow she swore she caught a glimpse of the White Eyes reflecting off the glass. She shivered.

Eager to continue the conversation, she asked: "How did you know the patient was a Bounder?"

Lucas shrugged. "I could feel hopelessness nearby, and it was not my own."

"Right . . ."

He laughed. "Let's just say it was a hunch. About what, I cannot say, other than I *knew* something was askew. After our pleasant talk with the Stewards, I was impelled to view the storm again through more penetrating eyes."

"The All-Sense?"

Her captain nodded.

The All-Sense was thought to be the most obscure, if not outright most difficult, of the four so-called "movements" that a Durationist could focus their power. It concerned the ability to interpret the past and forecast the future. Gemini frowned thinking at the thought, for although her slagging game was coming along, her other skills were woefully underdeveloped. Especially the All-Sense.

"It was through the All-Sense that I first saw the storm was not what it seemed," Lucas said. "But even back in Bedlam I recognized that, crucially, our stop at Black Beach was the moment on which the rest of the night would be determined."

"What do you mean?"

Lucas waved a hand back in the direction they had come. "Literally *hundreds* of possibilities were converging around that hilltop: the league's derision towards our presence, Metro Reef Watch's bluster towards you, the reorganizing storm, the presence of a Sleeper, so forth. When so many factors converge, this becomes a contraction of *Time*, of Duration itself, like a river that turns to rapids. These moments are ruptures in *Time*, for often it is what we do at these moments that determine the outcome, and even the smallest of choices has large-scale ramifications."

"Right..."

"For instance." He looked off to the side, twisted his hand in the air, as if to conjure his example. His voice picked up that rustling speed. "If Metro Reef Watch had goaded you into a brawl, perhaps the broken patient manages to shoot one of you. Or, if I am too late to get there, perhaps he explodes and everyone is killed. Just a simple sneeze or cough from one of the doctors present might have set the Thrall off earlier. But it is not just danger that characterizes a rupture. It is also the temptation to ... to go with the flow, to capitulate to inertia. Do you know what I mean by this?"

Gemini scrunched up her face, thinking hard. "Well ... if you're saying time's like a river ... and the river is going fast ... do you mean—do you mean it's like being tempted to just let go and get swept up by the currents?"

"Yes, exactly," Lucas smiled. "Now, given the elements at play tonight, where would we be right now if we *were* swept away by the currents? Don't think, just remember what we've seen so far."

Gemini remembered. She saw Lionel's curled lip, the heavy chain tugging at Bion's neck; she heard Dale sobbing over his stupid harp, her team being told to go home . . .

She said: "We'd be on the turnpike, heading home."

"Exactly! It's those moments where one can either stay within time or *break* out of it. Breaking out of the flow is dangerous, and many things work against you. But if you succeed, you will have succeeded in changing the flow of time itself in your favor."

She looked sharply at him. "And that's why you feel so strongly about doing this tonight. This is *our* chance to . . . to change the flow."

"Yes. That is what I sensed, Gemini. The contraction. The rupture. It was from there that I was able to sense out the Sleeper, and through the Sleeper's addled mind I was able to glean the severity of the storm. You will learn to see the history of a person, a place, a storm, shackled to its present. Duration is *always* going on, whether you or I are aware of it or not, and in ways a rigid devotion to slagging alone cannot divulge."

She flexed her gauntlet hand anxiously. "I wish I could use *Energy* the same way you use *Time*."

"*Energy* grants as much vision as any other Icon. You may see it through a different lens, but you will see the same river I see, just from another perspective. You master one Icon only to see how it blends with the others. Forget what you read in bogus playbooks, Gemini, or what you were taught in Spectrumore. The Icons are just points of access, different windows we may use to reach the same reservoir. The Sky Watch understood this, and that was how our league conducted business before we became beholden to the competition of the machifare. To this day, those of us still working for Echo Division recognize the truth: intuition is true contact with Duration, and therefore also how one senses where Duration is *weak and rotting*, such as with agents of the Echomar."

Gemini nodded slowly. She knew that if Lucas had his way, the Echo Division, the intelligence branch of Durationists colloquially known as the Sky Watch, would never have been subsumed by the Durationist League of Roslyn to begin with. Clearly, whatever knowledge the Sky Watch had that allowed them to root out and neutralize blighters was effective: she remembered how casually, how *easily* Lucas had thwarted the Sleeper from annihilating himself and everyone in his wake.

She shook her head. "I still know so little . . ."

"You are still so new to this game, Gemini. This is a difficult life; it takes decades to master the skills we're talking about. Do you think I mastered *Time* overnight? No, and I still don't know nearly as much as I need to. It never ends. You must have patience. Remember, there is a reason why you asked to first only practice the dedication you are called to, and why you must master slags before you can appreciate the other movements of Duration."

Gemini vividly remembered when she had first chosen her dedication. It had been a few years prior to her meeting Lucas. She had awoken one night in a cold sweat from a lively dream, one that involved her flying right into the sun, and by morning her gym trainer had confirmed her as a practitioner of the Icon of *Energy*. She had felt more relieved than anything else, as she had been playing in the amateur circuits for several seasons at that point and was worried she was going to be forced to consider a different career. Those who never heard the calling were asked to walk away from Duration.

Shortly after her calling, Gemini had pawed some used *Energy* playbooks off the market in Spectrumore. They had been written by Toledo U, the same school that Peppy had attended and the home of the eponymous Premiere team. Gemini had been hopeful that she could study up and one day impress some Cog Mind scout who happened to attend one of her scrimmages. It never happened, but she had held onto her playbooks, and she still used them to advance her knowledge and awareness of *Energy*. She thought she had been working pretty hard and was hopeful she could try to tackle some really complicated slags by next season, but she couldn't help but notice that whenever she came to Lucas all excited about some new move she had performed or some deeper level of *Energy* she had accessed, he seemed altogether unimpressed. She recalled that he had only grudgingly allowed her to keep studying from the books. Had she offended him somehow by choosing the texts she had? Or maybe he thought she wasn't getting it down fast enough?

As if he knew to quell such a thought, Lucas said: "You are learning your Icon at a satisfactory rate. It should be said that *Energy* is not the easiest of dedications. Your slags are exactly what a closer's attacks should be: swift and focused, with no frills."

"But my other skills are useless," Gemini said. "Especially the All-Sense. I'm just no good at it. They had a big amateur symposium for it in Londinium a few years back and I was just terrible."

"I agree, forecasting is not your strength. Fortunately, you are adept at Now-Sense, which is far, far more valuable."

"Really?" She looked at him doubtfully. "That's not what the league thinks. I've even heard Bion say that the Now-Sense isn't important to study, since really everybody uses it."

"I would respectfully disagree with our League Steward. Your average scofflaw, high on fixes and using a wrist booster to mind thought-tosses, is *not*, I promise you, engaging the Now-Sense. In fact, to truly sense the rise and fall of cogs around us is *exactly* how one engages the deeper sense of the future. It was only through mindfulness that I felt the Sleeper nearby. It was only through Now-Sense that I knew of Liz's warning, like a message in a bottle tumbling through choppy waters. Always live in the moment, for it's the moment that divides into past and future. You cannot see the distance without knowing the foreground."

Gemini stared at the floor, mulling it over.

"Remember," he continued, "there is a reason you must first practice only the dedication you are called to, in the specific steps around the cross. Duration does not let you navigate its secrets so brazenly, so devoid of discipline, without great cost. There are prices to pay, especially in charged situations. The Founders did not respect Duration when they first discovered it, and to this day the result of their reckless meddling is all around us. Look back to Black Beach. You think a storm somehow jumbled all those ships together? Or how about the skyline behind me. Is it natural for coral to grow so rampantly, to actually flourish up into the sky?"

The history of Roslyn sometimes made Gemini's head spin. "Well, no. But I . . ."

"Don't forget the Valley Forge. Can the Sky Ways or Sub Rosa just be the consequence of common geology? Or if you need an extreme example, the Echomar—"

"I get it, I get it." The less said about the Echomar, the better.

"Our world is a testament to the power of Duration, as well as the danger of it. You must take your time, for you can only make lucid contact with the Icons when you truly comprehend the enormity of what you will witness. Hastiness spells disaster. That is why you must be patient."

The rain grew harder, the wind harsher. Skyscrapers grew large in the window, then disappeared from sight as the skyrail turned directly towards the great central borough of Metro Reef City. A familiar feeling of dizziness overcame Gemini. She closed her gauntlet hand, so it wouldn't shake, and said, "I just don't want to let you down. Captain."

"I would not be taking you into this if I did not think you were ready. That goes for Peppy and Griffin as well." He gave her another shrewd look. "I take it that you do not approve of how I've handled our wingmates."

Gemini raised her eyebrows. "Why do you say that? I mean, I . . ." She faltered, then quickly added: "Griff has gotten used to playing guard."

Lucas leaned forward and smiled. "You did not answer my question."

"It's . . . not my place to disagree with you, Lucas."

He laughed. "You are my second-in-command, Gemini. I value your opinion. Speak freely."

". . . All right. Griffin's too loyal to you to ever admit it, but I think he still resents that you picked Peppy over him to be striker. I *know* it." She spoke in a hushed voice, for whenever Peppy and Griffin were held out-of-step, she was paranoid that they somehow could overhear Lucas and her talk. "And honestly, I get where he's coming from. He played right wing his whole career. I think he looks around and sees that other teams, good teams, have gotten rid of left wing altogether, they just go with a pair of strikers, and he wonders why we can't do that too."

The captain nodded. "I have my reasons for why I am sticking with the cross formation, and eventually I think Griffin—and you too—will understand what they are. For now, I will just say that I don't think you can punch the core of a Poacher Storm without a defender and expect to survive. But you know, the thing is, Gemini, both Griffin and Peppy really *would* be better off at right wing. Both have aggressive instincts. But *Alchemy* is a good dedication for left wing, and Griffin was once a Duke's League player because he's so adept at it; he is very good at slagging elements together to shield and obscure us. I decided I had to maximize his talent there. And, given that Peppy has become a skilled shot through the use of *Shapes*, which is much more useful for striking, I decided we would be better suited with him at right wing. But you cannot change a dog's spots, as it were. Griffin gravitates towards the position he'd rather play, and I agree with you: who can blame him? Mind you, it does not help that left wing is mocked so much in the amateur circuits for being 'soft' that it becomes almost a mark of shame to play the position.

"No situation is ideal right now, Gemini." He shut his eyes. "Griffin and Peppy are too similar as players; their way of seeing the game is redundant. But so long as the league restricts me to recruiting players from the bottom of our conference, we're going to be stuck with Durationists who have come out of the same systems, were fed the same playbooks, and had the same creeds jammed down their throats. Unfortunately for us, the league values allegiances over innate skill, and while this obsession might rake in the cogs, it has crippled our game."

Gemini sensed Lucas had a lot more to say on the matter, but he did not elaborate. The train was shaking, and the rain was so heavy that tower blocks and billboards faded out of sight.

Lucas opened his eyes and leaned back. "Do you hear that? Old Atlantic must be entering the field."

Gemini strained her neck in no particular direction, unsure of what she ought to be hearing. "Er," she said uncertainly.

"Over the codex," Lucas explained. "I can't even gather my thoughts without hearing their alma mater."

"Oh . . . right," Gemini said sheepishly, slumping back in her seat. She let her mind drift slightly, and just as Lucas said, the fight song for the Blood Work Society's second-ranked team filled her head.

> *O' Atlantic, Old Atlantic*
> *Watchers of the East Sea*
> *Guardians of the Revere*
> *Blessed county 'tis of thee!*
> *O' Atlantic, Old Atlantic*
> *Your slags keep our skies blue*
> *From Tremont Tower's heights*
> *You'll see the dark night through*
> *O' Atlantic, Old Atlantic*

Your slags keep our skies blue
You keep the weather true

Fernando wise and strong
Steadfast through the smog
Thom fierce and proud
Smiting blighter crowds
Ajay shields us all
From quaking thunderfall
And Sophia's wicked light
Shines through the night

O' Atlantic, Old Atlantic
A Yankee noble four
Your slags keep the skies blue
You keep the weather true

"Never cared for that one," Lucas said. "It's obnoxious . . . I guess there's some Old Atlantic diehards nearby."

"It's really dangerous of the league to allow that!" Gemini said. "I can't believe the Alumni Circle would be okay with fans being this close. Especially after what *just* happened back on Bethpage!"

"I agree. I think, deep down, Bion and Lionel dislike it as much as we do."

"They have a funny way of showing it . . ."

He laughed. "Don't let Lionel bother you. He was just trying to get me mad. Nothing unusual there . . . there *was* a time, a hundred years ago or so, where he and Bion would come out and admit how much they hate dealing with this kind of stuff. But the machifare are demanding more and more cogs from us, and in lieu of any major victories, they—*we*, I guess I should say—have to rely on fan rallies to keep everyone's halos nice and shiny. I imagine also the Blood Works Society probably wants a lot of fanfare backing Old Atlantic, just to calm everyone down after reports of what happened to Tremont United."

Gemini shook her head. "Well, maybe if they saw how bad Black Beach was they'd think twice about having fans this close to a storm! That poor urchin girl . . ."

"You know," Lucas said, as the sky car shuddered and groaned against an angry burst of wind, "she was a big fan of Old Atlantic."

"How do you know that?"

He shrugged. Fluorescent lights over his head blinked. "She was wearing their sweater."

"You know . . ." Gemini hesitated. "Something about her really bothered me. I mean, obviously it was a terrible way to go. But also, just . . . you know, something about *her* really hit home."

"Hmm. She reminded you of *you*, obviously."

Gemini nodded stiffly. Such a bald truth made her throat strangely hot. She felt there was something else about the urchin that bothered her, something elusive, but she didn't know what, and presently it was too difficult for her to figure out. Her spine tensed. She knew she ought to bring up the *other* topic worrying her, that now was as good a time as any, but much to her annoyance, the burning sensation had taken away her speech.

Strobes of lightning lit up the window behind her.

"Obviously, we met under similar circumstances," Lucas said kindly, as if to assure her she wasn't being ridiculous. "She, like you, was a very big fan of the game. She probably rooted for Old Atlantic just because of their closer. Like many urchin girls do, including you—"

"Not anymore," Gemini said flatly.

"—at one time," Lucas agreed. The floor shook beneath their feet. "Speaking of which, I must admit that I am curious to see Old Atlantic out in the field. Especially to find out *if* their star closer matches her reputation . . ."

Thunder shook the panes of glass.

"You know, I saw her once," said Gemini.

"Did you? When?"

"At the closer's conference they held in Spectrumore a few years ago. I wasn't invited, of course—only 'prospective' amateurs were, not some scrub like myself—but I found a way to sneak in. I really wanted to go, because she was talking at the pro panel, and since they were taking questions I knew I might have the chance to ask her something. She was everything I wanted to . . . I mean, I just really respected her back then—as a closer, you know? I wanted to meet her. But throughout the entire hour, she barely said a word. She just sat there the whole time, strumming her fingers against the table, rolling her eyes at the moderator's questions. She didn't give a shit.

"So the Q and A started, and I worked up the nerve to get in line. I was last. By now she was only giving 'yes' and 'no' answers to people. It was so awkward. After a long while I was gonna be next, after this little guy in front of me got his turn. Just some urchin, couldn't have been any bigger than that poor girl . . . obviously there was no way he was a Durationist. I think he must have sneaked in, just like me. Anyways, he says to Sophia, all eager, 'Hey, Sophia! I really want to ask you two questions. Is that all right?' She replies in this cold, bitchy voice, 'Well, you have one left.' The crowd laughs. It was an uneasy laugh, like the kind you hear after a bad joke, but still. The urchin's face turned red, but he just stammered on. I think he forgot whatever he was going to ask, and over all the snickering he just blurts out, 'I just want you to know I'm such a big fan, I think you're amazing. I love how you've stood by the Rishi all these years, how you helped expose the crimes of the machifare. I really think you're the kind of player who could stop the war and bring peace between the Echomar and Roslyn. I just wanted to tell you how much I believe in you, Sophia.' You know what she does?"

"What?"

"Her eyes light up. I've never met a Rishi with eyes that strong, have you? They're so intense it's hard to even look at her. Anyway, she rips into him. 'You have no idea what you're talking about. '*Peace*?' Idiot. Get the fuck out of here.' That's all she said. The worst thing was that the crowd kept on laughing. I remember the urchin just turned, pushed past me, and bolted for the exit. I never saw someone run out of a room that fast."

"Then it was your turn."

Gemini shook her head. "No, I . . . I just turned and walked away. Everyone was still laughing, I don't think she even noticed me to begin with. There was no way I could have asked her anything after that. I told myself that I wanted to catch up with that urchin, just to . . . you know, tell him how messed up all of that was. But really, I think I was just so scared I was going to get the same reaction. Maybe I should have stayed; he was gone by the time I got outside anyways. But her voice . . . it was like ice. And those eyes, Lucas! They're like knives. I just couldn't take it."

Gemini didn't tell Lucas what she would have asked had she stayed in line. In truth, she wasn't going to ask Sophia anything. She had a much more shameful intent that evening. She had been planning on . . . gushing. Being a fan, just like the urchin had. *Thanking* Sophia for being an inspiration to her.

Thank the Over-Soul *I didn't stay,* Gemini thought. *I would have given up the game then and there.*

A cluster of tower-blocks whizzed past Lucas's head, licks of orange flames flailing out the windows, a canopy of smoke mingling and melding with the clouds.

"I don't think anyone would have wanted to stay in line after that," said Lucas. His finger ran across his lips. "Well, we shall see. Even in today's league, I'd like to think that chivalry isn't lost among all the competition. If Old Atlantic joins the fray, they may end up being valuable allies."

Gemini frowned. "And if they want to rob us? You know as well as I do that if all the headlines tomorrow say Old Atlantic—*Sophia*—won the night, everyone's going to be rallying around her next week to have her own team . . . or worse. If there's any truth to these rumors—"

"Again, no matter what Londinium or the league offices desire, without a Token of Power, no one besides us has a claim. Nevertheless, your concern that Londinium will prop up challengers against us is astute. That's why it's imperative we punch the core ourselves." He clenched his gauntlet hand. "I've worked too hard—*we've* worked too hard—for this opportunity, Gemini. It's our time to prove our worth."

The train buckled so much that Gemini had to grip the edge of her seat just to keep from falling over. "Straight-line winds," Lucas murmured, cocking his head. "And hail again, by the sound of it. We don't have much time." Gemini really hoped that the skyrail could hold up to this kind of abuse. She swallowed. What exactly would happen if the tracks gave way beneath their warped train? Would they just crash into the city below, or would they keep floating on and on, lost out-of-step? Crib physics were a little beyond Gemini. She decided that now probably wasn't the time to brush up.

She was hoping now that Lucas would guess what was on her mind. It would just be so much easier if he somehow spelled it out for her. Wasn't that always the case? But he said nothing, and Gemini knew she was running out of time. Rows of skyscrapers surrounded them, as if the train was passing through the ribs of a skeletal beast. They would reach the Upper East Side any minute.

Lightning charged over the tower peaks.

She had to tell him. It would be stupid not to, if only to get absolution before battle. The dizziness returned a little. She squeezed her hand shut.

"Lucas . . . I, uh . . . I had a dream last night."

Thunder clapped. Lucas's expression remained unmoved, but his eyes grew sharp. He knew what she meant by *dream*. An Icon dream. She didn't have to explain that part to him. He wasn't a skeptic about this sort of thing, although right now she kind of wished that he was, that he thought Icon dreams were bullshit. That way she could blissfully forget whatever the hell it was she had seen last night.

"You should have told me sooner." It was not an admonishment. He said it delicately. "I always take a closer's dreams seriously. Would you scoop it with me?"

Thunder clapped. The lightning looked like a net being cast over the city. Gemini hesitated. "I—I don't know if I can totally recall everything for you. Just some of what I saw—"

"That will suffice."

She sighed and tried to relax. The skyscrapers grew dense around them; they were deep in the village now, close to their destination. She closed her eyes. At least it was easy to mind Lucas. His thoughts were so strikingly obvious compared to anyone else's, including her own. Like a lighthouse on a dark shore.

The minding began, and she shared with him what she had seen.

—*I was standing outside an old chapel, at night. The doors had been left open. There was a strange chanting, words I couldn't understand. A procession of women streamed out, maybe seven or eight of them. They were all dressed in dark, regal gowns. They walked in pairs, except for one who led the whole group. She was the most striking, the most elegant. She led the procession. They were all chanting.*

She swallowed, continuing to scoop him.

—*The leader's face was caked in makeup, way too much makeup. She looked like a doll almost. And she had a crown, too, like she was a queen or something, and she wore a shiny necklace or brooch that she had her hand clasped over really tight. She wore a glove, too . . . A silver-and-black glove . . .*

The train rocked. Thunder clapped.

—I watched them go past me, away from the chapel. Then the chanting was slowly replaced by this strange, labored breathing. It was coming from inside the chapel, so I went inside to find out what it was.

I walked down the hall. The panting just grew louder and louder. I couldn't stand it, it was sickening. But I wanted to know what it was. I came to a little alcove, with a spiral staircase that stretched beyond the ceiling. At the foot of the staircase, in the shadow of the spiral, I found the source of the breathing. It was . . . a man. No . . . a king, Lucas. A king.

Thunder clapped.

—He was in a heap of torn robes, a pool of his own filth. He was curled up, and his face was turned away from me, so I pulled on his arm to spin him around to see if there was anything I could do . . . and that's when I saw him . . . his face. His face was also caked in makeup, so much that it had turned solid on his skin, so that his jaws were locked, his eyes wide. His crown had been smashed into his head like shrapnel from a bomb. I couldn't see any blood, there was so much powder and makeup . . . the panting, Lucas. The gasping. I thought I'd choke.

Thunder clapped.

—I ran up the spiral stairs. I didn't want to abandon the king, but somehow I knew I was going to die . . . I ran and I ran . . . but his gasping was just so loud, and the stairs began to shake, the walls were crumbling, and the old chapel started to give way.

Thunder clapped. There was a whining noise in the distance.

—I fell with the bricks, Lucas, screaming, I couldn't hear myself over his breath. I fell . . . and then I died.

Silence, save for the whining sound. Gemini opened her eyes. Lucas's hands were folded atop his blade, eyes still shut. He was deep in thought.

Then the whine became a howl, and silver walls, metal chairs, and flickering lights shot through them. Another train. Gemini really hated that.

The train passed, and there was silence again.

Lucas opened his eyes.

"It certainly has Iconic elements," he said, slowly. "But for now, there's nothing else to say."

Gemini was perplexed. "Could it have something to do with tonight?"

"There's not much profit in marking deadlines for dreams to show merit, Gemini. We will find out what it means only when we are supposed to. You can't tease meaning out of a future that's yet to come." He smiled. —*But if it helps, the dream does not portend to your fate tonight. I'm sure of that.*

Gemini breathed, met his stare. —*How can you be sure?*

—*Well, I don't have any reason to believe the dream even concerns you, lest you are actually a grayskin in disguise.*

Gemini managed to smile. She didn't pretend to understand his reasoning, but she was certain that Lucas would not have minced words with her if he thought that she was in real danger. That fact, his reassurance, was all she really needed.

"Thanks," she said.

"Thank you for divulging," he said. Gemini thought there was still something distant in that shaded, incandescent gaze. But what it was, she could not say.

There was a screeching sound, and they were tugged back and forth as the train buckled against the wind. Outside, Gemini could see the translucent walkways abutting chrome skyscrapers on either side of the railway, crossing above and below them. They were deep into Metro Reef City now, in the Upper East Side corridor called the Electric Canyon. It was eerily empty.

"The station should be just ahead," said Lucas.

Gemini was about to remark that, all things considered, it had been a smooth ride, when a series of blinding red flashes lit up the northern sky. A second later there was a deafening boom, and she was thrown off her chair and onto the floor. She scrambled to her feet just as Lucas rushed into the control room; through the front viewport, she could see a smoking hole in the middle of the railroad, rapidly expanding as they approached.

Lucas jerked the brake lever back, but the wheels of the speeding train futilely screeched against the slick, rain-swept tracks. He planted his feet and threw his hands outward, fingers clawed, and the train shuddered and wailed as he tried to will them to a halt.

Gemini was aware of Peppy and Griffin appearing behind her as the captain released them to focus on the train. "Are we there—" Peppy began before hollering as he lost his balance, and he collapsed atop Gemini.

Gemini threw him off and clambered into the operating room. She ducked past Lucas's outstretched arms and slammed her fist on the control panel. Her halo and the blinking lights flickered in concert, and the engine abruptly died. But the train barreled forward, the twisted, smoking hole in the railroad growing larger and larger.

Lucas yelled out, pulling his arms back like he was yanking at some invisible wire. The train screamed across the tracks. The hole was less than a car's length away, and Gemini, Griffin, and Peppy began to scramble for the door to make a hasty exit—

A final shudder of protest, and the skytrain came to a harsh stop. Gemini, Griffin, and Peppy again fell to the floor. Hail hammered overhead. But as the captain helped Gemini to her feet, jangling thumps echoed off the side windows.

"They're here," the captain said, staring out the portal. "Shutting down the train must have put us back-in-step." Rain was bursting down, making it difficult to see; but as lightning cracked again, they saw a mob of leatherheads staring at them from the catwalks, pistols drawn, jumping and yelping in excitement.

"We'll have to fight our way north. Peppy, Griffin: take to the higher walkways. Play zone. Gemini and I will cut through the middle path."

Gemini raised her gauntlet hand and flexed it. Her halo brandished curves of orange fire, little spirals of molten lava that flowed from the burst at the back of her wrist. She felt the loading, the rush of cogs flow through her, and she reached into her coat for the grip of her kreisflyer.

The doors slid open. A terrible blast of wind and rain immediately pushed them back. Lucas from Slag Falls, no stranger to inclemency, tossed the scabbard back over his shoulder and drew his zeitblatt in a single flourish. The cobalt patterns enclosed in his gauntlet hummed crisp, cool, and sharp.

"Let's go," he said, then leaped off the train.

7. Fighting the Hordes

A PAIR OF KAPPOS raised their scrap guns at the stranded train. Lucas landed atop them in mid-slice, and their sparking heads went tumbling across the chiffon walkway. Ten more of the rickety critters swarmed him at once, firing pistols and swinging dirks wildly. Lucas met them with a whirl of slashes and thrusts. With each swing of the zeitblatt, the space between him and the Kappos seemed to contract, and from Gemini's view it looked as if the sword was forming ripples in the air, compressing everything towards her captain in a wavy, twisting blur. Just as the ripples grew dense, there was a brief absence of sound, then a deep, resonant twang reverberated across the chasm. Her captain emerged from a cloud of smoke and cinder. The severed limbs of all ten Kappos lay in his wake. Even to Gemini's eyes, he had moved impossibly fast. But the three Durationists did not have time to admire their captain's prowess. More clanging gunfire resounded off the side of the train, and together they jumped from the car.

Gemini grabbed the overhead portion of the doorframe and flung herself up and backwards, so that she landed on the roof of the train. Molten shrapnel ricocheted near her legs as Kappos from a catwalk above shot down at her. She deflected the fire with a few flourishes of her kreisflyer, then hurled herself towards a walkway on the west side of the street, opposite of Lucas and out of range from the Kappos' potshots.

Landing on one knee, she pushed her headband out of her eyes and looked down the vast corridor. The Electric Canyon was a wide gulf through which the skyrail gradually descended to run along the Jamaica Freeway tens of stories below. There was still some power here, and Gemini thought she saw the outline of stranded cars briefly illuminated by flickering streetlights, but otherwise they might as well have been traversing a bottomless cliff of glass and steel and fading neon lights. The tops of skyscrapers were all shrouded in a low ceiling of fog and rain, so that Bedlam Athletic might have been trekking through a shadowy cavern. The facade of each building held a veneer of shimmering, translucent color that seemed to ripple across the glass; occasionally an ad for a NERVE Company fix or the local Durationist teams bounced off the glass, like sea monsters trying to breach an aquarium wall. Translucent walkways adjoined each building, and it was these footpaths that Bedlam Athletic could take north to their destination. Gemini minded her map and radar, and she noted that the core of the storm was still idling offshore, churning angrily; but it had spewed out a front line that was now drifting directly over the Upper East Side. The TAN building was somewhere twelve blocks ahead, concealed by sheets of rain.

A shot whizzed by her. Eight Kappos hopped out of the mists, coats and arms swaying. They ambled towards her like a mob of demented urchins.

Gemini deflected their next round of shots with her sickle. She felt her gauntlet hand sizzle and throb. A surge of cogs burned through every cell of her body from the inside out. She imagined an inferno pulsing from her heart and through her veins, one lick in a limitless blaze, completely unseen and totally incomprehensible to someone not engaged with Duration.

Gemini saw the world as *Energy.*

Before the Kappos closed in on her, Gemini flung her kreisflyer at them, and as she did this she imagined a rope of sun-colored light unfurling between her gauntlet hand and the flying sickle so she could control its every turn.

The kreisflyer hurtled right through the first startled Kappo, ripping through its chest in a blast of sunlight. Gemini twitched her wrist, and the flying sickle proceeded to tear through the other leatherheads in a shower of sizzling fire.

One of the Kappos hopped sideways, losing its arm from the curved blade but otherwise unharmed. Its damaged limb burst with electricity, but it raised its leper gun in its remaining paw and aimed at Gemini's head.

Gemini didn't need to think about how to react. She twitched her fingers, ever so slightly, and again the kreisflyer obeyed her gentle tug. The rebounding saucer tore through the back of the Kappo's neck. Its head lopped backwards, while its flailing body toppled forward and skidded to a stop at Gemini's feet. Gemini's halo flared bright as the kreisflyer landed back in her gauntlet hand.

Something swooshed to her right, and she glanced over to see Griffin soaring down the corridor. His glider had materialized at his back. He took a swift turn under the skyrail and looped out the other side. The wind and rain howling through the city chasm was difficult for any ordinary person to walk in, much less fly. But Griffin had been practicing the Icon of *Alchemy* for hundreds of seasons, and for him, navigating the crashing gales was second nature; teasing out a lonely breath of air to rise at his back was nothing difficult. Thus he easily bent the violent gusts under his wing and moved too fast for the Kappos still shooting from the higher floors to reach him. He jetted all the way up to their catwalk, drew his zero-iron, and then with a wave of the wedge-shaped club he turned the stormy gusts against them. The Kappos squealed and toppled off the walkway, exploding against the railing or the road far below.

Crack. Gemini heard Peppy's scope shot echo down the steel corridor. He had lunged up to a sidewalk a dozen levels above her. His rifle was already out before he hit the pavement, and he picked off a score of Kappos two blocks away. The downpour did not affect his aim in the slightest, and crack after decisive crack signaled a sparking Kappo slumping over the railing. His halo-hand burned bright red, and the pupil of his eye, now infinitesimal, glinted ruby. In the moments before he squeezed the trigger, all he saw were hints of a grubby coat or a bobbing leather helmet, nothing else. Any Kappos that charged him he immediately mowed down with a careless flick of a pistol. All he knew was the crooked, scrawny shape of a Kappo; it was as if the storm, the city, and the world itself did not reach his eye.

A lone pair of leatherheads scampered out of the rain, and Gemini quickly dispatched them with a single swipe. She heard barking over her head: a dozen more scrawny, grinning figures came out of the clouds above, floating down on shoddy brown parachutes.

—*Look out down there!* she minded Peppy's warning. *Para-Kappos on their way!*

Three of the descending Kappos drifted towards her. She tossed her sickle up at them, cutting the parachutes out from them, and they crashed around her in squealing, sparkling crunches. Peppy dispatched four more, his shots ripping the parachutes right out of their hands, and gusts conjured by Griffin sent the rest careening through windows, shattering glass and agitating restless wall-ads.

Lightning forked over the skyscrapers, and the glare revealed a second batch of Kappos parachuting into the canyon. Gemini was getting ready to fling her sickle again when her moped appeared in front of her. Lucas's thoughts filled her head:

—*The Courier tells me there might be some stranded people just north of you. Get ahead and check it out. I'll be right behind you. Peppy, Griffin—keep playing cover.*

Thunder quaked through the canyon. Gemini hopped onto her moped and gunned the engine. But she had barely started moving when one Kappo landed right on the end of the bike, dirk raised high. She pivoted around her seat, kreisflyer drawn—

The Kappo's head exploded. It tumbled back onto the walkway bursting in flames. Gemini saw that Lucas had taken the shot from across the way, before he used the bayonet at the end of his grudge shot to impale another Kappo who tried to jump him from the side, while at the same time he used his sword to cut down two more . . .

Gemini zipped ahead, disappearing into an incoming horde. She could barely see the walkway before her, could barely keep her eyes open in the blinding gusts and stinging rain. It didn't matter. Instead she relied on the vibrations she felt in the handlebars of the moped, the tiniest of perturbations that told her when a slick spot lay dead ahead, or a dull beat that signaled the clumsy gait of an approaching Kappo. She followed these hints without hesitation, letting the Icon of *Energy* guide her as she swung her sickle back and forth and fearlessly ran over Kappos that tread in her path.

The role of a closer was to take risks, to be aggressive, to plunge forward into enemy lines; but Gemini was not alone. Griffin covered her from above, zigzagging back and forth across the chasm, the blunt end of his weapon turning raindrops to icicles that he tossed down at the Kappos swarming the walkways. The ice exploded into a thick, taupe-colored mist that filled the canyon, preventing the impish creatures from seeing where the Durationists approached. Any Kappo that crossed heedlessly through that haze was instantly struck down under Peppy's sharp eye. *Crack. Crack.*

Two blocks north, Gemini espied four redcoats taking cover under a storefront. The cops stood in front of a couple of civilians, and they were returning fire at a wave of leatherheads creeping towards them. Gemini wondered why they simply did not retreat back into the building when four Kappos smashed out of the windows above and joined their companions. They surrounded the redcoats, who stumbled backwards, weakened by the mere presence of the leatherheads. The Kappos raised their dirks—

Gemini gunned the moped and charged into the leatherheads, her sickle beaming with amber fire as she slashed through knives and guns and mechanical limbs. She chased down a Kappo who tried to hop away, then braked hard and turned back to the storefront. Five more had hopped out of the window; but by then Lucas had bounded across the street and was already upon them, his zeitblatt creating arcs of blue light with each slice, and after a few yelps of protest the Kappos were no more.

"Much obliged," one of the redcoats said. "We were trying to get these folks to Uptown Shelter."

"We're on our way to the TAN," Lucas said. "The shelter is across the street from there. We'll escort you." He said to the civilians: "Stay behind us and keep close to the buildings for cover." They nodded, their eyes wide at the sight of his gauntlet and cowl.

A jangling thump rang off the glass wall, and another wave of Kappos came clamoring down the street. Cracks echoed over the din of rain and thunder, and Peppy shot down half the horde; the rest stumbled into one another or fired way off the mark as they got lost in the icy haze Griffin was creating by swinging through the rain with his zero-iron as he swooped across the gulf, his staff transforming the showers into hailstones that crashed around the Kappos and sent up geysers of white mist.

Gemini rode into that mist and started hacking away. Her captain strode after her. Scores of Para-Kappos dropped down around him, but Lucas cut them down without halting, spinning his sword patiently between attacks, the air around him crackling with indigo ribbons. Each swing of his blade slowed the rainfall to a crawl, chastened the wind to gentle, aimless gusts. The cops and civilians gawked in disbelief as they crept past floating globs of water and drifting debris, a constellation of suspended inclemency. Anyone hiding in their flats who dared to peer out the window would have seen the eerie calm Bedlam Athletic left in their wake: rain drifted weightlessly, glass walls no longer rattled, and steam rose off catwalks littered with trails of sparking, smoldering Kappos.

But with each passing block the downpour grew heavier, the wind stronger. Wave after wave of Kappos still filled the canyon, flittering down the walkways and raining down from above. Determined to push through, Gemini mowed down line after line, her kreisflyer burning so hot that the corpses she left in her dust were pyres of burning scrap. She rammed ahead until the crackling of Lucas's blade and the snap of the redcoat's guns grew muffled behind her, and she reached where the east side of the canyon ended, so that the west side of the corridor now looked out over the Jamaica Sound.

Gemini could see the massive thunderhead brooding over the water. Lightning pulsated across its soot-covered surface. It was an insurmountable peak, its summit inconceivably high, the gales bursting from its base so ferocious that she could no longer steer straight. She gripped the handlebars tight as a gust whipped over her, and the glass wall to her left groaned. But the rainfall parted, and Gemini could see that just two blocks ahead the walkway ended at a dark, needle-shaped outline that stabbed deep into the overcast: the Tower of Allied Nations. They had made it!

Immediately she noticed that something was wrong.

—I can see the TAN building, Lucas. It . . . it doesn't look good. There are deep holes in its side, a lot of windows blown out. I think it got hit by the lightning . . .

A shadow overtook her. She squinted upwards. In another blast of lightning she saw more Para-Kappos jumping from a jet-black, flatbed ship. The size of a large truck, it chugged through the mists, a roaring propeller at its stern. The airboat zoomed past Gemini, then wheeled around so that its starboard side faced her.

—*Airboat!* Gemini warned her teammates just as a pair of buzz saw–shaped shadows jumped out of the vessel, which then ascended back into the stormy ceiling. The mean-looking shapes landed atop the walkway with heavy thuds.

—*Slasher Kappos!*

Gemini had keen memories of how fearful her old coaches back at the gym in Spectrumore were of Slasher Kappos. War Daddies, as they called them, were one of the greatest threats that the Echomar deployed in battle. Curled up into armored balls, they tore chunks of glass out the translucent pavement as they skidded across the walkway, flinging themselves at her. If an amateur Durationist saw those jagged boulders rolling towards them, the old coaches taught that the best thing for the novice player to do was to *run*. But Gemini was not going to run. She throttled the motorbike forward and threaded directly between the rolling attackers. She took a swipe at one with her kreisflyer, but the sickle bounced off a hard, charcoal-colored hide, the deflection ringing painfully up her arm.

She wheeled about, then whistled in dismay: three more airboats flew overhead, and as strobes of lightning beamed over the city, the glass bluff became riddled with the shadows of the fifty Para-Kappos swooping down into the canyon. Gemini had her work cut out for her. The leatherheads were no issue: Peppy was knocking them out of the sky at a rapid clip, and Griffin pummeled them with sheets of ice and fire, while their captain continued his unassailable march. But her teammates were occupied, which meant that the two Slasher Kappos, which had bounced to a halt and were now careening back her way, were gunning for her and her alone.

Undaunted, she again rode straight between the wheeling brutes. This time she tried to swing for a crevice in one assailant's serrated armor, but to no avail. As she came to a stop she saw that Lucas was three blocks back, the zeitblatt gleaming, the redcoats shooting down any leatherheads he managed to miss. Then the cloudburst grew dense, and Gemini could no longer see any of her teammates. She pivoted, ready to make another pass at the Slashers. But this time they didn't charge her.

Instead they bounced into the air and unfurled. Clawed feet crashed into the glass floor. Gemini flinched, not from the stinging wind but in revulsion. The Slashers were hunched and hulking, their gray-and-green scaly hide covered in armored plating. The plating was onyx in color and appeared heavy and foul, like it was made of bone. It was etched into most of their skin, from the tip of a thick tail that flicked in the air behind them to the back of their powerful necks and their wide, blunt heads that were adorned by round, slightly flared helmets. The Slashers' primal eyes narrowed as they stared Gemini down while forked tongues flicked behind toothy maws that protruded out and over their mouths, melding with their helmets like hideous face masks. Triads of long, curved claws flexed from their hands and feet. Each Slasher carried nothing except for a long, crude rifle slung over its back with a sickle-shaped bayonet atop the barrel.

Both Slasher Kappos crouched, lifted their rifles at the approaching Durationist, and fired.

The Slashers had better aim than their scrawny cousins. One blast singed Gemini's shoulder, and the other she barely deflected with a wild swing of her kreisflyer—but she had to pivot so fast to block the shot that she lost control of the moped. She made a last-ditch effort to gain control, still deflecting the Slasher's fire, but as she swerved over a slick puddle the handlebar jerked completely out of her grip. Gemini lunged out of the seat before the motorbike veered onto its side and slid towards the Slashers, sparks flying off the glass. One of the Slashers lazily kicked the bike aside, then it and its companion continued firing at Gemini, who had landed on one knee and then cartwheeled behind a storefront, her sickle reverberating in her hands like a gong from all the parried shots.

Her arms ringing with pain, Gemini kept her back against the frame of the storefront and caught her breath. When she risked glancing over the corner, she was greeted immediately by another round of clanging shrapnel. The Slashers were closing in. Lucas and the others were nowhere to be seen, lost in a deluge of rain and leatherheads. If she was going to survive, she had to act fast.

She took a deep breath, then threw herself back into the line of fire. The close proximity made it even harder to block the Slashers' shots, and it made her arms ache with every blast, shaking her to her core, but somehow she held her ground. As if emboldened by her efforts, her gauntlet hand glowed like a star, and her sickle shined like a yellowy crescent moon. Smoke rose from her grip, her legs quivered, and she felt sweat break out on her brow as she barely parried shot after shot. A few bullets got by, grazing her arms and legs, but she didn't back down. Her kreisflyer was now absolutely bursting with fire.

I am fire.

Distantly, she knew it was a silly thought, impossible and absurd . . . but no. Such doubts had to be quelled.

Another shot clashed off the sickle.

I am fire. I am fire.

The grip was so hot now that it burned her fingers. She could hear the Slashers growl between the gunfire, as if they were frustrated by her stubborn defensive stand.

I am fire. I am fire.

Her halo and sickle gleamed in unified sunlight, and in that instant, there was no doubt in Gemini's mind what she was.

With a heave, she threw the heavy, burning sickle at the nearest of the Slasher Kappos. It had no time to react, blinded as it was by the luminescence bursting between Gemini's gauntlet hand and the scorching eclipse launched from her fingertips. The kreisflyer cut through the Slasher's armored hide like a hot knife through butter. She caught a glimpse of the Slasher's protruding jaws opening in shock, its wiry tongues flickering as it let out a squealing howl before its entire body exploded with flames. The ensuing explosion nearly threw Gemini off her feet, and for a moment, there was nothing but dizzying golden light. Then the kreisflyer returned to her shaking hand, smoking but no longer ignited.

She fell to one knee, panting hard. The powerful slag had cost her dearly. Unfortunately, she didn't have time to recuperate. The remaining Slasher lowered its clawed hand, no longer needing to shield its eyes from the glaring light. It hissed at the charred husk that remained of its companion, then fired its rifle furiously at Gemini.

She quickly shot upright and parried the shots with tired, heaving swings. The sickle felt so heavy that she had to hold it in both hands. She didn't have the strength to mount another slag strong enough to cut through the Slasher's plating, but she could at least block its gunfire. The Slasher kept shooting at her, but she kept deflecting until at last the monstrous Kappo grew fed up. Growling, it held its bayonet out with one hand and flexed its claws in the other, then gave a guttural roar before lunging at her.

Gemini managed to parry the thrust of the Slasher's bayonet, but the hulking monster was so heavy that it easily shoved her onto her back. The clawed foot pinned her down by the shoulders, crushing her chest, and she gasped as the air was squeezed harshly from her lungs. She couldn't even try to wrestle free, and what little strength she had left she was using to keep the Slasher's bayonet away from her neck, but the blade was sliding down the curved edge of her kreisflyer, and it was now just inches from her throat. The armored monstrosity leaned into her face, snarling and hissing, its snakelike eyes in a leer; Gemini grimaced and tried to turn her head away as the protruding jaws opened and closed, but cold, oily smoke seemed to ebb and flow over her face, and a black, wiry tongue drew closer to her . . .

An invisible blast sent the Slasher rolling backwards. Gemini immediately sat up, gasping as if she had never breathed before, and she was barely aware of Lucas moving in front of her, sword at his side. The Slasher found its feet and roared at the new challenger. It started to swing its bayonet, but Lucas was already upon it, as if he knew in advance where to strike, and his blow was so sure that he cut the Kappo's rifle in half.

The Slasher Kappo threw the useless halves of its weapon at him and Lucas lazily batted them to either side. The Slasher took a few steps back, lowered its head, and hissed, its palms pointing upward as it curled its claws. Then it charged, swinging its hands in a frenzy, its maw snapping for the Durationist's neck. Lucas weaved in and out of the furious assault, but he held his zeitblatt low to the ground, and the Slasher Kappo seized the blade with a clawed foot and shoved it halfway into the glass floor. Now, apparently having disarmed Lucas, the Slasher gave a triumphant roar and reared up high over its enemy, claws reaching for his shoulders—

Lucas plunged the bayonet of his grudge shot in between the plating on the War Daddy's underbelly, and the beast screeched in fury. Arms flailing, it shoved its face into Lucas's, still hissing, inky smoke issuing from between its jagged teeth—

Lucas pulled the trigger, and the Slasher's head snapped back with a booming crack. Oily smoke was subsumed by a jet of fire, then white fumes. Lucas raised his boot, and with a kick he pried the Slasher Kappo free of his bayonet. It flopped onto its back, blackened and charred, curling up like a gigantic dead roach.

With little apparent effort, Lucas freed his zeitblatt from the surface of the walkway, casually shaking glass off the blade's edges. Then he withdrew his sword and helped Gemini to her feet. As he did so, Gemini felt a warmth run through her veins and noticed her halo flicker in sync with his; her captain was scooping cogs to her to help her rejuvenate.

"You will have to learn to be more economical with your slags," Lucas noted. "That said, it was a pretty impressive attack."

Gemini beamed. "Thanks," she muttered, and as her face burned, she felt her strength return to her. "First Slasher I ever killed. I wasn't sure if—"

—*Heads up!*

It was Peppy. They heeded his warning just in time to look back and see the trio of airboats again descend into the canyon, all the way back where their skytrain had stopped. The Kappos commanding the airboats were barking and yelping orders at one another; turret guns above and below the center of each ship started wheeling about, firing red projectiles in every direction.

Peppy and Griffin, who had been dispatching the last of the Para-Kappos along a walkway that connected the east and west sides of the canyon, dashed in either direction as the crimson fire ripped apart the catwalk. The redcoats and civilians shoved themselves through the door of the closed shop, bullets nipping at their heels. Lucas and Gemini blocked a round of shots, until Griffin, taking back to the air, slapped a disc of ice their way and a glacial wall jutted out of the ground, shielding them from the rest of the fire. Griffin then flung a few orbs of fire down at the airboats as he soared over them, and he managed to knock a few Kappos off their ships to squeal down into oblivion. But the airboats chugged on, and as they came level with Lucas and Gemini, a Slasher Kappo aboard the lead skiff barked orders to the gunners. The turrets swiveled straight ahead, and with a clanging blast, red orbs hurtled through the air directly at the tower looming over the corridor.

—*Peppy!* Lucas scooped as he dropped to one knee and opened fire. Somewhere behind him, Peppy joined in, and together they managed to destroy four of the fiery bombs before they reached their target. Two missiles smashed into the side of the tower and immediately erupted in volcanic bursts.

Lucas frowned, lowering his rifle. —*They're trying to take the whole TAN down . . . along with whoever is trapped inside. The ships are in my way now, I can't get a shot at the gunners. How about you, Peppy?*

—*Negative, Captain. I'm too far out.*

Lucas turned to Gemini. He pointed at the airboat nearest to them, its roaring propeller almost right over their heads.

"I'll give you a boost."

Gemini nodded. Her strength had returned to her, and after surviving against the pair of Slashers she felt elated that Lucas trusted her to finish the job here. She crouched low. The ground beneath her feet glowed hot, then she sprung high into the air, trails of smoke falling from her feet. It was dizzying, to be so high off the ground, with no support below—but through the Icon of *Energy* she could *feel* her destination ahead of her, felt the wind giving in to her ascent, and she had no doubt she would make the jump. Somewhere below, Lucas shoved his hands upward, and the invisible shove sent her even higher, until she was somersaulting over the railing of the airboat and landing on its deck.

Immediately the seven Kappos aboard screeched, reaching for knives and guns. Gemini threw out her sickle, and in one clockwise arc she decapitated all but the gunner. The gunner had ducked beneath her blade, but not before shooting at the wheel on the bow of the ship, ripping it apart.

Gemini realized the Kappo had all but ensured that the airboat would crash into the Tower of Allied Nations. The leatherhead stood and gave a hollow cackle, then made a move to draw its tin shot—only to realize that both its hands were missing. It stared at the fizzing, jagged stumps at the end of its arms in bewilderment, then whirled around to see that its hands were still clutching at the turret controls, then spun around again just as Gemini cut it cleanly in two.

Gemini pushed the upper half of the Kappo off the controls and threw aside its severed hands. Then she gripped the levers and turned the turret on the two boats hovering on her starboard side. The other Kappos, gleefully launching rockets into the tower, never knew what hit them. Only the Slasher Kappo helming the skiff closest to her saw it coming. Gemini squeezed the trigger twice and the two other airboats exploded in brilliant yellow flashes, debris raining down on the highway far below.

But the Slasher reacted fast. It lunged out of the fire, hurling itself like a cannonball, and landed next to her. Its sheer mass caused the entire skiff to tilt sharply to the side. Gemini grabbed hold of the turret, which spun wildly as the boat careened out of control. She heard the War Daddy roar, saw its maw snapping at her. She twisted the gun to aim at its face, pulled the trigger, heard it screech. Successive flashes of gunfire revealed mangled teeth, a pockmarked face, a clawed hand shading feral eyes. The Slasher snarled, threw its claws out at her. Gemini leaned back, pulled the trigger again. Another bright flash, and the Slasher stumbled onto its back. That was opening Gemini needed. Her yellow coat billowing behind her, she wheeled the gun around towards the bow of the ship and blew out the propeller.

The airboat began to careen out of control. Without thinking, Gemini jumped off the skiff and fell towards the earth. The Slasher Kappo, wounded but alive, threw itself after her; she felt its claws rip at her jacket, felt herself falling, falling towards a black abyss below. Then someone grabbed her by the hand. The Slasher plummeted past her, snarling as it vanished in the abyss. She looked up and saw Griffin, banking his glider to the side; somehow, he managed to carry them both back to the walkway to land next to Lucas and Peppy. Their captain had raised his gauntlet hand to give the crashing airboat a gentle shove, so that it did not collide with the Tower of Allied Nations but instead landed out in the water in a harmless blast of angry foam.

They stood silent for a moment, the cops and citizens tepidly catching up with them, everyone trying to get acclimated to the sudden calm. The sky above them had cleared. There was just a pungent sea breeze and a light, salty rain.

"Was that your first Slasher kill?" Griffin asked her, gesturing back to where the two dead Slashers lay on the sidewalk. She nodded, and he handed her a hunk of charred, bronze armor.

"I pulled this off the dead fucker. Stitch that to your jacket. That was some pretty nice work, Gem."

Her eyes started burning, so Gemini gave Griffin muted thanks and stared very hard at the ground as she pocketed the ore, embarrassed by how much her teammate's gesture had meant to her.

8. Tower of Allied Nations

THEY HAD REACHED THE northeastern tip of Metro Reef City, where an embankment of buildings overlooked a valley of gloomy slums. The glass walkway fed into a wide esplanade that grew diagonally out of the cityscape and ended at the entrance to the Tower of Allied Nations building. The base of the spire-shaped building was wrapped in a bewildering ribbon of highways. With all the smoke pouring out of the tower's battered summit, Gemini feared that the roadway system was the only thing still holding it up.

The thunderhead seemed to have shifted slightly towards the north, and red flashes could be seen deep inside the black anvil. Gemini wondered if the Poacher was fighting the Durationists led by Toledo U, or if it had simply chosen to pillage the northern borough first.

The uptown shelter was just a block west. The walls of blue ore gave the shelter the appearance of a glacier that had been carved into a massive oval. But something was wrong. Police sirens were flashing along the street beneath them, and whitecoats were rushing out of ambulances while people flooded out of the entrances. It looked as if the entire shelter was being evacuated. From Bedlam Athletic's high vantage point, Gemini could clearly see a deep, jagged hole in the roof, a plume of smoke pouring from the gap. Ridiculously, she thought of a gigantic cracked egg.

"Didn't think Poacher lightning could bust through sky glass," Peppy muttered.

The redcoats and citizens whom Bedlam Athletic had escorted to the shelter thanked them profusely, then scattered into the mob that was pouring out of the shelter's upper entrance. Gemini started to ask Lucas about the crack in the blue ore, but their captain had already walked back to the promenade that led to the TAN. He was kneeling down next to a small crater at the center of webbed cracks that ran through the glass. Something was submerged in the floor. Wisps of dark steam rose around a heavy, head-sized chunk of ruby-colored rock. Though its outer layers were a deep mahogany, a brighter scarlet shone at the rock's core, as if there was a flame dancing at the heart of the stone.

"This is what the airships were firing," Lucas muttered. Gemini, Peppy, and Griffin started forward, but he raised his hand.

"Do not come closer." He stared at the rock with a grim frown, his eyes burning fiercely beneath the cowl.

"Red ore of the Echomar. There is not a more dangerous substance in existence. I have never seen it weaponized like this."

Griffin furrowed his brow. "It's not the first time they've used red ore against us, though."

"Yes, that's true. They embed bits of it in their artillery. And red lightning, of course, travels through a prism of red crystals carried high in the towers of the storm . . . but this is *more* than that. Red ore this dense should be too unstable to even exist. Yet we just witnessed airships volleying whole missiles of it."

"Why should it be too unstable to exist?" Gemini asked.

"Because red ore is full of dark thought; it is shapeless, amorphous, sculpted only by the power of the Void. Whereas our blue ore, while also matter without form, is made purely of cogs, even the stuff ground into fixes. And because it is made of cogs, it is brought to life by those who carry the glow of cogs, and in Roslyn that gives it endurance and strength. Red ore is crystallized by the bonds of the Echomar. It's nothing but destructive, chaotic; it is the very *lack* of cogs. It should not be able to endure for very long, and certainly not in this large a quantity.

And it should *never* be able to break through a potent source of consolidated cogs, like blue ore—or the roof of a shelter. And yet . . ."

He trailed off and started to murmur some sort of unintelligible hymn under his breath as he waved his gauntlet back and forth over the crimson stone. Gemini shivered. She could feel something *wrong* emanating from the rock, icy but electric, like the heartbeat of something that should have been dead. It made the hairs stand on the back of her neck, made her feel cold and anxious.

"It sort of feels *a lot* like a cascade," Peppy muttered aloud, thinking the same thing. "But instead of just a lot of, uh, sad things . . . it feels—"

"*Powerful*," Lucas agreed. "Very powerful indeed. Stronger than anything the bonds ought to produce . . ." He resumed his quiet chant, his gauntlet hovering over the ore, until his halo glinted sky blue. The smoke was extinguished and the light at the center of the rock seemed to fade away, leaving just the dim tint of dry blood.

"There," he said. "Now it is safe to touch. We need to take this sample with us. It may hold clues as to what the Blood Poachers have been up to . . ." He seemed to make his mind up about something. "Gemini, if you don't mind, I need *you* to hold onto it until we get back to Bedlam."

Gemini tried not to let her face show surprise. She exchanged quick glances with Peppy and Griffin.

"Lucas, I—I don't know if I'm the best person to, uh, handle *that*. I'm sure you'd do a better job."

"No, Gemini, I cannot touch it. But it is quite safe now, for you. I trust you."

A cold breeze crossed between them. Gemini hesitated. Though Lucas still sounded calm, there was a slight edge to his voice. He had been deeply bothered by the discovery of this strange rock, something that went beyond just the strategic threat of the Blood Poachers' new weapon. He sounded impatient, angry . . . or was it something else?

She picked up the ore; it fit comfortably in both hands. It was cool to the touch, yet it made her fingers tingle uncomfortably. And even though its power was subdued, something about it still stirred unsettling things on the edge of Gemini's mind.

"Captain." She offered it to him. "I—I've never handled something like this. Why can't you—"

"*I cannot touch it*," Lucas said sharply. His eyes flashed, and for a moment his gaunt face was lit in a horrific pattern of green and gold.

A smattering of thunder echoed dimly from far away. Peppy and Griffin threw each other startled looks. Gemini, taken aback, stared questioningly at their captain.

—*Lucas . . . ?*

He sighed, and after a moment he met her gaze.

"Sorry," he said in a calmer voice, and his face softened. "For anyone who has spent too much time in the Thunder Nation . . . whatever is in that ore does not bring up any pleasant memories. Let's just leave it at that."

His eyes again glinted, like floodlights in an abysmal fog; but this time Gemini only nodded, and with a wave of her hand, the red ore disappeared from beneath her palm.

An ugly, high-pitched rattle echoed from inside the tower, growing louder and louder until Gemini feared it might be a voice. It sounded like a hoarse scream.

"What the hell was that?" Griffin asked.

"We'd better find out," said Lucas.

The sky blinked with crimson light as peals of thunder drummed across the water, and a bitter wind pierced through the esplanade so that the flags of Roslyn and its allies across the globe snapped rigidly to their sides.

Lucas strode towards the entrance. Gemini, Griffin, and Peppy lingered behind for a moment, looking nervously up at the shattered windows and ragged holes, before they followed their captain into the tower.

The three teammates didn't exchange a scoop, but Gemini knew they were all thinking the same thing: what had happened to the other Durationists who were supposed to meet here?

The scene in the lobby was as bad as they feared. The bodies of redcoats and stripe-tied staffers lay all over the marble floor. Looks of terror were etched upon their faces and their hands were locked against their ears, rivulets of dried blood running over their fingers. Each face was strangely blurry and absent of detail, as if it all had been washed away, and everything about them—their bodies, their clothes, their eyes and halos—were devoid of color, so that all the corpses appeared black and white. It was as if all warmth had leaked out of them before Bedlam Athletic had arrived.

"Sick," Peppy said. "Real sick."

"It would have been impossible for an ordinary person to survive a lightning storm like this," Lucas said. He looked down at the fatally stricken, then up at the riddles in the windows above, where the lightning had crashed through and the sky beyond still flashed. "Not good. Not good at all."

The sight of the dead was enough to chill Gemini to the bone—but even more foreboding were the jagged stalks of bloodstained glass that rose out of the floor like bloody crystal trees. These were stained-glass effigies of steel and stone, melted down and fused together by the Blood Poachers' lightning. Trails of dense smoke billowed from their top branches and sunk along the floor to tangle at the Durationists' feet. A fountain at the center of the lobby, which Gemini knew had once displayed statues of the Founders of Roslyn, had been almost completely blown away, a miniature forest of red stalks subsuming the plinth where the sculptures once stood. Only one statue remained, a Durationist from antiquity, his cape risen appropriately over his face as stalks wrapped around him like a twister of glass lightning.

The floor creaked beneath their feet. A still escalator led up to a balcony lined with lifts and entryways into the Allied Nations main hall. Instead, Lucas led them down a separate stairway that went into a chamber with a vaulted ceiling.

"Whoa," Peppy said. The far half of the chamber was filled with a great aqua-blue expanse of sky glass.

"The TAN storm shelter," Lucas murmured. "If there are any survivors, they'll be in here."

Thunder rumbled outside. Faint strumming resounded beyond the walls as rain splattered across the tower.

". . . I'm . . . not minding anyone on the codex," Gemini said uncertainly.

"No, neither am I. Unfortunately, I think they're trapped inside . . . and if you look up, you'll see why."

Gemini gasped. A pool of lava seemed to have filled the top of the once-pristine glass, and it was sinking and spreading through the blue ore like a toxic spill at sea. Molten rock was seeping down into the shelter.

"It must have been struck by lightning," Lucas said. "The sky glass is all warped. Instead of keeping whoever is inside safe from the Poacher

Storm, it's now infected with dark thought . . . there are still people alive in there. Including one of us."

"How do you figure?" Griffin asked.

"A Durationist skilled with *Ore* is staving off the effects. I bet it's Ajay from Old Atlantic; there's not that many *Ore* users to begin with. But he's held it off for as long as he can."

"How do you know that?"

"Because otherwise this entire wall would be red by now."

The crimson cloud sunk deeper and deeper. Another hoarse cry quivered across the room, and Gemini realized it was from the red ore eating away at the sky glass.

Peppy shuddered. "Man, that's *wrong . . .*" He didn't finish his thought, but he didn't have to; Gemini felt it too. It was the same ominous, slightly dizzying feeling they had just experienced with the red ore out on the promenade, only much more intense—so intense that no one besides Lucas dared to get close to the glass.

A hand slammed against the inside of the glass. Gemini, Peppy, and Griffin all jumped backward. Another fist pounded against the wall, then another. Lucas continued forward as the wall filled with groping, clawing hands, dozens of people desperate to escape. The red smog slowly descended upon them like lava rolling down the side of a hill, gaining speed, and their fingers started to slide towards the floor as a hideous curtain fell over the shelter that was now a tomb.

"It's going to suffocate them!" Gemini cried.

A crack of thunder shook the tower. Lucas stopped right in front of the glass. He brandished his zeitblatt and pointed its tip at the deepest swirl of crimson, which was now almost level with his pallid face. Hands within the wall reached towards him.

—*Get back!*

His thought was strong enough to penetrate the barrier, and the hands darted away like a frightened school of fish. Lucas drew his sword back, his halo-hand sizzling cobalt, then he plunged the zeitblatt into the heart of the blood rock.

The ruby sea halted. A hissing noise, like the sound of vanishing ice, spat across the chamber. Lucas gently twisted the blade back and forth, and the fiery rivulets started to contract and shrink. Hoarse screams and hisses turned to shrill wailing and whining. The crimson cloud suddenly imploded upon the submerged sword, which shuddered madly as Lucas smoothly churned the hilt of the weapon, his halo bursting electric blue. Ribbons of red converged, faster and faster, until a final, inhuman scream caused Gemini and the wingers to cover their ears and shut their eyes.

When they again dared to look, they saw that the blood rock was gone. Lucas's sword glowed blue and white, and a vertical line formed from the floor, through his sword, and up to the high ceiling. The sky glass quaked and receded to either side, and steam rushed from the passage that slowly formed.

Lucas stowed his still-lambent sword as people stumbled out of the shelter, coughing and gasping for air.

Rain drummed patiently against the tower.

The ambassadors to the Allied Nations were deeply shaken. Their halos were faint, and two execs from the NERVE Company were out cold from shock, but otherwise it could have been far worse. Gemini, Griffin, and Peppy helped them to benches along the wall, while Lucas approached the three Durationists who emerged from the shelter. One player pointed a grudge shot at Lucas until he could see through the steam, then he hastily lowered his weapon.

"Sorry, Captain, just a little jumpy." Thom from Tremont, the striker for Old Atlantic, smiled wearily. "You're the last player I expected to run into. But after the beating we just took, I guess it's anyone's game tonight." Blood trickled from beneath Thom's wide-brimmed hat, and one of his eyes was puffy and black. The jersey beneath his jacket featured an interlocking *O* and *A*, the letters of Old Atlantic. Standing to either side of him were two players Gemini did not recognize, but judging from their orange-and-black sweaters, they were from a Cog Mind county team. The less experienced duo were shaking badly, their halos weak of color; they looked almost as bad as the civilians they had been stuck with. Both county players gawked at the sight of Lucas.

"Is your team all right?" Lucas asked Thom. "Where is Fernando?"

"We've . . . well, we've been better. He's over here." Lucas and Gemini followed him into the shelter.

As they crossed into the gloomy room, Gemini was suddenly aware that she was trying her very best to remain hidden behind her captain's shoulder. Her feet seemed to be willfully working against her, as if her boots were full of lead. It was like an invisible line had formed between them, a marker that Gemini was certain, if she crossed, would expose her as an impostor who didn't belong in a field this dire. Her heart rate quickened. No, it was not Thom nor even Captain Fernando whom she was intimidated by seeing, though of course she loathed to trust them all the same, given their treatment of the Meta-School over the years. No, it was, much to Gemini's embarrassment, *Sophia* whom she dreaded to meet. Somehow she had imagined that this day would not come until much, much later in her career, when she was a Duke's League player, for instance, and no one would dare question her—nor her captain's—bona fides. Yet here they were, and try as she might, Gemini could not shake the foul memory of that closer seminar back in Spectrumore.

As it turned out, she had nothing to worry about. Sophia was nowhere to be seen.

The shelter was a twilit twin of the antechamber, with a vaulted ceiling, benches, and walls made entirely of sky glass. Shafts of dim light cut through the sea-shaded air from holes torn in the arched roof, and chunks of ocean stone littered the floor. Trickles of rain pattered down on the three of them as they walked under the breach.

"We just got here when the lightning went off," Thom said. "So much you couldn't even tell that it's nighttime. Wasn't like any Poacher lightning I've seen before. Usually you can resist its effect, you know? Not this shit. Felt painful to even look at. Damn lucky we didn't get killed."

A Durationist lay on the bench to their left, a dark man with gnarled gray hair and the wrinkled face of a grayskin. He was out cold but breathing. His gauntlet hand was over his heart, his bronze-colored halo very faint. His other arm was floating awkwardly over the floor, where a shard of night-colored sky glass dangled from a bracelet wrapped around his wrist. Gemini recognized him as Ajay from Jumano City, left-winger for Old Atlantic, one of the most famous first-wave players in the sport and a pioneer in the Icon of *Matter*, which meant he was highly adept at slagging ore to his will. Once again, Lucas's prediction was correct.

"He'll be okay," Thom said. "Although I dunno how. He did this crazy shit where he stopped the red rock from spreading through the whole room. Nearly killed himself doing it. Slag was starting to wear off before you got here. He's stable; I gave him a few fixes, and—hey boss, look who's here!"

In the back of the room, a man in a long black cloak stood over a figure cowering at his feet. His gauntlet hand rested on the handle of a whip at his side, and despite the siege of the shelter, his golden wrist was still bright. Gemini noticed four rings around his halo, and not because this man flaunted his fortune in any way, like Dale from Goethal Heights had done, but simply because this Premiere Class player *commanded* attention through his wealth. The cloaked man turned as they neared.

Fernando from South Tempest had a stony face and dark eyes that were framed by curls of black-blue hair. He did not visibly react at the sight of Lucas. He only said, in a voice that was perfectly clear in its loathing: "You have got to be kidding me."

"No, I am not," Lucas said.

It was no secret to anyone that Fernando and Lucas hated each other; or, at least, it was known in league circles that Fernando despised Lucas. Gemini had never heard Lucas utter a bad word about the captain of Old Atlantic, but she knew the story as well as anyone else: Seven seasons ago, Fernando had challenged Lucas to a one-on-one duel to take the Token of Power off his gauntlet hand. There was no requirement to accept this challenge, and many had assumed Lucas would refuse. Instead, much to everyone's shock, he obliged. The duel reportedly took place right in the erstwhile abandoned arena that was now the Meta-School's own gym, in Bedlam City. No one really knew what happened; Lucas had forbidden the press from covering the fight, and neither Durationist had spoken a word about what had gone down in the seasons since. But what was known was that Lucas still wore the Token of Power, and Fernando had never dared cross Lucas again.

"Are you trying to get expelled, Captain?" Fernando asked. "Didn't the Stewards tell you to go home?"

"We had reason to believe the storm was worse than what Bion or Lionel realized," Lucas said. "We figured you'd need help."

Thom shrugged. "Well, he does have a point there, boss."

Fernando glared at his striker, then shook his head. "Bringing this mediocre talent out here . . . putting lives in danger. That's the Lucas from Slag Falls I remember. What a disgrace."

"Respectfully," said Lucas, "I'd say it's to your benefit that my 'mediocre talent' happened to find you. I don't yet know how the Poachers are corrupting our shelters, but clearly you would not have survived much longer being trapped in here."

Fernando grunted, as if it was a point he was happy to ignore. "Well, since you're here, Captain, maybe you have the right—ah, *sense*—to talk to this man. He won't tell me anything."

Lucas's eyes descended on the man whimpering behind Fernando. He nodded in comprehension. "Ah . . ."

Gemini looked at the cringing man. He was a bald grayskin. Faint brown lines ran across the back of his head. A leather glove covered his halo-hand, and he was dressed entirely in black save for a locket of red ore around his neck.

Griffin entered the shelter, stopped dead, and cried: "Aha! I knew it!"

Ikoff Minor, high ambassador to the Echomar, was crying hysterically. "I—I know nothing! You can't prove I had anything to do with this!"

"We can by the lump of shit hanging from your throat," Fernando spat.

"You can't arrest me! Detaining me due to my nationality is an act of—"

"We damn well can arrest you," Fernando said. "The diplomat of a hostile nation can always be detained until his homeland negotiates for his release. You know full well that's in the Treaty of Camulodonum. Now, once more: what are your masters planning to do next?"

"V-Vlaz Gal had nothing to do with this! This—this is the work of radicals, not anyone affiliated with the Fathom!"

Griffin snorted in disbelief. Gemini was inclined to agree with him. Nothing happened in the Echomar without the Fathom, the shadowy citadel at the heart of the Thunder Nation's capital, knowing about it. Only crackpots thought that the Vlaz Gal government wasn't controlled by the Blood Poachers, since only the most loyal, ardent of the Thrall could possibly survive in a place so wicked, and so clearly a source of the Blood Poacher's power. A common joke in league circles went like this: *never accuse the Fathom of anything until the Fathom denies they did it.*

Fernando flexed his fingers as he stared down at the ambassador. "Considering what you've done tonight, I really don't mind doing this the hard way," he said.

He raised a hand. Ripples of hot air flowed from his palm and over the ambassador, who howled as the skin on his arms and face began to sear. Gemini shifted uncomfortably; even Griffin held his breath.

"Please! Can't you tell I—I know nothing!"

"Let's try again," Fernando growled. He splayed his fingers, as if to intensify his slag.

"Enough," Lucas said. "He's telling the truth."

Fernando paused. The Thrall panted and looked up at the Durationists with pitiful eyes. Fernando glared at Lucas.

"The Icon of *Time* giving you a hint, Lucas? Or maybe you just have the right *eyes* to know?"

Gemini started to speak, but Lucas raised a hand. "The Fathom would *never* be sloppy enough to make a diplomat their agent. Besides, I doubt this talentless fellow has the cunning to be the Thrall we're looking for. I recommend you detain him of course—it is per custom, though I doubt the Echomar will bother to negotiate for his release . . ."

Fernando muttered to himself, furious that Lucas had made salient points.

"I'm innocent!" the ambassador blathered. "I swear—"

"Shut up," Fernando said, and with a flick of his hand the ambassador's head slammed against the wall, and he fell silent. The captain of Old Atlantic began to pace back and forth, still grumbling to himself.

The pattering of rain grew rampant. Lucas looked around at the Durationists in the room.

"There should be more of you . . . where is your closer?"

"She split on us," Thom said bitterly.

"Split?"

Fernando spat at the ground, but he did not elaborate, so Thom continued: "She minded a commotion down in Harlo Valley. The local militia was overwhelmed by Kappos, and all their shelters are overcrowded. So she decided to jump down to protect one of her people's goddamn temples, just as the lightning storm started up here . . ."

"We had orders," Fernando whispered. He clenched his fists. "She'll pay this time . . ."

Gemini looked at Griffin. Neither seemed to know what to make of this news. Part of her was relieved she did not have to deal with Sophia, but the idea of a player—even a rival player—ditching her own team was just plain offensive. It simply went against the conduct a player in the Durationist League of Roslyn was expected to show. That Sophia would actually abandon her team in the middle of a storm this bad seemed outright treasonous.

Lucas, though, simply looked thoughtful, and he moved on without further comment. Instead he threw Gemini a furtive look.

—Do you feel it? This is another rupture!

Gemini looked within, but she felt nothing except her own nerves. She frowned. She didn't need the All-Sense to understand why Lucas thought this was another crucial moment: here they were, in a tower shellacked by the storm, with a dozen high-profile civilians and the Blood Poacher leering down, and their rival team's star closer nowhere to be found . . .

Then, Gemini's eyes grew large. It was like a door in her head had briefly opened and shut. When she considered everything going on, the dull maritime colors of the room seemed to intensify; the shards of broken rock glistened, and for a very brief moment she was acutely aware of the bundled masses of cogs that comprised the other players around her, the halos of each ebbing and flowing like the very breath from their lungs. And suddenly, for reasons she could not explain, Gemini was certain that *something* was missing here, an element that would make itself known imminently.

Just like the Thrall back at Black Beach. Something will force our hand here. But what?

Lucas beamed at her, as if he was aware what she was thinking, or perhaps just pleased that she had achieved some deeper glimpse of what was going on through her use of Now-Sense, just as he had predicted. Then he turned to one of the Cog Mind players, both of whom looked completely overwhelmed by everything happening around them.

"Shepherd from Old Hollow, Captain of Great Revere, correct?"

The county player nodded. He seemed taken aback that Lucas even knew who he was.

"How did you get separated from your team?"

The wind screeched and groaned against the tower.

"We were part of the company that Toledo U led down from the Revere," Shepherd explained in a quavering voice. "The Blood Poacher attacked us in New Bronx. Our club got separated from the others. The Blood Poacher..." Thunder clapped, and his face went white.

His teammate, Kat from Sin City, finished the story for him. "Our closer, Ronnie from Londinium, got impaled by one of its tails. Then our left wing, Noam from Chambersburg, he got struck by lightning..." She recited her teammates' deaths matter-of-factly, but her hands were twitching uncontrollably, and she was staring at the floor. "Shep and I were trapped on the freeway. I knew enough *Alchemy* to wire a car, and so we drove down here. We just got here when the lightning hit."

Drumming rain turned into thumping hail. Fernando, apparently untouched by the story of two players being murdered, scowled and rolled his eyes.

"So let me see if I have this right: we nearly risked the lives of everyone here just to hold the shelter door for two Durationists who were running away from the storm and clearly in over their heads. Don't know what Kip was thinking, bringing scrubs like you out into a fight like this."

Kat frowned. She did not get angry, but she also didn't back down against Fernando. "Captain, you don't understand. You weren't there. None of us stood a chance against this thing. Even Toledo U was falling back... I've never seen Kip that scared in his life."

The Old Atlantic captain turned away from everyone. "What a night this has turned out to be," he grunted. "Supposed to rendezvous with the Premiere teams. Instead stuck with some county scrubs and the league's rejects."

"You'll have to make do, Fernando," said Lucas. "The storm will be upon us any minute. We have to get ready."

Screaming gales gnawed against the walls.

"No," Fernando said. "*No.*" He turned around, rubbing his hands together, then nodded with certainty. "What *we* have to do, Captain, is get the hell out of here and back across the river."

"What about the city?"

"Our mission was to get the ambassadors and execs to safety, and that's exactly what I'm going to do. Half my team is either unconscious or MIA. I have no interest in suicide."

"Tremont United could still be out there," Thom pointed out. "Plus, we don't know if the other Cog Mind teams got out okay."

Fernando threw his teammate another nasty look, which Gemini was sure was coupled with a scoop that told Thom to shut the hell up. Then he said: "The alum told me Red Tide is leading a fleet that should be here by dawn. They'll handle rescue and recovery."

"There won't *be* anyone to rescue if the people here have to wait that long," Lucas insisted. "There must still be a hundred thousand down in the valley slums. The storm will kill them all—*unless* we activate one of the coastal beacons."

"It's so nice to see that you care, Lucas. Maybe you *should* stay. If I'm being honest, you probably react better to red lightning than the rest of us. Almost as well as the ambassador, I bet . . ."

Gemini and Griffin both started to shout at Fernando when Peppy barged into the room.

"Somebody's coming!"

Everyone except Thom, who kept watch over the unconscious ambassador, rushed out into the antechamber.

The rupture, Gemini thought. She tensed.

The diplomats and high-necks were pointing and shouting at a broken window that faced the east. Beyond it, a small square ship was careening clumsily towards the tower.

"Kappo airboat," Peppy said. He started to raise his scope shot, but Lucas held out his arm.

"That's *not* a Kappo."

The boat grew larger and larger, then it veered right past the window. All the civilians and the two members of Great Revere hit the floor, but Bedlam Athletic and Fernando rushed upstairs and back outside, just as the boat crashed onto the esplanade, churning up glass in its wake and braking to a whining halt at the center of the concourse. Smoke and flames rose off the stern engines.

A short, compact woman with dark, spiky hair and dressed in a long maroon sweater stumbled off the skiff. She had scrapes and deep cuts all over her arms and legs, including an ugly-looking gash in her left shoulder. Her carmine-colored halo, usually so bright, was now so weak that its shine could barely be seen through her gauntlet hand. Her broad face, which so often flashed a careless grin beneath knowing eyes, was twisted in anguish and exhaustion. Hail pelted her as she staggered towards them.

"Liz!" Lucas cried, rushing to her side.

Elizabeth from Ogunquit, the Premiere Durationist, closer for Tremont United, collapsed in his arms.

"Lucas . . ." She groaned. "Lucas—thank the *Process* you're here . . ." She gave a shuddering gasp.

Gemini had never seen such a great player, one of the finest in the history of the sport, so utterly spent. It frightened her.

"What happened out there, Liz?" asked Lucas.

"It's . . . it's bad, Lucas. You have no idea . . ."

Fernando cleared his throat. "Elizabeth," he said. "Where is the rest of your team? I have been trying to reach Captain Ahmed for hours now."

"Ahmed . . ." She sighed and slumped against Lucas's shoulder. "Ahmed . . . is broken. He is a Sleeper Thrall. He betrayed us to the Blood Poacher." She would have collapsed then and there, had Lucas not been there to keep her steady.

They went back down into the antechamber. While Lucas bandaged Liz's shoulder and scooped her some of his strength, Liz explained how her captain had betrayed them all to the Blood Poacher, how her wingmates Benjamin and Kim had met their end at New Bronx Seaport, and how she had narrowly escaped the Poacher's storm cruiser.

"Killer Fives was able to throw lightning like I've never seen a Blood Poacher do before," she said. "It flew off to chase after Toledo U, I think. Otherwise there's no way I would have escaped alive . . ."

Fernando shook his head in disbelief. "Are you're *sure* Ahmed didn't just go mad from all the red bolts?"

"No, he . . . he changed as we punched the core. His skin had inroad lines all over the place. His eyes caught on fire. That's when he pulled his sword on us and . . ." She trailed off.

Lucas exchanged looks with his team. Nobody spoke. For Elizabeth from Ogunquit to be this alarmed spoke volumes. Even worse, Gemini knew, was that Lucas's fear had proven correct: one of their own had betrayed them to the Echomar—and not just any Durationist, but Captain

Ahmed, leader of the league's flagship team. It was shocking, horrifying news, the kind of awful truth that made Gemini's halo flicker to even think about.

The thumping hail grew louder and louder.

"Well," said Fernando in a thin voice. His face was very pale. "That settles it. We're leaving now. You all, help me usher out the civilians."

"We're not going anywhere," said Lucas. "We have to buy the city enough time for the Red Tide fleet to arrive."

A line of thunder became a steady roar.

"Lucas, let me be very clear with you: I am *not* going to sacrifice *my* team to entertain your insane delusions about becoming a real player again."

The room was still. Lucas walked up to Fernando until they were about a foot apart. Lucas was a head taller, and though his face remained serene, his eyes glowered beneath the cowl. Fernando swallowed but held his stare.

"I *am* acting like a real player, Fernando. *This is our job!* We *can't* run. One of our own is responsible for tonight's events. It's *our* responsibility to make up for that. As powerful as Killer Fives is, the army it brought tonight is not strong enough to take on that many Durationists. We just have to hold out until morning. And if we activate one of those beacons, the odds will be in our favor. There's a chance we might even be able to take out the storm ourselves. But the fact is, if we do not activate one of those storm shields, an untold number of people in this city are going to die tonight."

The windows flashed with crimson light.

Fernando was still unmoved.

"Grant's Lighthouse is currently right under the heart of the storm. Now look, if you want to try to swim over there just to turn on the storm shield, I'd be *more* than happy to see you try."

"What about the Harlo Dam, then?"

"It's not worth the risk!"

"Fernando, you know Killer Fives as well as I do. You know full well that if that dam's shield is left inactive, Killer Fives will try to destroy the floodwall. Which means that if the lightning doesn't kill thousands of people, the flooding will!"

Something rattled upstairs.

"Lucas, listen to me." Fernando folded his arms, looked down, and sighed. When his face met Lucas's again, he looked tired. "Half my team is out of play. Truthfully, we were lucky to survive—and *yes*, I admit we have you to thank for it. But I still have a chance to fulfill the objective set before me, and that's what I'm going to do. I did not get this far in my career by flaunting league orders whenever I felt like it."

"What's going on tonight is beyond the league," said Lucas.

"Yes. It is. Which is exactly why storm hunting is not on my agenda. Think about it! If the storm killed these people, the damage would be immense! *I* have to make sure that doesn't happen. If you want to argue that ten thousand rabble are more important than a couple affordaires, you're entitled to your opinion. But I am a captain of a Duke's League team. I can't afford to traffic in moral quandaries."

"It's not about morals, Fernando. It's about justice. It's about fighting back against our enemy until nights like these never happen again."

Fernando shook his head. He let out a chuckling breath. "Ah, still the Lucas I remember. You know, this is exactly why the league wanted to ban you for life—"

"You'd be dead if it wasn't for us!" Gemini shouted. Lucas shot her a warning look, but right then she just didn't care. They had come this far, had saved everyone here, and she was not going to let this accomplished, arrogant player slander them or her captain.

Fernando sneered at her.

"We're all going to end up dead anyways if we listen to your self-righteous captain a second longer. Can't you see, girl? He's leading you all on a death march to try to validate his crackpot *school*. It's absolute insanity, but I won't stop you. The *Over-Soul* bless you! But I will not put *my* team at risk! Once again, my mission is to get these people to safety. And that's exactly what I'm go—"

White-hot pain shot across everyone's foreheads. The eastern sky burst with fire, and a terrible wind blew through the plaza.

—*Durationists.*

Something shrill and foreign dug itself deep into Gemini's head. Her hands shot to her temples, and she cried out as she felt pangs of fire clash against the inside of her skull. She looked out the window, and though she could not see the storm, the light coming through the shattered glass was now hauntingly white. The diplomats and execs broke out into screams. Some fell to the floor, faces twitching uncontrollably, limbs jerking with spasms. Somebody retched. Around her, the other Durationists were moaning and cringing. Only Lucas and Fernando managed to endure the Blood Poacher's words with just a grimace, but not even they were ready for what happened next.

"*Durationists. You cannot win.*"

Hearing that voice was like a blizzard of spitting whispers that stabbed into her ears to form a bloodcurdling scream. It made Gemini's heart stop, made her spine squirm like it was trying to rip itself out of her back. Squinting through her fingers, she searched for the source of the spoken word. It did not come from the sky. She saw that her captain and Fernando were looking up the stairs, and so she tracked their gaze up to the lobby, where the floor was rattling and the ghastly corpses were still strewn about.

"*Give us your fascists.*"

Gemini's stomach roiled; she thought she was going to be sick. She caught sight of a body hanging from the stairs. The corpse's jaw clenched as it moved.

The Poacher's speaking through the dead . . .

"*Give us your fascists. Give us your fascists or your* ghettos *will* drown in fire. *Your* fascist psychic masters *are weak. The end is coming. Death to Roslyn. Mind the Void, Durationists . . .*"

Then there was a passing cloud, and then the glow faded, and the pain in Gemini's head receded.

They worked to bring the civilians back to their senses; at least two of them had died. The thumping of hail had ceased, but jangling thunder and vengeful wind still rocked the tower.

After they tended to the fresh round of injuries, Fernando immediately started to round everyone up, his mind clearly made up more than ever. Much to her own shame, part of Gemini wanted very much also to leave, because she never wanted to feel that electric jolt slash through her mind ever again, and also because she feared that no matter how optimistic Lucas was, Bedlam Athletic stood no chance against Killer Fives.

"We're out of here," Fernando said. "You heard him. I'm not handing over our people just to satisfy that bastard's blood lust."

Much to Gemini's surprise, this time Lucas only nodded and said: "You're right. We need to get the ambassadors and execs to safety, and your wingers are in no condition for this fight. Take everyone back across the bay. My team will stay here and defend the people stuck in the valley."

Liz stood next to him. She leaned on his arm to steady herself. "I'm coming with you," she said.

9. Silver Bullet

THE GARAGE DOOR OPENED. Seven Durationists stared out at the empty, windswept freeway. They could just make out the glowing hill of New Bronx across the valley. Gemini wondered how many of those lights really were fires. Above the northern borough, the slate sky was ruptured by stains of scarlet and bone.

A smudge of violet smoke appeared over the road. The plasma grew refulgent as the Courier minded them.

—*An entire Kappo swarm has taken over New Bronx. They will march south just as the storm makes landfall over the valley.*

"How many, five thousand?" asked Lucas.

—*More or less.*

"And any word from Red Tide Fleet?"

—*Nothing since they departed the reach. They should be there by sunrise.*

A rumble of thunder. "Let's hope so. Thanks, Courier."

—*Good luck, Captain.*

Lucas watched the lightning for a moment longer. Then he turned to the other six players. While Old Atlantic—or at least the two members of their club who hadn't been knocked out or gone missing—hurriedly escorted the convoy of diplomats out of the city, this small company led by Bedlam Athletic would dare to punch into the core of the storm.

"Our goal," Lucas said, "is to buy everyone out there enough time until the Red Tide fleet gets here."

"How do we know the Poacher won't just try to knock the fleet out of the sky?" Griffin asked.

"Because the Blood Poachers are not staging a serious invasion of Metro Reef."

"They're not?"

"No. There are probably less than ten thousand Kappos out in the field tonight."

"That sounds like a lot to me."

"Two swarms are not enough for a prolonged insurgency. There's no sign on radar of another storm brewing off coast, so I think we can be certain that this thunderhead, vicious as it has been, is the lone cell the Echomar has dispatched tonight. Which means, again, this event was simply meant to be a demonstration of power. Which also means they'll retreat once the siege becomes more trouble than it's worth.

"But still, anyone stuck down in the valley is in grave danger. What few shelters they have are poorly designed and overcrowded—though as we've seen up here, storm shelters are no guarantee that anyone is safe against *this* storm. The local militia is probably overwhelmed fighting Kappo mobs in the streets. But leatherheads are the least of their troubles. Killer Fives will want to take as many lives as it can before sunrise. We can't let that happen."

He raised his gauntlet hand, and the other six Durationists imagined a map of the valley floating over his palm. The wide basin of gloomy slums and muddy fields was just a few miles across, a miserable shadow between the big city and the northern neighborhoods. A miniature replica of the storm hung like an anvil over the edge of the map.

Lucas pointed at the snaking river that ran through the middle of the valley.

"The Harlo River runs right under the center of the freeway, right where these suspension towers are. Now, there's a major shelter along the river, just east of the bridge . . . this oval building *here*. That's also the headquarters for the Harlo redcoats, and it's probably where a good chunk of the population is spending the night. If they aren't under attack yet, they will be once the storm rolls in. Unfortunately, the storm's still blotting out the codex, so we need to be close enough to warn the militia. Once we're out there, we need to give them cover while they get as many people west as they can."

Gemini eyed the anvil warily. "If the storm overtakes them while they're making a run for it, they could be sitting ducks."

"There's a way to keep them out of the storm's sight," said Lucas. "See these tunnels, right under the shelter? They run along the river, so the people can take them west. Plus, all the other shelter points are along that route, so everyone can spread the word as they go and get as many people away from the sound as they can."

"There could be Kappos in those tunnels," Griffin pointed out.

"That's a risk we'll have to take. I'd rather the redcoats tangle with a mob of leatherheads than have to deal with any red lightning. Still, that horde coming down from New Bronx could be a problem. They might overrun the shelter before anyone has a chance to get out. And, from what our friends here with Great Revere have told us, as well as Liz, it sounds like the redcoats have been in a firefight with blighters up in these northern neighborhoods all night. We have to help them hold the line until our people are in those tunnels. I want two of us to go directly to New Bronx. Shepherd, Kat." He nodded to the two county league players. "Are you up for a fight?"

"You can count on us," Shepherd from Old Hollow said. Both he and his striker, Kat from Sin City, had chosen to come along—perhaps, Gemini thought, to try to avenge the death of their teammates. The prospect of battle had apparently done well for them both: their halos were glowing a lot brighter than they had been just a while ago.

"Just so you know, Captain," said Shepherd, "I think there were a lot of people still trapped in the northern neighborhoods. It didn't seem like things were going very well up there . . ."

Lucas nodded. "Work with the redcoats to rescue as many as you can. There won't be enough time to save everyone, but if even one person is saved, that's a victory. Now, while you hold the line up north, and while the militia evacuates people out to the west, the rest of us will create a diversion to keep the White Eyes focused on us."

Gemini raised her eyebrows. "And just how are we gonna do that?"

"Kill as many Kappos as we can." Lucas smiled grimly. "I know Killer Fives. Given the chance, it will always go out of its way to kill Durationists. Always. Well, we will give it a chance, all right. Once it engages us, we'll head to the east side of the freeway. It's sparsely populated there, mainly just sand dunes and abandoned buildings. That way we'll keep people out of harm's way, and it's a good place to play cat-and-mouse."

Thunder growled.

"Any, uh, tips?" Peppy asked.

"Never directly engage a Blood Poacher. You *cannot* block red lightning, so don't even try it. Don't directly attack it. Just take potshots and kill as many Kappos as you can. That will get it angry, thus distracting it even more. Otherwise, just keep moving. If we get a good shot at the damn thing, Gemini, Liz, or I will take it. Otherwise, our goal is to just keep it busy. *Don't* try to be a hero! If you do, you'll be dead before you realize you made a mistake."

He looked at Elizabeth from Ogunquit. "Sorry, Liz, I should have deferred to you. Does all that sound right?"

Elizabeth smiled. "I couldn't have said it any better. Especially the last bit . . . there is one other danger, though."

"Flooding?" Lucas said.

Liz nodded and tapped at the source of the river. The land here rose sharply on either side of the watercourse to form a ravine. The ravine was well below sea level, and the only thing that kept it shallow was a tall dam that separated it from the sound.

"If Killer Fives blows up that dam—"

She waved her hand, and the wall disappeared. Water from the Jamaica Sound rushed through the narrow river glen before crashing atop tower blocks and streets, quickly inundating the valley in a catastrophic flood.

"If it pulls that off, it doesn't matter where anybody hides. No one's going to survive."

Peppy let out a low breath. "Gutless way to win a fight," he said.

"Killer Fives *loves* to fight dirty," Lucas said, frowning.

"There's a way to stop it," said Liz. "Somewhere inside the dam there's a mind box that can project a storm shield. One of the old city beacons."

"A beacon?" said Kat from Sin City.

"Storm beacons were part of an old defense program," explained Lucas. "They're projections of sky glass meant to repel Poacher Storms. Since the Echomar hasn't staged an attack on the interior for a long while, Londinium decided that all the ore lying around was better suited for fixes or weaponry, so most of the beacons have been decommissioned. But two still stand right here in Metro Reef: Grant's Lighthouse and the Harlo dam. Fernando was right: we're not getting to the lighthouse now, it's right under the storm. But the dam beacon's another story."

"Why hasn't anybody turned it on by now?" Gemini asked.

"It was our job to do it," Elizabeth said darkly. "I guess it was Ahmed's *real* job to make sure that we never got around to it. Judging from the work the Poacher's done to all the shelters tonight, the shield might not be foolproof. But it is made of some really pure ore, some of the finest we have, so at the very least it will take a while to chip away, a lot longer than the dam itself would take. It should buy us enough time until sunrise, I think."

"There is also a chance that if we turn on the shield with the Blood Poacher close by, we could incapacitate it," said Lucas.

"Just as long as it doesn't blow up the dam first," said Gemini.

"We'll have to cut it close," Lucas said. "We'll split up. Gemini, Griffin, and Peppy, you three will go turn on the shield, while Liz and I distract the Poacher."

"You sure you want to do that job by yourselves?" Griffin asked.

"Don't worry about us," said Liz. "Although, since you mention it, Lucas, there is a chance that you and I will also have to go separate ways. Kappos will probably try to march down the freeway. We can't let them or they'll be sniping down evacuees all night. Not to mention they might try another attack on the city. It's probably best if I hold them off solo while you keep Fives busy."

"I don't like the idea of everyone splitting up," Griffin said, and Gemini was inclined to agree.

Lucas scratched his chin. "Once the beacon is up and the evacuees are secure, we can regroup. I'll stay with Liz as long as I can, then I'll figure out a way to draw Killer Fives away from everyone. It will think it has us on the run, that it's forcing us to separate. If we hold the northern lines, and if I keep it distracted long enough. Yes . . . *yes*." His eyes glowed with triumph. "We have the damn thing beat!"

"What is it?" asked Liz.

"I'm going to make the Poacher think there's a ton of people trapped in this high-rise on the other side of the river. It should have been abandoned hours ago. If we can fool the storm into believing otherwise, that should draw a lot of Kappos—not to mention Killer Fives—as far off the scent as we can take them."

"How are you going to do that?" Gemini asked.

"Leave that to me. As long as you three activate the shield just as the storm passes over the dam, the beacon will catch the Poacher off guard and cripple its fleet. At the same time"—he pointed at the high-rise he had in mind for a decoy, on a ridge overlooking the sound just south of the dam—"if I can keep Killer Fives interested in this building long enough, the Poacher will be close enough to the beacon that we might be able to stun it. Maybe even long enough to kill it."

There was a calm silence. The other Durationists struggled to accept the enormity of Lucas's plan. If the final part worked, the battle might be over before reinforcements even arrived, and they would be able to claim something few teams in conscious history ever could: that they had vanquished a Blood Poacher!

But it was a big *if* . . .

"If there are no questions, then let's get ready to move. Red Tide will be here at dawn. At the very least, we just have to make it until then. Before we go, Liz—if you could come back upstairs with me for a minute, we need to collect as much untarnished blue ore as we can. Now that I think about it, I need your cribbing skills, too."

If Liz thought this request was unusual, she did not show it. She simply nodded, and they started upstairs.

"One last thing," Griffin called after them. "What if the Poacher breaks the dam before we get to it?"

It was Liz who spoke.

"Just leave that to your captain and me."

The Durationists prepared for battle. Lucas had cribbed Bedlam Athletic's transportation into the garage. Shepherd and Kat, who had lost their vehicles during the Blood Poacher's attack, jump-started an abandoned militia ATV. Gemini checked to see if the damage to her moped had been erased. Then she sat down on the floor with her legs crossed and started her battle meditation. As she began, she noticed Shepherd and Kat start their own pregame ritual, murmuring a list of mantras under their breath.

"*The Icons are my windows to the world. They are my eyes, and Duration is my being. The Icon of* Alchemy *will guide my striker, and the Icon of* Force *will—*"

"I think you missed a line," Kat muttered.

"Ah, shit," Shepherd said. "Did I ever tell you how much I hate the new code? Too much to remember. Why can't we just take some fixes? You see the Blood Works players? Just pop a few pills and you're ready to go."

"You know, I was talking to Lucas's left-winger. He uses *Alchemy* too. He used to play for the Blood Works Society, and apparently they gave him a pill for every slag. Like, if he just wanted to tap into air pressure, all he had to do was take a fix. So jealous . . . oh well, we're the idiots who walked into a Cog Mind gym."

"No kidding—Hey, Gem, what kind of routine do you guys have?"

Gemini shrugged. "Really, all Lucas asks us to do is just think about our dedication."

"Think about what?"

"How it connects us to Duration, stuff like that."

"No lists? No memorizing lines? See—the only people who have it worse than us are the damn Last Church players. I'd rather recite some shit about how my Icon helps me see the world than pray to the Barra any day."

Kat urged him to stay focused, but as they resumed their mantra, their eyes lingered on Gemini for a few seconds, as if they hadn't totally believed her explanation for the Meta-School's ways and were hoping to glimpse some hint of what Lucas really had in store. But Gemini just sat there, hands in her lap, eyes half open, until they finally turned away.

She could not blame them for being curious. Anyone who hadn't automatically dismissed Lucas from Slag Falls as a crank really did wonder what kind of gist he had in mind for the Meta-School, what his secret methods were to tap into Duration, and just what kind of techniques he had imparted to his fledgling crop of players. Now and then a reporter from one of the many fancasts out there showed up at their gym and started snooping around, asking players just how the Cowl had them training. As campus administrator, Gemini had made it one of her personal assignments to personally shoo off any talkie that showed up uninvited on their property.

She frowned. Outside of a few cryptic hints, Lucas had never bothered to explain to her exactly what his overarching plan was. She had been honest with Shepherd and Kat: all she had done in her battle meditation was just imagine how the Icon of *Energy* burned within her, how everything was made of bounded flames and waiting for a practitioner of *Energy* to free them. All Lucas asked from his players before combat was to internalize the powers of their aspect, to feel how everything else in Duration partakes in their chosen Icon. He even permitted his players to keep using techniques they had learned from past affiliates, perhaps knowing that the average Durationist was loath to relinquish habits that he or she had grown accustomed to over the seasons. And while both Gemini and Peppy had been all too happy to discard the mind-numbing itineraries of the Cog Mind, Gemini was certain that if she looked over her shoulder, she would see Griffin take a light fix to aid his meditations. And if he or Peppy felt any less confident in their battle meditations than she, they had never said a word to her; she was sure that the exercise left their gauntlet hands glowing just as bright at hers.

Still, Gemini was troubled. Did Lucas not want her or anyone else to know what his designs for the Meta-School really were? Did he not trust her with the strategies he intended to use to fight the Blood Poachers? Or did he think that their affiliate's gist was already obvious and didn't need explaining?

She closed her eyes, took a deep breath, and dismissed the thought. Such worries couldn't help her at the moment, and one thing Lucas had insisted to her, explicitly, was that her battle meditation ought to leave her *knowing* her place in the here and now. *Always live in the moment,* he had told her back on the train, *for it's the moment that divides into past and future. You cannot see the distance without knowing the foreground.*

Another breath, and she whittled her mind of concern. She fell deeper and deeper into her trance, her eyes closed, her face screwed up in concentration, until her halo blossomed like the high sun. Her heart was filled with the prickling sensation of a match being lit. A serene calmness overtook her, and her expression softened as she imagined herself drifting apart. As she dove into her Now-Sense, she felt as if her eyes and ears were floating away, so that she was in one place but many other places, and then and there she became acutely aware of what everyone else was doing.

Up in the lobby, Lucas and Elizabeth had finished piling chunks of sky glass that had fallen out of the shelter's ceiling into a mound. They had gathered a lot; the pile was a head taller than Lucas. He and Liz raised their hands and murmured a few words, and a second later, although Gemini thought she saw the pile was still there, she decided it must have just been a trick of the gloomy light, because the floor was now bare.

Their work done, Liz and Lucas now stood together by a hole in the wall, watching the rain.

"I'm sorry about Kim and Benjamin," Lucas was saying. "Ahmed, too. Whenever it happened, he died then."

"It's okay," said Liz. "I'll be okay." Gemini was surprised to see her take Lucas's hand.

"I'm just glad you're here, Lucas. At least something good happened tonight."

"You're probably—no, definitely—the only Steward who would ever say that."

She laughed. "Zeno loves you too."

"Oh, yeah. I keep forgetting he's one of the alumni . . ."

Suddenly feeling very indecent for eavesdropping, Gemini forced her mind away from them and back into the garage. But instead of returning to her own head, her focus settled upon Peppy and Griffin. The wingers were double- and triple-checking their equipment.

". . . still can't believe it," Peppy was saying. He shook his head as he reassembled the barrel of his scope shot. "When do you suppose he defected?"

"Who knows." Griffin was adjusting the loft on his zero-iron. He seemed distracted.

"Probably years ago, I bet. You can't break a Durationist in one night, can you? Didn't the captain say some Sleepers stay in denial about it for years until they snap? Maybe that's what happened . . ."

"Yeah, maybe—listen, does it bother you the captain doesn't want us to take a shot against the Blood Poacher?"

"Huh? No, not really. I mean, he probably figures only he or Liz have the experience to handle that kind of thing, right?"

"He said Gem could, though."

"Oh, yeah. Well, I mean, she is our closer. That's what closers do, yeah? Kill Blood Poachers."

"I know, I know. And nothing against Gem either. She was awesome back there. I'm just wondering . . .—"

"What?"

"Well, don't you think the captain's overthinking all this? Is all this old-school stuff really gonna matter when shit hits the fan? I was talking to that chick from Great Revere. Did you know most of the Cog Mind teams don't even teach the differences between wingers and closer anymore? Even Toledo U just uses the different position titles out of tradition, nothing else—did you know that?"

"That right?" Peppy said while checking his ammunition.

"And then there's all those county league teams I was telling you about. The ones using three or five players instead of four."

"Uh-huh."

"I'm just saying . . . why's the captain so sure diamond formation is our best bet on a night like this?"

"I dunno, Griff. But like I said, I'm sure the boss has his reasons."

"Yeah . . . I guess."

"—love to know how you were able to get it back."

Unabated, Gemini's mind had turned back to Lucas and Liz. They were walking back downstairs and had paused on a landing while Lucas inspected Liz's stormhammer with an admiring eye.

"It's an old cribbing trick I figured out years ago," Liz said. "Can recall items that are precious to me, even if they were stolen or lost. I don't know why I never explained to you how to do it . . ."

Lucas handed back the weapon and gave her an appraising look.

"You say that like you won't get the chance."

She shifted uncomfortably. "Lucas, there's something else bothering me about tonight. Something's off."

"What do you mean?"

"I don't get what the Fathom is trying to do here. They weren't worried about anyone finding out Ahmed was theirs. Hell, Killer Fives *told me*, and told me it wanted me to tell everyone. Think of all the intel they must be throwing away. Ahmed must have told them loads about the league, about the Blood Works Society. It's all over now. It just seems like a big piece to waste just for a hit-and-run attack."

"Well, they *did* knock out our best team," Lucas pointed out, not without sympathy. "The Blood Works Society's hegemony will take a big hit, and the country's going to be a real mess until Open Season is sorted out. If nothing else, a lot people died tonight, and many more will be scared to even leave their homes. All victories for Vlaz Gal."

"And they would have accomplished all that even if they had never blown Ahmed's cover. All they had to do was kill me and no one would know a thing! Ahmed could have even pretended to survive, and he would have been able to keep spying on us. Instead they kept me alive with the intent of letting me talk. Lucas . . ." She hesitated, then looked at him. "The only way this makes sense is if they have another Sleeper they think is more important than Ahmed."

Rain dribbled down a window. Lucas tugged at his beard for a few moments and said nothing.

"If that's the case," he said at last, "it would have to be somebody who could offer them everything Ahmed did. In terms of intelligence, in terms of influence. Maybe even more. But who would be a bigger prize for the Fathom than the captain of Roslyn's highest-ranked team?"

"I don't know," Liz said. "It could be someone high up, or it could be someone the Fathom believes will rise during Open Season. But if I know one thing about the Blood Poachers, it's that they don't look at us the way we see ourselves. They don't care about our rankings or what league we play in. They only care about how much damage someone can do if their halo was to go toxic. And wealth doesn't always show how many lives we touch, does it, Lucas?"

She looked away from him. "Just make sure Simon and the others know, okay? If the league's this badly compromised, they'll need Echo Division more than ever."

"Once again, you talk as if you won't be coming back with us."

"It's . . . going to be a long battle, Lucas. I'm just making peace with what could happen."

Gemini listened on, her heart racing. Ahmed's betrayal had been disturbing enough. The idea that *another* Durationist could have turned was unthinkable. She tried to picture what Durationist could join the Thrall, but the moment she asked the question, a heavy weight pressed on her shoulders, and she was rooted on the spot. She felt something strike her in the heart and she let out a small gasp. She opened her eyes, but she was no longer in the garage: all she saw were the terrible images of a triumphant queen and dying king. The death rattle grazed her ears. Gemini thought she would lose her own breath from shock.

She exhaled. The king and queen vanished. In their place, she pictured a wall of dancing, spinning flames. She welcomed the light to her eyes, enjoyed the heat against her skin, but something was still wrong. Within the raging inferno was a lone flame a shade cooler than the rest. It quivered and spat, and as Gemini focused on the writhing lick she grew overwhelmed with anger and fear. Whether it was her own emotions or someone else's, she could not say. All she knew was her own frustration at questions left unanswered, her own dread that what she saw portended to her own doom . . .

"Gemini."

She opened her eyes. Lucas had reentered the garage and knelt down beside her.

"Before we go, there's something we have to talk about."

"How to kill the Blood Poacher." Her voice sounded dreamy from the trance. She didn't know how she knew, other than the fire must have told her.

"As the closer," her captain said, "you may have that opportunity. It also may fall to Liz or myself. But if you have a shot, your kreisflyer alone will be useless. None of our conventional weapons will do any good against it. Only one thing will . . ."

He produced a silver ball the size of a marble. Despite its diminutive size, Gemini was in awe. It was like staring at the deepest, darkest night sky that held an infinite amount of stars—except Lucas was holding that vast power between two fingers.

"Do you know what this is?"

"A silver bullet," she breathed. Anyone who had ever dreamed of playing closer dreamed specifically of this moment, when they were bestowed with the one weapon that could kill a Blood Poacher. Gemini felt another pair of eyes gazing at the small but immense projectile. She threw a glance behind her and saw Griffin quickly look away.

"A silver bullet is made of the highest grade of ore known to man," Lucas said. "It is so dense, so packed with pure cogs, that this one bullet alone has more raw power than every other Durationist weapon ever combined. Silver bullets are very rare, which is why each team only carries one. But a true shot will destroy a Blood Poacher outright."

"Have you ever used one?"

"Yes. At Dixie Reach. That's how my grudge shot earned its nickname." He patted the butt of his rifle. Etched onto the side were the words *Storm Killer*.

"So . . . if I think I have a shot . . ."

"First, summon the bullet. Then—show me your kreisflyer . . . see that notch at the center of the blade?"

"Yes."

"Place the bullet in there and throw."

Lightning struck the valley. The garage glowed a brilliant red.

"Then what?" Gemini asked.

Lucas laughed. "Then think of a good nickname for your sickle." He got to his feet, patted her on the shoulder, and went over to check on Peppy and Griffin.

Thunder clapped. Gemini stood up. Her legs were very weak, and this time she was sure that it was her own fear she felt. She had always known this moment would eventually come: by the very nature of the position, the closer punched the core of the storm more daringly and more recklessly than any other player and thus was often the one with the best shot against the Eyes of Thunder. Yet somehow, stupidly, Gemini had never expected her chance to come on a night like this, when things were so dire (*when were they ever* not *dire during a Poacher Storm?*) and when the fate of hundreds of thousands of lives might depend on her not-always-brilliant aim (*but was there such a thing as fighting a Blood Poacher when the stakes were low?*).

"Don't overthink it."

Liz stood across the bike from her. She smiled sympathetically.

"When you're a closer, you can't worry about the burden. You just gotta trust that you know what you're doing."

"But how can I do that," Gemini said, a little helplessly, "when so many people might be counting on me?"

Liz still beamed at her. Despite her youthful face, her dark eyes conveyed all the wisdom of her six-hundred-year career, a career twice as long as Gemini had even been in Roslyn.

"I'll put it to you this way. Trusting yourself is all you got left. All those worries and cares won't do you a damn bit of good when the going gets tough. Find a way to believe in yourself now, because there's going to be a moment in the battle where you'll need it."

"When?"

"When you stare down the eyes of the Blood Poacher," Liz said. "When you see the White Eyes up close, you won't even remember any of the other fears you've ever had, believe me. And only one thing can save you then."

"What?" Gemini breathed. The garage, everyone else, seemed very far away.

"Your instincts," Liz said. "Trust them, trust yourself out there no matter what, and you'll make the right choices when it counts."

"Final words, everyone," Lucas called out. "Then we're hitting the road."

"One other thing," Liz said. "When you get to the beacon, you may have to answer some questions to activate it."

Another thunderbolt struck close by. Another blinding flash of red. Another boom of thunder.

"Questions?" Gemini repeated numbly.

"Yes. It was built by the Last Church, so the mind box that controls the dam might contain some riddles related to their lore. I'm sure it's nothing you don't know, but if it is, again—remember. Trust yourself. Do that, Gemini, and I think you'll do just fine."

The Premiere player winked at her before going over to console Shepherd and Kat. Gemini watched her walk away, feeling better about herself and yet not entirely confident she could follow Liz's advice, whether or not she could trust herself to ... well, trust herself. She sighed, then walked over to her teammates.

Lucas started pacing in front of them. "Now listen," he said. "Over the years I've always told my teams to ignore the press. Also, I have never been one for big pep talks. But here's the deal: no one thought we'd be here tonight. On this night, on any night. All the experts wrote us off a long time ago. They wrote you off, they wrote me off. I bet people don't even believe we're really out here, that it's some kind of joke ...

"Well, here we are. And each of you deserves to be out here, because you earned it. You ignored the noise and put up with all my coaching these past few seasons, and you earned the right to be out here on a night like this. I've worked too hard—you've worked too hard—to let it slip away." The golden cuff gleamed on his wrist. "Tonight, we prove that we're here to stay."

Gemini swallowed, listening with rapt attention. Peppy and Griffin stood absolutely still. Lucas's voice was cool, but there was something in his inscrutable eyes that she had only seen a handful of times before, moments where something fiery inside him broke through and the color of his eyes lit up his gaunt face.

"The most important thing I can tell you, my friends, is this: Stick to your roles. Play your position. Be disciplined." As he said this, he gave Griffin a significant look, and Gemini wondered if their captain had an inkling of their left-winger's reservations. "Only a team that works in concert can destroy a Blood Poacher. No, we can't block the Poacher's attacks. But if you stick to your assignments, if you play within yourself, Duration has a way of keeping you safe, of making sure that you stay out of harm's way. I know this. I've seen it too many times for it to not be true. The bane of a Blood Poacher's existence is a smart, disciplined Durationist team. That's what stands before me. And no matter what happens, I am proud to have fought with the three of you, and I will back whatever decisions you make out there.

"Stick to your roles. Stick to your roles, and by sunrise we will have taken the field. Win tonight, and they can't write us off anymore. Do you understand me? Win tonight, and we prove that we are here to stay."

His three teammates nodded, speechless. The thunderhead snarled.

A lump had grown in Gemini's throat, but as she walked back to her bike, her legs no longer felt so weak, and though her heart still beat fast, there was now a warmth in her chest.

"Liz," Lucas called. "Ready?"

"Yes," Liz said, breaking out of a huddle with Shepherd and Kat. All three of them had bleary eyes, and Gemini had the distinct impression they had been exchanging tributes and vows to avenge their fallen teammates.

Lucas got on his ATV. Liz sat behind him. Shepherd and Kat started up their vehicle, while Peppy kicked his bike to life and Griffin got under his glider. Gemini swung atop her moped and gave the starter a sharp kick. The garage rumbled with purring engines; thunder clapped outside. The road ahead led to a mountain of smoldering soot and zigzagging fire.

"All right," Lucas said. "Let's roll."

There was a series of whining growls. Gemini gunned the throttle, and the next thing she knew she was shooting out of the garage and onto the highway.

10. Punching the Core

THE SKY FLASHED. ABANDONED cars were scattered across the road, many with their doors still hanging open and lights still turned on. Lucas and Liz took the lead and weaved between the stranded vehicles, Shepherd and Kat right behind them. Gemini brought up the rear, with Griffin soaring overhead. As they crossed over the southern end of the valley a vicious, stinging blast of wind tried to wipe them off the road. Lampposts on either side of the overpass groaned and bent. The entire freeway was shaking beneath them, as if the earth itself dreaded the storm's impending landfall.

Beneath them were clusters of tower blocks and shanty villages that dotted the muddy slopes. Many structures had been damaged in the first wave of storms, with windows blown out and roofs torn off. People were still on the streets, openly panicking, throwing one another aside in their rush to reach any kind of sanctuary. Gemini heard screams in quick bursts as they zipped over the slums, but she also minded the scoops of people trapped under rubble or running from blighters.

Lucas did not look back at anyone, but his scoop answered what the other six Durationists were probably thinking.

—*We have to keep going. If we don't punch the core, no one's going to survive anyway.*

The entire sky was shrouded in inky darkness, but the crimson strobes that flashed across the east betrayed the outline of the thunderhead that loomed closer and closer to the coast. The storm towered over the sound like a churning cliff of granite and fire. All the northern neighborhoods had vanished beneath a sable curtain, and the beam of the lighthouse was completely smothered. Though the White Eyes remained hidden, Gemini was certain that they were being watched. She was still afraid, but there was now also the thrill she always felt before battle, like the excitement before a big scrimmage, only a hundred times greater . . .

—*Watch out! Airboat right behind us.*

Not a second after Lucas's warning, red streaks hurtled by, cutting down streetlights and blowing up huge chunks of pavement. Peppy barely swerved out of the way of a falling lamppost, while Gemini wheeled past a crater that blew open in front of her. She glanced over her shoulder and saw the skiff fly out from behind the TAN building, turrets blazing. Another round of strafing riddled the highway, and the Durationists wound between and around abandoned cars and trucks so that the missiles hit them instead. Gemini felt a great heat lick at her back from the ensuing explosions.

—*Griffin, do you have a shot?*

—*I'm on it.*

Gemini felt him jet past her, then watched as he pulled up in a steep ascent and went behind the rest of the company. There were more thumping shots from the skiff's cannons, but no strikes hit the road. Gemini glanced back and saw that Griffin had come out of his somersault behind the Kappos. They swiveled their guns at him and were trying to knock him out of the sky. Gliding between their fire, Griffin sliced the air with his zero-iron, and a swift gust blew three of the leatherheads right off the deck. Griffin barreled away from more gunfire, then caught rain on the blade of his weapon. He swung the zero-iron before veering sharply away from a volley of red rockets. A chunk of ice embedded itself in the airboat's engine. The Kappos on board started yelping in panic as the propeller screeched to a halt, and then the boat plummeted nose-first into the road below. Griffin zipped past the resulting fireball and rejoined the rest of the company.

From the front of the group, Lucas gave a thumbs-up.

—*Good deal, Griffin.*

Thunder growled disapprovingly, as if the storm were vexed by their march. The rain intensified, and the downpour became so heavy that Gemini did not see the suspension towers until they were practically driving beneath them. They had reached the center of the freeway. On the other side of the highway, a dozen Kappos with crooked rifles and scope shots were taking turns firing down at the oval-shaped building next to the bridge. It was the storm shelter! Its curved roof rose just over the freeway, and it was shattered with a dark, smoking hole. Gemini grimaced. Lightning must have hit this shelter too.

Lucas jerked the wheel of his ATV, and he and Liz did a flying roll over the island at the freeway's center. They landed flush on the other side of the road. A trio of Kappos looked his way just before he ran them over. Before he even came to a halt, Liz jumped off the back of the kart and brought her sledgehammer down on three more grubby combatants, who could do little more than gawp before her weapon collided with them. With a screaming clang and a miasma of blistering colors, they crumpled into cinder.

Shepherd and Kat joined the fray. Shepherd swung at the Kappos with a wooden bat, his skill with the Icon of *Force* multiplying the impact of each blow he landed so that he bowled over a bunch of Kappos at once, while Kat threw out her hands and conjured wisps of orange fire that bounced across the pavement and burned down the rest of the mob. By the time Gemini, Griffin, and Peppy came to a stop, all the Kappos had been reduced to smoking scrap.

Lucas kicked aside a sparking carcass. Then he peered down between the hangers of the bridge. A hundred feet below, a squad of redcoats were holed up by the entrance to the shelter. Several civilians were peering out behind them. The cops lowered their weapons. One of the redcoats waved up at Lucas. It would have been ridiculous to shout over the howling wind, so instead he minded them.

—*Thanks for the help, Captain. We're kind of in a jam here. The lightning did something to the shelter; it was making people talk funny. We crammed everyone into the lower floors, but the red shit started spreading down here. We were trying to figure out where else we could go when those blighters started shooting at us.*

—*Unfortunately, it's about to get worse,* scooped Lucas. —*The Poacher Storm is going to make a direct hit here.*

Lightning flashed. Gemini looked the opposite way, eastward, where the barren wastes rose to meet the sound, and the shallow river entered a narrow ravine that ended at a stark, gray wall. The Harlo Dam was just a practice field away. The storm was still offshore, though growing closer by the minute. They had time, but they needed to act fast.

—*What are your orders?* the redcoat below asked.

Just then a bullet whizzed by Lucas's head. He didn't blink, but the other Durationists took cover behind a cluster of cars, and more Kappos began to march towards them from the bridge's north end. Peppy started sniping them down while Gemini tossed her sickle in a great loop, and before she even caught the rebound a pair of Kappo heads tumbled out of the fog. Kat kept slinging fireballs down the road. A sudden flash signaled whenever she connected with a blighter.

Lucas remained by the side of the bridge, occasionally deflecting a shot with his sword without even raising his head.

—*Start evacuating people into the tunnels along the river,* he told the militiamen, *take the sewers as far west as you can go. Alert any shelters along your way to do the same. How many people do you need to move?*

The redcoat was already waving his men to action.

—*A few thousand. Plus there's still a lot of people trapped uphill . . . hordes have been pouring out of New Bronx all night. My men are doing their best to try to keep blighters from creeping down into the neighborhoods. But there's just too many.*

Thunder crackled over the gunfire. Lucas glanced back at the storm, which was growing closer and closer to landfall, then blocked a shot before responding.

—*Have you had any word from the eastern valley?*

—*Nothing for a few hours. They got hit hard early on. We heard a rumor that a lone Durationist was helping them escape . . . but nothing else.*

—*I'm sending two of my players down to help you hold the northern ridge. The rest of us are going to give you cover while you evacuate. If you have any men to spare, and if they're brave, I need help with something important. But it's very dangerous.*

No sooner had Lucas cribbed Shepherd and Kat down to the riverfront than Gemini felt something sting on the back of her neck. It was only then that she noticed vapor rising off the pavement around them. Except it wasn't vapor, for water vapor didn't sizzle and writhe into the air as this rain did. Nor was rain supposed to smoke or burn. She noticed little puffs of smoke rising from the sleeves of her jacket. It was singeing her clothes, boring into her skin! The other Durationists winced as they realized what was falling on them.

"Acid rain!" Peppy exclaimed.

Liz pointed a pointed a finger upward and the acid ceased to hit them, instead burning atop the invisible shield she had conjured over their heads.

"Right on schedule," Lucas muttered with a frown. He knowingly looked east, a moment before a line of fireballs appeared out of the iron sky.

"Look out!" he shouted.

Everyone ducked for cover just before everything around them exploded.

Bridge cables snapped apart; parts of the road went flying. Gemini threw herself away from a car, and a moment later it was struck by a fireball and went hurtling off the overpass. Below them, cops shouted and pushed people back into the shelter just before the burning wreckage crashed onto the street. When the blasts finally subsided, Gemini dared to look up. Gaping holes riddled the freeway. Fires had broken out in the tower blocks below. Lucas helped her to her feet, and they looked out towards the sound.

A long, obelisk-shaped smear emerged from the storm, lights blinking along its surface. Gemini realized it was cannon fire. She felt rooted on the spot at the sight of the monstrous Echomar warship. A small, passing cloud receded against the thunderhead, like a tiny iceberg breaking before the hull of a colossal ship, and the White Eyes of Thunder surfaced through the smoky slate, leering at them menacingly.

The wind was screaming, the thunder unyielding. Another round of red rockets exploded around them, followed by more gunfire from up the road. A fresh horde of Kappos appeared, riding aboard a clanking tank. Slasher Kappos rolled past, and Liz ran out to meet them, while Peppy began sniping away at the smaller enemies aboard the tank.

Lucas, Griffin, and Gemini took cover behind a truck. The clouds around the White Eyes stirred. Something massive was unfurling, and Gemini thought she saw the shape of horned wings before the clouds burst with webbed lightning that raced to stretch out over the entire valley. Everything shook madly. Wherever Gemini looked, buildings erupted in flames.

"Get to the beacon!" Lucas shouted at her and Griffin. He grabbed them and shoved them aside, just before something struck the truck and blew it sky-high. Peppy rushed over to them while strafing at the incoming Kappos.

"I can't crib you down there," Lucas said. "It's too risky now. You're going to have to make the jump. We'll find you after you get the shield running. Go!" He drew his zeitblatt and raced out to meet the charging Kappos.

Gemini, Griffin, and Peppy looked at each other and nodded. Gemini got back onto her moped with Peppy hitching on behind her. Griffin slipped into his glider, dashed for the edge of the bridge, and jumped. Gemini took one look at the riverfront below, then sped for a hole that had formed in the side of the road and throttled into the air, the sky bursting red all around them, the Blood Poacher watching their descent until they fell through a blanket of mist and out of sight.

The fog gathered under the bike's tires as they plunged towards the earth. Gemini couldn't see Griffin, couldn't see anything except a constant strobe of red light. An endless screech of wind and thunder filled her ears. The clouds were spinning madly, and the gales threatened to pitch her dangerously off course. Peppy gripped Gemini's waist so tightly she thought she was going to choke.

Refusing to let herself panic, she pulled the handles up to keep the nose of the bike above her. Then she focused on the fog, willing it gather under the wheels, to wrap around the frame of the bike, using it to slow her fall.

The moped shuddered against gravity, wrestling in the ethereal net Gemini had conjured with the Icon of *Energy*. The haze stopped swirling, the wind around her calmed, and she could distinctly hear explosions and gunfire breaking out all around her. The bike steadied, and she held her breath as they emerged from the bottom of the fog.

She found herself falling towards the river. Gemini hit the throttle and made a nosedive for the path along the bank. But the wind, as if doing everything it could to thwart the landing, pressed down on the bike, threatening to send them crashing into the embankment . . .

Peppy stretched an arm past her, his eye on the pathway. "I got it, I got it!" he yelled. In that moment, all even Gemini could see was the gravel road, as if nothing else had ever existed—

She grunted and rammed against the handles of the bike. Peppy swung forward into her. They had landed right on the edge, with the rear wheel of the bike caught on the embankment. Gemini gunned the engine, and with a squeal they skidded onto the unpaved road.

Immediately they saw a pack of Kappos running down a man and woman. The Kappos were hopping onto the man, knives drawn. The man started to scream, and the color around him faded, inky smoke rising into the air. His partner struggled to crawl away, but already the ragged leatherheads were overtaking her—

Three Kappos tottered into one another, heads and limbs erupting in fire as the kreisflyer ripped right through them. Three more fell in rapid succession under the barrel of Peppy's tin shot. As Gemini caught her weapon, the four remaining Kappos started to flee towards the dam in retreat. But a sudden gust sent them against a brick wall along the road, crushing them into a flaming heap. Griffin landed next to his teammates, zero-iron drawn.

Gemini hopped off her bike and rushed over to the fallen man. The woman was sobbing hysterically next to him. Gemini grabbed the man's halo-hand and tried to feed him some of her strength. He looked as if he was smeared in shades of gray. His face was vacant and blurry. The oily shadows kept rising from the wounds in his chest. Griffin hailed a pair of redcoats over to them just as the man took a shuddering breath, and the smoke escaping him finally started to thin.

"Take him to the shelter and get him down in the tunnels!" Gemini told the cops as they placed the man on a stretcher. She swallowed hard as she watched them head back under the bridge, the woman still sobbing, puffs of smoke still flowing from the man's chest as they disappeared behind a curtain of rain.

She shook her head and turned to her wingmates. "Come on. We gotta get there before the Poacher does."

She and Peppy hitched back onto the motorbike and started towards the ravine. Griffin glided low alongside them. Rain whipped in all directions.

It again started to singe their clothes, and so Griffin, leering out from under his shaking glider, raised his zero-iron in front of them, and a forking wind summoned by the blade of his staff kept as much of the downpour away from them as possible. Gemini glanced upward and immediately felt vertigo: through the lightning, she found herself gazing up at the thunderhead's face, all the way to its overshooting top. A harsh, flattening burst of air fell down upon them. The storm was almost directly over them now.

They were on the very outskirts of the valley, riding alongside the fetid river and down a rolling road amid fields of dead grass and sand dunes. Gemini risked looking back. She saw the prismatic flare from Liz's hammer, could see the distorted bubble that formed around her captain as he halted leatherheads in their tracks. Liz and Lucas stood side by side on the bridge. Wave after wave of leatherheads and Slashers were charging at them from either direction. The two Durationists were moving frenetically, the air around their weapons sizzling with maroon and cobalt. Scores of sparking Kappos fell from the bridge, their flaming, broken bodies piling up along the river below. Then a dark swell of clouds reached out from the thunderhead and swallowed the freeway, and the shelter, the bridge, and Lucas and Liz all vanished in bloody mist.

"They'll be fine," Peppy said from behind her. "They've have handled worse than this."

They rode on. Another Kappo mob hopped out of the alleyways to their left, and they cut, shot, and blew them down without braking. An airboat passed by, and a dozen more Kappos floated down towards them on parachutes. Peppy started picking them off. Griffin eyed the power lines that crossed the river just behind where the Para-Kappos were descending.

"Gemini, you know if those wires are still live?"

Gemini reached out through *Energy*, felt up the atoms of the electrical towers on either side of the river, all the way up to the conductors hanging from their crossarms. At once she felt a deep thrumming.

"Live!"

Griffin ascended in another spiraling somersault, and as he came level with the Para-Kappos he sliced the air with his zero-iron. A huge wave of wind sent the entire horde flying back into the power lines. There was a series of shrieks, flames, and bursting fires. A few smoldering corpses landed around the trio as they drove by; the other Kappos remained hanging from the power lines, swaying in the wind.

The sky flashed endless red now, and buildings on desolate hills rising on either side of the river were aflame. Shouts and sirens clashed with the thunder and rain. People were screaming in the distance, and the smell of smoke filled the air. An eerie glow seemed to emanate from somewhere behind them. All of the valley was ablaze. Up the northern ridge, Gemini could see a column of redcoats rushing out into a distant square to meet a mob of Kappos, and she could just make out the flames spewing from the hands of Kat from Sin City before rainfall obscured the scene. She could hear Kat's thoughts, too, before the Poacher Storm swallowed them.

—Shepherd, I'm going in. I think there's p-people trapped up in th-that sh-shop . . . C-come . . . g-guys, l-let's-

As they shot past the scorched dwellings along the slopes, Gemini saw men and women who were dashing for shelter being helplessly jerked backwards by the forceful wind. Or at least she assumed that was what was happening. Ludicrously, she almost perceived clawed, whiplike tentacles grabbing their shoulders from behind to drag them into the fog . . .

We have to hurry, she thought.

The gusts were so intense now that Gemini was forced to swerve back and forth as to not topple over. The sounds of thunder, wind, and rain had merged into one blaring roar. Gemini did not dare mind the radar, but if she did, she suspected she would find that they were now almost in the heart of the storm.

She, Peppy, and Griffin were punching the core.

"I can't even see the ravine!" Peppy said. "It's gotta be coming up, right?"

Gemini squinted into the gloom, trying to discern the dam. But as the sky again flashed crimson, all she saw were white, ravenous eyes looking back at her.

Volleys of electricity erupted around them, causing them to careen wildly. It was only due to Gemini's calm grip on the handles that she did not go completely out of control. The thunderbolts that struck nearby were so focused, so powerful that they jutted up dirt and sand, scorching it instantly and leaving tall stalks of glowing glass in their wake. They had no way of knowing where the red lightning would strike, had no means of shielding themselves from its terrible red glare. All they could do was zigzag back and forth, reacting to the jagged shards that erupted in their path. Whenever the lightning hit—which was almost constantly now—Gemini could see hideous shapes all around them. The valley was gone, leaving red eyes and sharp claws to stalk them.

"This is fucking insane!" Griffin shouted as he struggled to keep his glider from crashing.

But then the clawed shadows to either side of them disappeared, and for a moment the fog parted, and they at last saw that they had entered the ravine, and the blank wall of the Harlo dam rose before them.

Peppy looked up and shouted: "It's coming back!"

Streams of jagged lightning ripped into the gulch; vivid crimson flames erupted everywhere. Griffin's glider burned apart, and he let it go and fell to the ground. Lightning struck right in front of Gemini. Thunder rang in her ears as she veered completely out of control. She and Peppy leaped off the moped right before it slammed into a stalk of red glass.

A nightmarish shadow hovered somewhere over them, and the bloody lightning gouged the ravine again and again. The world was spinning; Gemini couldn't even get up. She had no idea where Peppy or Griffin had wound up. She wasn't sure if she or any of them had been struck, or whether her teammates even existed anymore. The lightning was so intense that she no longer could feel anything, could no longer think anything, and her halo seemed to drain of all color beneath the endless glare of deep red and pale white. She saw Kappos parachuting down around her, saw lightning crash into the dam, cracks starting to form. A rotating column of jet-black clouds descended over the ravine, and submerged within that violent updraft of smoke and ash were the White Eyes and a pair of crimson wings, and each time the crimson wings snapped, more red bolts flung down into the gulch.

—Kill! Eat! Have fun!

There was an icy screech somewhere above them, chilling to the bone, rattling their brains, and in that moment a thousand horrible thoughts crashed through Gemini's skull and she knew that they would die, that as much as she desperately wanted to move, there was no point, there was nothing she could do—

The shadow left them. Gasping, Gemini looked back down the path they came. A truck full of redcoats was bouncing down the opposite bank before turning around a corner. She saw Lucas standing on the bed, sword pointed at the dark blot in the sky swooping down at him.

—*Gemini! Hurry!*

The shadow descended after the truck, and the clouds engulfed her captain. At the same time, somewhere nearby, a chorus of prayers pleading for help abruptly broke out.

—*Help! We've been trapped in the Bayside Suites all night. Anybody, please help!*

—*Please . . . I have connections in the NERVE Company . . . I can reward you. Just help. Please . . .*

—*This is the ambassador to Kairos. Please, is there* anyone *out there? Save us!*

Then she heard her captain's response.

—*This is Lucas from Slag Falls, Captain of Bedlam Athletic. I'm leading a platoon from the local militia. We're o-on . . . w-way. J-just h-hold-*

Silence. The Blood Poacher had left to chase after her captain. Whatever his diversion was, it seemed to be working.

Lucas's appearance brought Gemini back to life. She struggled to get to her feet; Griffin gave her a hand. Peppy was firing away at the descending flock of Kappos. An airboat was hovering over the river, its cannons pointed at the dam. Something sprayed water over the top and shook it from the other side. More cracks formed along its facade.

"That's gotta be artillery from their storm cruiser!" Griffin shouted.

"The dam won't hold much longer if they keep hitting it like that!" Gemini cried. "We have to get moving!"

"Forget it!" Griffin said. "They spend a few more rounds and this whole thing is coming down! Peppy and I will draw their fire."

"How—?" Gemini started to ask, but Griffin had already lunged towards the river, spinning his zero-iron beneath him so that the abrupt updraft sent him hurtling all the way up to the skiff. He was batting away at Kappos before his feet even hit the deck. Peppy shrugged to Gemini, then took a crouching leap after his wingmate, the Icon of *Space* letting him land right next to him with ease. They quickly dispatched all the leatherheads aboard, most of them plopping into the river below. Then they commandeered the airboat and headed east, past the dam and out of sight. The rumbling of cannons stopped, and Gemini surmised the wingers were doing their best to distract the Doom Ship.

Now Gemini was alone. She saw a stairway at the foot of the dam, which led towards the top. She hurried for it, slicing through three Kappos who landed in her way. The rain resumed eating into her coat and skin, and she clenched her teeth in pain as she scurried up the creaking steps. They wound back and forth in a steep ascent. The whole dam was quaking, perhaps from the angry sea, or maybe from the wind or thunder, or maybe because it had already taken a lot of damage. She passed under one of the cracks formed by the Poacher's lightning, saw a stream of water trickling from it. She moved faster.

The stairs rocked madly under her feet. As she reached one landing, the entire dam groaned and shuddered and she braced herself against the railing, trying her best to not go flying off the side. She forced her feet to stay planted to the floor, a red heat bursting between the soles of her boots and the metal. She shut her eyes, summoning *Energy* to aid her.

She gasped. The flame in her heart was still burning from her battle meditation, and so she saw fleeting visions from her peers in the midst of battle.

Somewhere, off to the north, Shepherd and Kat were leading the Harlo militia into the Kappo hordes, mowing down any blighters who came their way, searching door-to-door for people still trapped in their homes—

—out to sea, Peppy and Griffin took a dangerous turn past the cannons of the sleek black storm cruiser, its fire coming precariously close their tiny airboat—

—as Lucas tried to grab the arm of a flailing soldier, but to no avail, and the spiked tail dug deep into the man's torso and pulled him off the back of the truck—

—and Elizabeth stepped over the mountain of dead Kappos as the figure approached her, a pair of War Daddies rolling to a halt at either side of the newcomer.

Elizabeth said nothing to the man. She scooped no thoughts, but Gemini was suddenly overcome by the sorrow that she felt.

The figure reached for a broadsword at his side. His hand was encased in a silver-and-black glove, though his halo was the color of burnt wood. His face was cut with jagged lines . . .

Gemini blinked, and she found herself back on the shaking stairway. She kept moving.

The rain was tearing at her; she felt it starting to sear her scalp. Smoke rose from the guardrail and the steps. As she rounded another flight, one of the steps gave way beneath her. She jumped onto the next landing, reaching for the guardrail, but it too broke away. Panicking, she started to run, not daring to look down as she felt the steps giving away under her feet at every turn. The dam quaked. She hopped over steps already crumbling. The acid rain ate away at everything. The entire stairway was coming apart!

Gemini swung around the final landing just as lightning slashed the wall close by, and in a blinding flash, the entire carriage sloughed apart and everything gave away. Gemini fell, fell away from the alcove, pieces of railing and carriage tumbling along with her. The gloom coiled in around her, pulling her and the debris down—

For a split second, she found footing on some piece of metal. She went rigid. With a shout, she thrust herself upward. She heard the clatter of debris against the dam, felt the heat of sparks beneath her feet, and the very next thing she knew she felt the air squeezed from her lungs as the edge of the alcove collided with her waist.

Desperately she groped at the floor to hold on. Her hair was burning from the rain; smoke was rising from her back and shoulders. She took a deep breath, then pulled herself up into the entryway. For a second she just sat there, panting, grateful for shelter. Then she looked back at the valley. Everything had been washed away in rain and fire; but suddenly Gemini saw a lot of things at once . . .

Lucas and the handful of redcoats still alive had their backs to the entrance of the apartment tower. A terrible shadow hung over them. Inside the building, Gemini could hear the thoughts of people still pleading for help. They sounded oddly hollow yet familiar, but there was no time to think about it, because—

Somewhere east of her, the Doom Ship was firing madly at Griffin and Peppy, who were taking potshots at the Kappos on the deck of the great ship. One red rocket slashed through the engine of her wingmates' airboat, and they started to veer out of control.

Hammer and sword clashed again and again as Liz and the Thrall battled atop the broken bridge. The Thrall seemed to have the upper hand

. . . it was driving Liz towards the edge of the road . . .

And northward, something had gone very, very wrong.

—*Shepherd, can you hear me? It's Kat. I just rescued a couple, but something's wrong with them. Their skin is all funny, they're talking strange . . . and something's throbbing in their chests.*

—*Get away from them! They're Thrall! Get away now!*

—*You heard him! Everybody, get away! Get—*

A terrible, sickening red flash crackled over the northern hills. Then there was only silence. A second later, Gemini could feel the scampering footsteps of blighters now charging down into the valley.

She had to hurry. She had to get the beacon running.

Gemini pulled herself up, opened the blank, steel door, and went inside the dam.

11. The Beacon

GEMINI KICKED THE DOOR shut behind her and peered into the pitch-black room. She couldn't see a damn thing, so she willed what dismal light there was in the room to be whisked straight into her eyes. Her pupils dilated at once, and she could at least make out the barest outline of the room.

She crept down a short flight of steps, then crossed the square-shaped chamber to a dais on the opposite wall. The whole room was groaning against the wind and rain; periodically there was a deep rumble, and the back wall throbbed, and water leaked out of its bracings. Not wanting to know what would happen if a whole panel gave out, Gemini hurried up the dais, where a head-sized silver cube sat on a pedestal. A gray-and-white mandala hung from the wall above.

She stared at the cube uncertainly. How was she supposed to turn it on? Liz had mentioned it was a mind box of the Last Church, which the mandala's presence confirmed. She said it would ask her questions . . . but how? Her personal mind box back in her office in Bedlam activated on a whim. This one lay dormant and oblivious. Stupidly, Gemini thought of scooping Liz or Lucas to ask for help. But there was no way they could hear her now. If they were even still alive . . .

She shook her head. She couldn't think that. Not now. She just had to act.

Thunder pealed outside; the wind still howled. Gemini started to place her hand on the mind box when she paused. Out of the corner of her eye, she thought she saw shadows stir. She looked but saw nothing. Everything was still. Maybe it was just the dam rocking, she thought. She didn't have time to find out.

She placed her hand on the mind box and closed her eyes.

Immediately, like she knew what to do all along, she thought of what she wanted.

—*I need to activate the beacon to save the valley and stop the dam from breaking!*

The box quivered slightly beneath her fingers.

—*Only a True Pilgrim of Roslyn can access this box. To have your request granted, you must prove that you are a True Pilgrim.*

Gemini frowned. —*How am I supposed to do that?*

—*You must answer a question that all True Pilgrims know the answer to. The question is this: How did you die in your past life? If you are a True Pilgrim of Roslyn, then you will know the answer . . .*

Gemini's heart thundered in panic. How on earth was she supposed to know that? As far as she knew, *no one* remembered how they had died before coming to Roslyn. Most people, save for the very rich, couldn't even remember all the years of their New Lives, much less what had happened *before* them. Was it possible that the very wealthiest people in Roslyn had gleaned such memories from their Past Lives? If so, then Lucas and Liz really had screwed up by sending her to turn the beacon on, because Cellar-dweller Gemini couldn't even remember her first hundred years off the boat, never mind whatever had killed her before she ever got here.

—*I . . . I'm sorry. I don't know the answer.*

—*All True Pilgrims know.*

There was a loud bang to Gemini's right. She jumped. A wall panel was bending badly, and a shower of water was now flooding the floor.

Panic knotted in her throat. "Please!" she cried desperately. "You have to turn the shield on or everyone here will die!"

—*You must answer the question.*

"But how can I? It's ridiculous. No one knows—"

She stopped.

The Past Life . . . what did the Last Church of Roslyn teach about the Past Life?

Her heart pounded. The walls throbbed. The answer came to her like it had been there from the start.

"It doesn't matter what my Past Life was," she said. "What matters is that I was reborn here."

The box hummed approvingly.

—*And what is the purpose of the New Life, Gemini from Bedlam Ghettos?*

"To serve the Barra. To rediscover the *Over-Soul* and restore Roslyn to glory."

Nothing happened. The walls were caving in. Gemini had been so focused on answering the question that she only now realized water had raced over the dais and was up to her ankles. She held her breath.

The box hummed again.

—*Well said. Activating beacon.*

Gemini opened her eyes and took a step back. The mind box had risen a few inches off the pedestal and was starting to rotate. The mandala on the wall blossomed into spring colors and started to spin in place. Blue waves shot out of it, coruscating across the entire room and beyond. There was a fizzing noise, like the sound of a bubbling pool, and a bright, sky-colored sheath stretched out over the walls, filling in all the breaches and calming the entire dam. The water drained from the room. The sky glass was doing exactly what it was supposed to.

Feeling extremely pleased with herself, not to mention relieved she had not gotten herself drowned, Gemini espied a stairwell to her left. Eager to see the full results of her handiwork—and with no other path out—she made her way up the steps. As she left the control room, she again noticed a stirring behind her from a passage across the room. But just then, she didn't care whether it was real or imagined. She wanted to see if the beacon was helping to turn the tides, and if the others were okay.

She emerged on top of the dam. She was on a road-sized walkway between two parapets, all now entirely encased in blue ore. Some kind of tower made entirely of sky glass now jutted out of the dam and rose high above it. To get a better view, Gemini ran all the way to the southern ridge.

Angry waves lashed at her from the sound, but none threatened the dam's integrity. She walked out onto a pebble path between sand dunes and turned around. A giant mandala made out of sky glass towered over the dam, slowly revolving in place. It resembled an enormous ice sculpture, except it radiated an intense, vivid heat, one Gemini found revitalizing just to be near, and her halo bloomed gold; but the foul weather seemed repelled by the beacon, and clouds and wind seemed to flee from the coast. Gemini realized it was no longer raining. A cool beam of light shone down on her from a hole punched in the clouds above. It might have been from the moon.

The beacon had cut a hole through the center of the storm!

She let out a cry of joy, then looked out to sea. The fearsome Doom Ship had retreated from the coast. It was now somewhere behind the lighthouse, whose beam once again flickered intermittently through the mists.

A shame they couldn't power up that beacon too, she thought. That would probably break the whole storm.

A trail of black smoke emanated from the shoreline on the other side of the dam, and Gemini realized it was from the airboat that Peppy and Griffin had hijacked. She couldn't feel their presence in the wreck. She didn't know whether that was a good sign or not. She was about to head that way to investigate when a glittering explosion erupted behind her.

An apartment tower overlooking the coast surged with brilliant blue flames. A blot of dark clouds over the building recoiled, and Gemini glimpsed a pair of monstrous wings shading feral eyes from the burning blue ore, and she heard a loathsome screech.

Whatever Lucas had done had worked! The Blood Poacher had taken her captain's bait, and the explosion, which Gemini figured had somehow been caused by the beacon, had confused the White Eyes, incapacitating it. The vortex that contained it was quivering, no longer spinning, leaving it exposed . . .

Gemini saw a handful of redcoats lying dead around the building. There was no sign of her captain. He must have survived. But why wasn't he taking a shot? She swallowed, feeling emboldened, and drew her kreisflyer.

—*Lucas,* she thought, never seeing the buzz-saw shape hurling towards her. *Lucas, can you hear me? It's working. The Poacher's stunned. I have a clean shot. Scoop me the bullet and—*

The Slasher Kappo slammed into her back, knocking her flat into the ground. It must have landed past her, because she was able to roll over. Coughing up sand and seeing stars, she grabbed her kreisflyer and scrambled to her feet.

The Slasher was crouching atop a dune, its armored hide burning with blue fire. Its jaws and face were mangled by bullet holes. Gemini's stomach dropped—it was the same War Daddy she had fought on the skiff back in the Electric Canyon. Apparently, it had survived its fall and been stalking her since. She recalled, glumly, that Slasher Kappos always pursued opponents that failed to finish them off. If this disfigured monster had been what Gemini sensed lurking inside the dam, then the activation of the beacon had badly wounded it. It leered and hissed at her. It was going to die trying to take her with it.

Then it gave a shrill yelp and jumped forward. Gemini twisted out of the way and turned around. The Slasher landed right behind her, claws flared. It wasn't going to let her back to the dam. It raised its rifle at her and fired.

Gemini parried the first thumping shot with her sickle. She backed down the slope away from the coast as the Slasher fired again and again, hopping from dune to dune. She blocked shot after shot, her arms burning in pain. The Slasher was shooting indiscriminately, and somehow this made it harder to deflect all its fire; Gemini missed one shot and it grazed her left shoulder. She winced, but only for an instant. Then her eyes grew wide as the burly monster lunged right at her. She threw herself backwards, and its clawed feet dug into the sand where she had been a moment previous.

The Slasher jabbed at her with its bayonet. Gemini parried the blow, but her opponent was so strong that she ended up falling backwards and rolling down a dune, only to come to a halt against a wooden fence. She found the strength to stand up and plow through the rickety barrier just as the Slasher raised its rifle.

There was a cracking thump, and the pickets next to Gemini exploded with shell fragments. She felt the shrapnel of the Slasher's second shot fly past her. She ran towards another dune, desperate to gain the high ground, then heard a loud crash behind her as the Slasher flung itself through the fence. Gemini reached the top of the dune and turned to meet the War Daddy as it hurtled towards her. Just as it unfurled, she brought her sickle low to the ground and thrust upwards, hoping to cut right through its underbelly—

The Slasher caught her swing with the barrel of its rifle, jamming it against her neck. It flung her backwards and she tumbled down the summit. Somewhere above she heard the clanking of the Slasher coming to a halt. As soon as Gemini reached the foot of the dune, she realized she was in grave trouble.

The ground ended. Her body began to fall off an incline and into open air.

She had reached edge of the ravine!

Reaching wildly and blindly for something to prevent her fall, Gemini dug her hand deep into the sand above her. The fact that the rain had made it muddier gave her some traction. But the change in momentum caused her body to slam hard against the cliffside, and her kreisflyer slipped from her grasp and dropped somewhere far below. She feared she'd soon be following it.

Lightning flashed. The toxic rain started to fall again, eating at her exposed hand. The Slasher Kappo stood over her and snarled. Her fingers slipped.

The Slasher bared its teeth and raised its rifle—

With a cry, Gemini fell from the edge. The Slasher yelped, but before it could fire an echo cracked across the ravine, and in a blur Gemini saw it flee from the cliff, bullets bouncing off its hide. Then Gemini lost sight of it as she tumbled through the air. She yelled, but wind and thunder drowned out her cries. She tried to summon Duration to somehow brace herself, but it was no use . . .

Then her free fall started to slow, as if an updraft were granting her a few extra seconds of life. Without understanding why, Gemini found herself in a crawling descent, and soon her body no longer tumbled, her hair and coat weren't flailing behind her, and she could again breathe normally. As she began to near the ground, the wind no longer reached her, and the sulfur drops in her midst halted to mere bubbles floating around her. She and everything close to her were weightless. Only as her feet gingerly touched the damp rubble of the basin floor did Gemini see the tall, hooded figure with his hand outstretched, blue halo beaming.

The feeling of weight returned to her, and her coat and hair fell back around her. Lucas lowered his hand, and he and the five redcoats who were still with him walked up to her.

"Good deal," Lucas said. He handed her kreisflyer over to her. "Next time, just make sure the coast is clear before you try hunting big game."

"The Poacher," Gemini chided herself. "I almost had a shot—"

"It's all right. We'll get another crack at it. To be honest, my trick wasn't as clever as I thought; the ore didn't fool it very long. I think it knew right away that it was my voice in the rocks Liz and I cribbed over from the TAN."

Gunfire whizzed by them, and the Durationists and soldiers hid within an alcove along the ravine wall. A dozen Kappos were gamboling towards them. Lucas and Gemini drew their weapons to deflect the next barrage, while the militiamen gunned down a handful of the leatherheads. The rest were swiftly dispatched by sniper fire coming from the opposite ridge.

Gemini looked up, and her heart leaped with joy.

"Peppy! Griffin! I thought you guys were done for!"

"No Doom Ship can kill us!" Peppy declared between shots.

Griffin swung his zero-iron, filling the valley with wind that pushed the next wave of Kappos onto their heels. Then he jumped down next to Gemini.

"Nice going with the shield," he said. "That scared the shit out of them."

"I'm just glad you guys are all right," said Gemini.

"Same." He put a hand on her shoulder. "Hey, I'm proud of you, Gem. You're growing up tonight. Keep it up!"

Gemini beamed at him as he jumped back onto the ridge.

—*Captain Lucas, can you hear me? It's Shepherd from Old Hollow.*

Lucas was clearly relieved to hear from the Great Revere captain. Deflecting fire to give the militiamen cover while they shot down the incoming Kappos, he responded. —*Good to hear from you, Captain. Are you guys okay?*

—*I'm fine. Kat is . . . well, she'll live, I think. I'm sorry, Captain. The Kappos cut through our lines pretty badly. They're heading down your way, if they're not there already.*

—*No problem, Shepherd. We'll manage. You did the best you could. Take what's left of your troops and go help the evacuees.*

—*We're on our way. Be aware, though, there were two Thrall up here. I'm pretty sure only one of them, uh . . . took itself out. The other might be moving towards you.*

—*We'll keep our eyes peeled. Thanks . . .*

Lucas addressed his team. —*Peppy, Griffin, you heard him. You're going to have a scrum up there pretty soon. There's a catwalk up ahead that you can cross to the south ridge. You'll have better firing lines from there. The rest of you, pick off as many Kappos coming our way as you can. We need to keep the Blood Poacher focused on us. Go!*

They marched out of the shadow of the dam and towards the approaching Kappos. Peppy and Griffin strafed from the catwalk above, while the redcoats took shots from behind Lucas and Gemini. Gemini slung her flying sickle out at the Kappos who managed to evade the soldiers' fire, a ray of sunlight tethering her halo-hand to the whirling blade as it tore through leather helmets and bolted necks. Any Kappos who managed to escape her slags were quickly dispatched by the twanging ripple of Lucas's zeitblatt.

Once Peppy and Griffin got to the south side of the gulch, Griffin cast a fresh blast of foggy wind through the ravine's mouth, blinding the Kappos pouring forth. But it was as tricky for the people to navigate as it was for the Kappos, Gemini thought. The ravine was riddled with red stalks of glass from the Blood Poacher's lightning barrage, which made aiming difficult. Shattering pops echoed out of the ether from Kappos shooting at the red glass. A redcoat nicked one of the stalks while trying to shoot down an approaching leatherhead.

"Watch your fire!" Lucas warned. "The blood rock in them might not be toxic enough to damage the dam, but they can still hurt us."

It was true: each time a Kappo's errant shot hit one of the stalks, it exploded with a loud pop and sent a cloud of shrapnel everywhere. Lucas raised his hand to slow the descent of one such cloud so that Gemini and the soldiers could safely walk under it.

They hadn't made it far before Kappos started leaping down from the northern ridge. Lucas cut down scores of them before they even planted their feet on the gully floor. Ten, twenty, thirty Kappos fell before him, knots of sizzling blue light mapping his sword's path. Peppy mowed down dozens more from across the gap, while Griffin caused such a disturbance in the air over the ravine that many Kappos were simply swept off the bluff and fell harshly to the floor, smashed to pieces.

A pair of War Daddies bounded across a catwalk towards the wingers, and Gemini tossed out her kreisflyer and cut the bridge's trusses apart.

The Slasher Kappos plummeted to the earth, landing hard on their backs. Before either could spring to their feet, Lucas swiftly impaled both. While this went on, another dozen leatherheads charged at them, but the Harlo redcoats quickly gunned them down.

Gemini was about to compliment them on their shooting when an airboat zipped overhead, rockets firing. Red glass exploded all around them; one redcoat was standing too close to a stalk, and he barely had time to scream before a bloody cloud engulfed him, and he vanished. Lucas was about to leap into action when someone lunged from the northern bluff onto the skiff. There was a high-pitched clang and a technicolor flash, and then the entire airboat caught on fire and careened towards the next batch of Kappos headed into the ravine. The leatherheads flailed and panicked before the skiff crashed into them and exploded.

By then Liz had landed next to Lucas. She had a furious look on her face.

"I fought him, Lucas! He's still out here!"

"Ahmed?"

"He was leading a batch down the freeway. I should have killed him! I had the chance, but he ran off when the beacon went up . . ."

"Don't think about it," said Lucas. "He'll turn up again, if he's not dead already."

Lightning struck nearby. The din reverberated off the ravine walls. One of the redcoats fell to his knees and howled from pain unseen, and before anyone could help him he pitched onto his face and lay limp.

A volley of red rockets rained down from the sky and crashed into the dam. Gemini's stomach turned, but as the smoke cleared she sighed in relief—the missiles had barely dented the sky glass. Then there was a heavy buzzing noise, and the mile-long Doom Ship rose out of the clouds and prowled along the southern rise of the valley. It did not dare to get closer to the beacon. At the same time, a rotating mass of volcanic plumes materialized over the freeway. Wings that spanned the suspension towers unfolded, throwing forked lightning over the Durationists' heads to lash against the shielded dam. The White Eyes cast their pale glow across the river. In the fog below the bridge, hundreds of Kappos appeared, ambling along either side of the river and in the shallow water itself, headed right for them.

"Well," Lucas mused. "We have its attention. Let's keep it that way. It's just a little longer until dawn." He pointed his zeitblatt at the approaching horde. "Everyone, stay in formation. Peppy, Griffin, if you can give us some cover from the Doom Ship, that would be fantastic. Gemini, Liz, officers: with me!"

Lucas jumped over to the north bank of river. Liz, Gemini, and the remaining pair of redcoats stayed to the south. A trio of War Daddies hurtled past the horde of their smaller kin, knocking a few out of their way as they engaged the Durationists. Lucas, Liz, and Gemini each took on one of the Slashers. Gemini jumped down into the water to meet hers, the murky water barely reaching her shins. The War Daddy unfurled twenty paces from her, and once again she saw the distorted face snarling at her.

Gemini leered at the Slasher and pointed at it with her kreisflyer. This time, she would finish it off for good.

It bounded towards her. But as Gemini rushed forward to meet it, she focused on the edge of her sickle until the blade was smoldering hot. She cut the Slasher's grudge shot in half, then jabbed at its midsection.

The Slasher hopped backwards, clawed hands swiping her sickle aside as it tried to bite her neck. Gemini recoiled from the snapping jaws. Muddy water splashed all around her.

Across the way, Liz obliterated the Slasher that had taken her on with a single slam of her sledgehammer, a multicolored shock wave briefly consuming the Kappo before rendering it into a charred husk. Meanwhile, Lucas had never let his War Daddy fully unfurl, instead raising a hand as it came out of its roll. The Slasher's armor emitted groans and sparks, its plating bent as if hidden wires were yanking it backward, keeping it rooted on the spot. The Kappo yelped in bewilderment as it slowed to a crawl, flailing its arms blindly, but it was unable to reach its assailant, for its attack had been blunted by Lucas's mastery over the Icon of *Time*.

The space between Lucas and the War Daddy seemed to compress, as if *Time* were strangling the air between them, but while the Slasher Kappo was caught in the distortion and struggling to unfold against the weight of its armor, Lucas moved in that contracting bubble with little resistance, as if nothing could slow him down, as if *Time* was on his side and his side only, and with rapid motion he jutted his sword into the empty air in front of his opponent. A moment later there was a twanging crash, and everything expanded, and the Slasher sprung forward and gave a gargled squeal. It dropped its rifle, Lucas's sword deep in its throat. Lucas waved his blade to the side and threw the slain Slasher Kappo to the ground.

Gemini nearly tripped as the War Daddy's foot clung painfully to her ankle. Clawed hands grabbed her arms, and the Slasher hissed at her, coiling to strike—

Gemini spun her wrists, and her flaming blade cut across the Slasher's ruined face. It let her go, yelping as it staggered backwards, and its lower jaw fell into the water with a plop. It waved its arms and screeched, ghastly smoke pouring from its severed mouth—

Gemini slashed it across the eyes and fire burned through the War Daddy's skull. It pitched onto its side with a splash and died.

Before her opponent even fell, a Kappo jumped at her, daggers in both hands. Gemini wheeled around—but a bullet struck the creature right in the head, and rawhide and metal pelted the river as it landed next to Gemini with a splash.

"Thanks!" she said to one of the soldiers up on the bank behind her.

The hordes kept coming. Griffin slung another net of icy mist down at the mob, but the Blood Poacher waved its wings and a piercing gale tore through the valley, breaking apart whatever slag the left-winger had conjured. Red rockets from the Doom Ship exploded across the southern bluff, and the ground beneath Griffin gave way. He almost fell before Peppy grabbed his hand and pulled him up. Another volley headed their way, and so the wingers took bounding leaps back across the chasm. There was a watchtower here, and Peppy vaulted up to its top.

—I got a good look at the Doom Ship from here. I'm going to try to take out some of its turrets.

He added an extra barrel to the end of his scope shot and began sniping at the cruiser miles away. Another round of red rockets resounded across the horizon, but Peppy fired a round of shots in rapid succession and Gemini saw the missiles explode prematurely across the skies. Meanwhile, a horde of Kappos scampered up the ridge to attack Griffin, swinging their daggers blindly. Griffin impaled his zero-iron in the ground, and the entire ridge shuddered. Rocks beneath the Kappos' feet jutted out of the earth, throwing them onto their backs. Realizing that might be a nice substitute for the icy fog, Griffin pointed his zero-iron at the horde about to enter the gulch and jabbed the ground beneath him. This time, a rush of dirt spread out from the blade of his weapon, running down the cliff face and past the other Durationists—right into the Kappos. The ground beneath the blighters undulated, and they crashed into each other, tripping over their own feet and impaling themselves on the red stalks of glass that littered the entire watercourse.

This made things much easier for Gemini, Lucas, and Liz, who waded into the confused mob and began cutting down as many as they could.

Gemini had never been in a fight so fierce. She was surrounded by too many leatherheads to count, weaving golden arcs all around her as she spun the kreisflyer furiously over her head and into the Kappos, cutting through their dirks and scrap shots, shattering the cursed machinery inside their patched limbs and frayed necks. Geysers of sparks erupted all around her. On the bank to her left, Liz was swinging her hammer left and right, and after each high clang and rainbow flash, the ground around her feet was littered with flaming Kappo parts.

Lucas worked his zeitblatt with calm determination, often cutting down three, four blighters with a single swing, once again leaving blinking arcs of indigo light in his wake. Just like in the Electric Canyon, Gemini noticed the rain and wind behind them seem to calm to an unnatural pace, so that raindrops drifted sleepily into the canyon walls, and the sky was noticeably lighter behind them; it was as if Bedlam Athletic and Liz had defined the very line between freedom and the Poacher Storm with the sky glass beacon at their backs, the leering Eyes of Thunder on the bridge ahead.

—*What's good about this,* Lucas scooped his team as he decapitated four Kappos and stepped over their bodies, *is that we're pinning the storm out of an easy escape. Red Tide will come from the west. If we're lucky, we might trap Killer Fives here. Just another hour or so . . .*

But the Blood Poacher would not be contained so easily. Just as the Durationists reached the mouth of the ravine, where the bluffs on either side steeply descended, a terrible screech echoed from the freeway. The White Eyes snapped its translucent crimson wings, flinging a web of red lightning out at them. Gemini braced herself, but the electricity scoured the walls of the canyon, tapered in the air, and slashed harmlessly into the beacon. The Poacher's wings snapped again; this time one of the soldiers fell during the blast, clutching his head, and a Kappo shot him in the chest. But the Durationists remained unscathed. Even Peppy on his tower had been spared. It seemed Lucas's prediction—that Duration would protect a disciplined team from the Poacher's wrath—had been correct.

Perhaps frustrated by its ineffective attacks, the shadow of the Poacher ascended from its perch, its infernal wings spread wide, and lightning was already spewing forth by the time it swept towards them.

"Look out!" shouted Liz.

Everything went black as the great shadow moved overhead—but the Blood Poacher was not aiming for them. Instead, webs of red lightning lashed out at the dam wall, leaving red stalks impaled harmlessly into the sky glass. The spiral of cinder and smoke that the Blood Poacher hid in came to a halt before the beacon, and it let out another horrible screech as the mandala rotated before it. The molten clouds shuddered, and the White Eyes wavered as if the sight of the beacon had paralyzed it. Griffin, who was closest to the listless inferno of wings and claws, stared at the Poacher with his mouth agape. He raised his zero-iron uncertainly, as if he realized he might have a shot to make but didn't know where to begin—

"Griffin!" Peppy shouted from the tower. "Incoming!"

The Doom Ship had launched a huge battery of rockets, a barrage of comets flying towards them. Peppy shot at them as fast as he could; many of the missiles exploded before making it halfway to the ravine, but there were too many for him to take on alone. Snapping to his senses, Griffin waved his zero-iron and conjured a dozen flaming discs in front of him. He swung at them all in rapid succession, sending them to hone in on the missiles.

He hit almost all of them, and they exploded right over the gully; the few he missed crashed into the dam. By the time the threat passed, the Blood Poacher had snapped out of its odd lull and ascended back into the clouds, its shadow sweeping over the north in an arc as it came around to make another pass.

"Did you see that?" Liz called as she smashed a few Kappos.

"Yeah," Lucas murmured. "Doesn't make sense . . ."

"What's wrong?" Gemini asked as she threw her kreisflyer into a crowd of Kappos, bowling them over.

"The Poacher's attacking the beacon," Lucas said. "Not us. Even most of the cruiser's artillery is aimed for the dam. But why? With that amount of sky glass, there's no way they can break it by morning. Killer Fives *has* to realize that. Unless . . ."

"It knows of a weakness we don't," Liz said.

The Poacher was coming back for them now, passing over the freeway.

—Griffin, Lucas thought, *keep your eyes open for any attacks on the dam. Knock out any more rockets coming your way. We don't know why the Poacher is still attacking the beacon, but we can't take any chances.*

Griffin did not respond right away. Gemini looked up and saw him staring at the incoming Poacher with that same uncertain expression.

—Griffin?

— . . . Yes, Captain. You got it.

Griffin deftly knocked more missiles out of the sky, and his ground slags kept stunning the Kappos that tried swarm the ravine. But Gemini was worried. She knew that look in her teammate's eyes all too well. It was the same longing look he had furtively shown when Lucas had shown her the Silver Bullet, and it had been the same wistful gaze he had often displayed when fantasizing about smiting a Blood Poacher. Seeing the Storm Devil so close while it was seemingly so vulnerable had made those fantasies real. Once more the Blood Poacher flew over them, and what little lightning it threw down at the Durationists missed the mark; again, the brunt of the lightning struck the beacon; again, the White Eyes halted before the spiraling mandala, as if it were both arrested and repulsed by its ethereal glow. Once more Griffin stared at the writhing cloud, but this time his reverie did not last as long, and he moved to swiftly dispatch the incoming missiles while the Blood Poacher flew away and again circled around the valley.

Feeling a little better, Gemini turned her attention back to taking down as many Kappos as she could. She, Lucas, and Liz held the line at the mouth of the ravine, while the only redcoat still alive took shots from behind a groove in the cliff face. The swarm of Kappos had become so dense, the blighters practically climbing over one another to try to attack them, that the Durationists were now swinging their weapons nonstop, cutting down Kappos from all sides, mountains of dead, leathery mechanical imps growing under ribbons of blue, arcs of yellow, and flashes of rainbow.

The battle raged on. The last redcoat went down in crossfire, but still, Gemini thought their chances were pretty good. The sun would be at their backs soon. Then Red Tide would come, the Poacher would retreat or die fighting, and victory would be theirs. They just had to hold the line . . .

She doubled her efforts. Lucas was in the middle of cutting down an entire mob when an urgent message reached him.

—*Captain Lucas! This is militia command. Are you there?*

—*Go ahead, Commander. Is everyone in the tunnels?*

—*Yes, sir. Something amazing just happened. There's a lot of Kappos down here—*

—*Don't worry, Commander. The fleet will be here soon.*

—*But we're already saved, sir. It's Sophia from Belmont Chapel! She is routing the blighters right now!*

Lucas threw Gemini a leery look, then responded. —*Glad to hear you're all right, Commander. We'll keep the storm busy until Red Tide gets here.*

"Well," he muttered. "As long as she's helping . . ."

The Blood Poacher flew past the highway and towards the ravine for a third time. Lightning rushed over the Durationists' heads and whipped the dam, and once again the Blood Poacher came to a halt before the beacon. This time it let out a low hiss, and its wings seemed to crumple under the glare of the sky glass. Its form within the cloud seemed to be pulsing.

Lucas suddenly stopped fighting. Alarmed, he reached into his coat pocket and found it empty. He looked up at Griffin.

"Griffin, no!"

Gemini only understood what had happened when Griffin raised his bare hand. A small, silvery orb floated over his palm, so bright that anyone standing on the gully floor could see it as clear as a star in the sky. How Griffin had purloined the Silver Bullet from their captain, Gemini didn't understand; then she realized that a shard of ore that dense, that powerful, was not *truly* carried by one glove alone, that an entire Durationist team collectively held it out-of-step, and that Griffin had summoned it to his hand because he was convinced he could slay the Blood Poacher here and now.

"It's okay!" Griffin shouted, letting the Silver Bullet float in front of him as he swung his zero-iron over his shoulder. The pulsing, quivering

Blood Poacher turned slowly towards him, almost feebly, as if it knew it was about to be dealt a lethal blow. "I got it, trust me!"

"It's a trick!" Lucas yelled, and now Peppy too was screaming at his wingmate to come to his senses, and Gemini and Liz looked on, horrified, as Griffin paused, his face pale, his body and the ground around him glowing deathly white, and Gemini realized he was staring right into the Eyes of Thunder. He flinched, as if his nerve had left him. Then, with a cry, he started to swing—

Red rockets exploded all around him and the Blood Poacher roared back to life, and its wings spanned the entire ravine as a cage of blood-stained lightning erupted all over Griffin, who screamed and fell onto his back, writhing; the Silver Bullet vanished, and his zero-iron tumbled down into the gulch. There was a terrible, scorching flash, and Gemini had to turn away to shield her eyes, but she still heard Lucas yelling, briefly saw Liz holding him back to stop him from jumping up to try in vain to save his defender . . .

Then the lightning stopped. The Blood Poacher was again flying away. Gemini scrambled to her feet and looked up at the southern cliff; it was covered in needle-shaped glass. Griffin lay on his back. His gauntlet hand lay limp over the edge. Thick black smoke was rising from his chest. There was no color in his wrist.

The ground was starting to shake. The shards of red glass all over the ravine and dam started to glow red hot, as if death had ignited them. Black smoke chugged from their tips. Gemini wanted to act, wanted to do something, but she was caught between cutting down Kappos and staring up at Griffin. The whole sky went pitch black, even over the beacon, and burning rain started to fall again, and Gemini had this horrible feeling that, somehow, their left-winger's fatal miscue had broken something deep within Duration, something that could not be fixed, and now their indelible march would be halted—and at great cost.

A figure stepped onto the bluff. It was a man dressed in ragged clothes. Gemini couldn't see his face, but it looked like his eyes were bulging. His hands were burning, and the ground beneath his feet seemed to smolder. His frame went rigid as something fiery glowed at his heart.

"Vlaz Echomar!" the Thrall shouted over Griffin's body. "Vlaz Echomar!"

Then it ran towards the dam, and with a gleeful look on its face, it threw its arms out and hurled itself off the cliff.

"Peppy!" Lucas shouted. "Shoot him!"

From the watchtower, Peppy raised his rifle at the falling man. Gemini thought he was about to squeeze the trigger when she heard a howling sound rush over her head, and the last thing she saw of her teammate was how he barely had enough time to look over his shoulder and raise his eyebrows in surprise before a red rocket from the Doom Ship slammed into the tower. The entire thing exploded in a huge fireball.

"No!" Gemini screamed.

"Vlaz Echomar! Vlaz Echomar!" the falling Thrall still shouted again and again, his entire body burning red, until he slammed into the middle of the dam wall and was immolated in a flash of bloody fire.

A series of bangs echoed down the chasm as every stalk of red glass exploded, zigzagging electricity shooting out to meet at the point where the Thrall had erupted in crimson flames. A column of fire rose through the base of the dam and ripped through the mandala. Each shard of blood rock that was embedded in the beacon exploded in unison. Everything turned white-hot, and with a screaming flash the sky glass was instantly vaporized. The explosion was so massive it shook entire dunes down into the gulch. Much of the ravine, including where Griffin lay, vanished in chutes of fire and ash. Smoke and dust were all that remained.

Then a different roar drowned out the sounds of the detonation.

What little granite was left of the dam crumbled away as the sea gushed forth and the floods were unleashed.

12. Rising Earth, Dancing Sun

THE WORLD HAD GONE mad, and Gemini could not accept that she had just seen two of her teammates die in the span of seconds, but right now she had less than seconds before she joined them. The surge tore through the ravine, ripping into rock and sand, trying to engulf as much of its new terrain as it possibly could. She could feel the sea spray hit her in the face; the earth was quaking in fear, and every fiber of her being was screaming the same thing.

Run! Run! Run!

Lucas and Liz had jumped down into the river. But instead of fleeing, they withdrew their weapons and walked past her, towards the flood. They stopped and stood side by side, equal looks of determination written on their faces. Something unsaid seemed to have passed between them. What it possibly could have been, and how could they could act so calm in the face of the deluge about to crush them, Gemini had no idea.

Killer Fives had landed back atop the freeway. It let out a hissing laugh. Its troops had joined it around the bridge to enjoy a view of the Durationists' imminent death. As if to guarantee the outcome, the Blood Poacher snapped its wings and flung lightning at them. It barely missed them, ripping up the embankment.

"Gemini!" Liz said. "Try to give us some cover!"

Without thinking about what she was doing, Gemini flung her kreisflyer at the power lines that hung between them and the freeway, dead Para-Kappos still hanging from the wires. The sickle cut through transformers, and the wires all ignited to form a wall of fire in the sky. She heard the Blood Poacher hissing in the distance, and as she caught her weapon she knew the flames wouldn't stop the White Eyes from seeing them for very long—but it was *something*. Besides, how long did they have?

"Gemini," Lucas said quietly, his voice somehow carrying over the deafening roar racing towards them. "Hold them off for as long as you can. Stay behind us."

Gemini didn't know what to say; there was no point. She would never abandon her captain, and she prayed to the *Over-Soul* that he and Liz, against all odds, somehow knew what to do . . . but how could they possibly hope to survive? Her body still screamed at her to flee, to get the hell out of there; but the acid rain was pouring all over her, causing every fiber in her body to ache, and the wind seemed to pin her to the spot. Even if she wanted to run, there was nowhere to go. The flood would crush them, would take the poor people hiding in the sewers too . . .

The roar was immense; the ground convulsed. She did not dare look back. Instead she looked up, but she could no longer see the sky, just a massive crest of water about to crash down upon them. Her heart stopped. The wave would overtake them in a second. Lucas and Liz stretched their hands out in some childish protest; she could hear the Blood Poacher and its kin snarl and bark, as if laughing.

Lucas and Liz closed their eyes, hands still splayed in front of them. White foam rushed over Gemini's head. She felt the cold water race up her arms and legs, and she cried out and shut her eyes.

But she did not see darkness, nor did she feel her body be torn to pieces by the currents. Everything was so silent, so calm, that for a moment Gemini wondered if she had been killed instantly.

There was only one way to find out. Slowly, she opened her eyes.

She gasped. She no longer saw Liz and Lucas, but instead two effulgent, glittering pillars of fire, red and blue stars burning so bright that nothing else, not the valley, the Blood Poacher, or the flood itself, could be seen. So dazzling were the two stars that Gemini thought they might have been one, brilliant spirals of carmine and indigo, suffusing with an interlocking pattern that kept spreading, filling all the blackness around Gemini and the spaces in between, until finally there was a flash like a shooting star, and Gemini found herself still standing in the riverbed, cringing from the impending wave . . .

Lucas and Liz had their fingertips on the calm sheet of water in front of them. Their feet were dug into the mud, their muscles flexed, their mouths in a slight grimace; otherwise they looked absolutely tranquil, their eyes still shut, as if they had done this a hundred times before and no effort was necessary; and even to Gemini, who was distantly in complete shock by what she was witnessing, it all seemed so easy, as if she knew all along that this was possible. Without fear, but with her mouth agape to betray the part of her that was absolutely in awe, she raised her head and saw that the cresting tide no longer moved. Waves atop the suspended surge tried protesting by spilling over the top, but then they—along with the acid rain—froze in place.

Both Liz and Lucas continued to trace their fingers in gentle circles across the water, and Gemini saw that both their halos were incandescent with red and blue swirls, forming the same pattern she had glimpsed through the Icon of *Energy*. Their heads were bowed, their expressions calm. Not even the sound of the Blood Poacher screeching in outrage could break their concentration.

A band of Kappos approached, and Gemini, feeling more emboldened than she ever had in her life, gave a furious cry and charged into the fray, cutting through blighters in an endless whirl. She paced back and forth behind her captain and Elizabeth, fervently slashing and hacking down any Kappos who dared approach, deflecting their gunshots, slinging her kreisflyer into their ranks. Even beyond the black clouds, the sky was starting to lighten, and Gemini knew if they could just hold out for a few more minutes, against all odds, they might still make it . . .

The Blood Poacher hissed in disgust at the Kappos failing to break through Gemini's defense. It flashed its wings, and Gemini barely dodged a thunderbolt that ripped through the dying embers of the power lines and tore up the earth. Jagged red forks caused both electrical towers to crumple. Lightning lashed at the water, nearly hitting Lucas and Liz, both of whom somehow didn't break their focus. Gemini gritted her teeth as she cut down another Kappo mob. The Poacher wasn't likely to miss a second time. But she had no means to block that kind of power. Lucas and Liz were quite defenseless, and it occurred to Gemini that as magnificent as their current display was, they could not hold back the flood forever . . .

"Lucas."

It was Liz who spoke. Her voice was so peaceful that it frightened Gemini to hear.

"I have to let go. I have to hold off the Poacher."

They both opened their eyes to stare at each other's reflections in the water. Gemini was overwhelmed with the sense that this conversation was not for her ears, that it was awful for her to even listen, but as she kept cutting down Kappos, she could not help but hear.

"I can't do this without you," Lucas said.

"My power is yours now. You can finish this. I'll keep Killer Fives busy for as long as I can. Lucas . . . I'm sorry that I was never there for you, back then. I want you to know that."

"Liz, don't do this now—"

"There won't be another time."

Lightning struck nearby, causing water to spray over them. Gemini desperately wished there were enough thunder to drown out their voices.

"Can you tell my *islamor*—"

"Of course."

"Lucas, just promise me one thing . . ."

She took a hand away from the water and leaned close to him. Whatever she whispered in his ear, Gemini didn't know, but as she beheaded another Kappo, she turned and saw Liz step away from the water, and she saw that Lucas looked stricken.

"Gemini," Liz said quietly, her head bowed. "If you get a shot, take it."

Gemini was about to point out that they had lost their Silver Bullet, but in the same instant she felt something tiny but heavy fall into her pocket. Either Griffin had left them the bullet before he died, or it had returned to the team on its own.

Elizabeth drew her sledgehammer. She raised her head, a solemn look on her face. Then, with a crouch, she sprung upwards, vaulting through clouds and rain, bounding past gunfire and lightning, until she landed on the broken bridge—right in front of the Blood Poacher.

Again there was no time to process what had happened. Another wave of Kappos swarmed the riverbed, and Gemini cut them to pieces. But the sounds of the battle happening above them even made Lucas raise his eyes. Gemini strained to see what was happening through the layer of gloomy fog that had settled over the river, but something glimmering out of the corner of her eye made her look over her shoulder.

Every time a thunderbolt ripped across the sky, the harsh, intermittent light cast shadows from the drama taking place on the bridge onto the wall of water, so that Gemini and her captain could watch the battle unfold. Gemini busily deflected gunfire from the incoming batch, but she could not help but look over her shoulder and behold what was happening. On either side of the bridge were Slasher Kappos, jumping up and down as they watched the duel transpiring at the passage's center. Elizabeth flourished her sledgehammer with steely precision, sending prismatic blasts towards the monstrosity swooping over her, blowing apart chunks of the whirling smoke that concealed her opponent. What could be seen of her assailant was a ragged, freakish horror. A flurry of claws and sickles cut a swath through Liz's strikes, and the wings spat red bolts at the Durationist, setting the bridge ablaze.

The ignited light illuminated the water at once, allowing them to glimpse full reflections. Liz's eyes were as calm as ever as she found her footing and thrust the head of the hammer towards the Blood Poacher's chest. But a long, serpentlike tail lashed at her, and she reeled backwards as the long scythe cut into her arm. Flames and Kappos danced around her. She was in trouble.

She was so transfixed on the battle that Gemini nearly missed the five Kappos that sprang out of the shadows. She lopped the heads off three of them with a single swipe, then wheeled around to see the remaining pair lunging for her captain. She started forward; but Lucas had seen their skittering forms reflected in the water. With his bare hand, he reached for the hilt of his sword, and with a stony glance over his shoulder, he slashed a diagonal, crackling blue line across the Kappos' chests. They screeched, exploded, and crumpled to dirt.

"Gemini," Lucas called as he withdrew his blade. A look of grim determination was strewn upon his face. "Stay close to me."

Gemini did as told, basically staying back to back with her captain while blocking gunfire. His fingertips still subduing the storm surge,

Lucas twisted his hands slightly while digging both boots further into the sand beneath him. A rumbling issued from the earth, and Gemini staggered as she felt the ground beneath them begin to rise. She looked to her left and right. A long sheet of rock that spanned the entire ravine was starting to rise towards the top, with Lucas at its center, barely aware of the ascent. His eyes were fixed upon Elizabeth's struggle, and he was desperate to get there in time to help her.

But while Killer Fives was occupied, the rest of its forces would try to stop them. Gemini cut the hands off the Kappos who tried to grab onto the ledge of their newly formed slate. As they passed through the low-lying fog, a series of thumps issued from the south. The Doom Ship had opened fire, and a circle of red rockets screamed right for them. Gemini stepped to Lucas's side and tossed out her kreisflyer, willing it to fly in a clockwise motion. Her weapon slashed through all but one of the missiles, destroying them, but the final rocket honed right in on her and Lucas. Gemini frantically clutched her gauntlet hand against her side, willing the sickle back to her as quick as she could . . .

Come on, she thought. *Come on.* The rocket's howling filled her ears, growing larger and larger in front of her as it drew close . . .

Then it exploded, less than ten feet away, the flames so bright that Gemini almost missed catching her sickle on its rebound.

Meanwhile, Elizabeth refused to go down quietly. The Blood Poacher's wings were folded and it was slowly stalking towards her, and she back-pedaled while swinging at the clawed whips tangling around her. Her hammer must have glanced one of the Poacher's gangly tails, for it gave a snarl and reared back, now standing almost upright. Its midsection was exposed, and Liz gave a cry as she raised her hammer over her head, ready to rush forward and slam her weapon into the Poacher's chest. But she couldn't see what Lucas and Gemini saw: one of the Blood Poacher's tails slithering under the bridge, to erupt out of the road behind Liz and lunge straight for her back.

—*Look out!*

Elizabeth wheeled around just as the tail snapped forward and the sickle caught the blunt end of her hammer, sending a wave of rainbows in all directions. The indirect blow was still enough to cause Killer Fives to snarl and take a step back. But Elizabeth was tiring. She held her weapon low, panting . . .

Lucas was flexing his legs all he could, as if by preparing to jump he would get there sooner. They were nearing the top; the wall of water was only three times Lucas's height now, so that the bridge and the bottom half of Elizabeth had disappeared from view. But they could still fully see Killer Fives, who had suddenly launched into the air and floated behind its opponent, and now its tails were swinging downward, their spikes pointed right for Elizabeth's back.

Elizabeth began to spin around, but one of the Poacher's tails wrapped around her arms and legs, holding her in place. Another tail swiped for her head, but with a valiant cry, Liz flailed her bounded arms and managed to bash the spike into the road. The Poacher reeled from the technicolor light that coursed up its spine. A whistling screech, like the winds of a passing storm, resounded over the valley, and the column of violent clouds blew apart. Completely exposed, the Blood Poacher let out a furious roar and snapped a third tail forward, and the scythe plunged through Liz's heart. Her head jerked forward and she let out a tortured gasp.

"No!" Gemini shouted. She did not dare look at Lucas, but his silent despair rang in her ears.

The tip of the tail ripped through Elizabeth's back before protracting, and then she fell out of sight.

The Silver Bullet vibrated in Gemini's pocket. So mortified was she that it only slowly dawned on her that the Blood Poacher did not notice that she and Lucas were rising and nearly level with it. Its shadowy form was vibrating oddly, and Gemini could see glimmers of rainbow light from Liz's final blow still running up its outline. It was stunned. Gemini reached for the bullet and placed it in the groove on the inner edge of her kreisflyer, just as her captain had shown her. With no hesitation, without daring to let doubt creep in, she raised her arm and prepared to throw.

Just before she let go, the sky erupted, and a web of lightning flashed, and in that moment Gemini somehow knew that a bolt would split off and strike her captain. She had a clean shot at the Blood Poacher, but she knew that while she took it, the lightning would hit Lucas, and he would die . . . and even if that thought didn't already mortify her, the fact that the dam he was conjuring out of the earth would remain unfinished, thus allowing the flood to resume and inundate the entire valley, did. She also knew that her ordinary weapon could not stop red lightning. But when fused with a Silver Bullet, maybe . . .

Without thinking it through, without fully understanding the choice that she had made, Gemini cried out and threw her sickle. It went high, far too high and short a trajectory to hit the Blood Poacher. Instead it spun, in an agonizingly slow arc, until it slowed right over her and Lucas's heads. At the same time a zigzag of crimson fire shot out of the darkness, intercepting the kreisflyer.

There was a crashing echo, like a thousand gongs going off at once, and then a glimmering explosion as her weapon was instantly incinerated. But the forked electricity stopped dead, and Gemini knew it had worked, that despite the choice she had made, it had all been worth—

A blinding red flash, then a bone-crushing blast. Something hot and prickly hit her right in the heart. The whole world spun; she saw nothing but stars.

She never even heard the thunder. Whether the second thunderbolt had hit her directly or simply somewhere nearby, Gemini didn't know. She was vaguely aware of falling on her back and nearly tumbling off the rocky ledge, so that she lay with her arm hanging off the precipice of the stone wall. She heard Lucas cry her name. Black oily smoke began to rise from her chest. She tried to lift her head to see, but instead, something very strange happened. She felt as if she were leaving her body, that her eyes and mind were drifting along with that dark plume rising out of her, and though part of Gemini's mind was terrified, though she wanted to shout back at her captain for help, desperately wanted to stay in her body, she couldn't, and a kind of strange quiet overtook her. She couldn't move, couldn't do anything but watch.

Lucas ran out of water to see shadows with, and he let go of the sea as his barricade of earth at last grew level with the conquered flood. He fell to his knees, exhausted. Gemini saw that his halo was no longer infused with special color: it was now only blue, and its glow was very, very faint . . . though not as faint as her own. He crawled over to her, grabbing her hand, again calling her name, and still Gemini wanted to call down to him, but it was like being in a dream she couldn't wake up from, one that was only growing deeper with each passing second, as if it would never end, and she could only distantly watch herself, her body lying so awkwardly, her eyes half open, while her captain slowly stood and turned to face their enemy.

From her top-down view, Gemini could not see the Blood Poacher, but she heard its guttural hiss and the deep barks of the Slasher Kappos as they taunted her captain.

"*SURRENDER.*"

The voice came from two sources, and it registered to Gemini that although she was no longer in her body, her mouth was twisting to speak.

Lucas drew his zeitblatt and pointed it towards the bridge. His arm was shaking badly. He was in no condition to fight.

"Do not use them to speak," he said. What dwindling part of Gemini that remained was alarmed at how weak he sounded.

"*THEY BELONG TO US NOW. SURRENDER.*"

Again Gemini saw her mouth move. Her vision was starting to spiral as more dark wisps leaked from her body, and she started to feel very sleepy, as if soon none of this would matter . . . but her last remaining ounce of awareness struggled against nothing, writhing to be free, to stay here . . .

Her captain placed his hand over her head. There was a rustling sound, and colors and shapes started to mix and meld with one another. Everything was a blur, and in the next instant Gemini found herself . . . seeing, not quite from Lucas's eyes, but not quite from behind his head either. She was with him, but she was not there at the same time. From her captain's perspective, she saw that he—*they*—were staring at the spot where her body had just been lying.

The Blood Poacher and Kappos hissed and barked at him, and as Lucas again lifted his sword, Gemini saw that his halo was even dimmer now. She wanted to tell him to let her go, that he could not fight while exhausted *and* holding her out of harm's way, that he had no strength left. But Gemini could not speak or even think, and so she merely watched as Lucas defiantly stared down the White Eyes of Thunder.

The Blood Poacher hovered over Liz's body. Its long, spiked tails slithered across the bridge. It was a nightmarish form, a living shadow, twice the size of any man. A final layer of swirling black clouds formed a tattered cloak the bleak color of ash, and two pale, skeletal hands folded over its chest. The huge, horned wings were but thousands of shards of red ore, expanding and contracting on either side of the motionless specter. The shrapnel seemed to flow in and out of two blindingly white wedges that abutted the shoulders of the Poacher: these were the White

Eyes themselves, huge and lidless, the epicenters of dark thought, their light so blinding that they washed out all detail of the Blood Poacher's head. Long, narrow horns grew out of either shoulder, flanking an abyss draped by a heavy hood. But within that shadow, Gemini felt *something*, something vicious, gazing at them, locking onto Lucas with a cold and calculating precision.

Lucas looked to either side. Kappos had jumped out onto the sheet of rock and were hopping towards him. The Slasher Kappos standing to either side of the Poacher all had rifles pointed at him.

Liz's slack jaw moved in fits.

"*EVEN AMONG DURATIONISTS, THERE ARE FEW WHO COULD BE SO CLOSE TO DEATH YET STILL HAVE THE STRENGTH TO LOOK* ME *IN THE EYES.*"

"I am no ordinary Durationist," said Lucas. "I have dwelt in the darkness that you call home."

Lightning struck at the center of the stone wall, and the cruiser fired a missile into its base. Lucas braced himself against the impact, but there was very little vibration; the entire slab seemed to absorb the strikes without as much as a crack. So long as Lucas stayed alive, the wall would not break . . .

"*YOU WILL RETURN TO THE VOID. BUT WITH YOUR SOUL IN PIECES. TO FUEL OUR MACHINE.*"

Lucas steadied his hand as he pointed his sword at the Blood Poacher.

"You will have to hunt me down."

Abruptly there was a terrible screech, warped and obscene.

Kappos lunged at him from either side. Lucas thrust his sword back and forth, and Gemini watched a flurry of leather helmets and rickety arms go hurtling off the wall.

Another screech. Then, in stilted motion, the Blood Poacher attacked.

A tail snapped forward. Lucas ducked under it and bolted across the wall, towards the northern cliff. The Slashers started opening fire, and Gemini heard the bullets bounce off the rock under her captain's feet. Lucas lamely swung his sword to the side, but he no longer had the strength to deflect any of the fire. He cut down more ragged shapes scurrying towards him, but a second swipe of the Poacher's tail knocked him off his feet. He had to do everything in his power to land on his shoulder instead of bouncing off the edge. As he rolled onto his back, Gemini saw a spiked tail striking for his legs, and Lucas curled up as the jagged line ripped into the rock right where his shins had just been. Then he leaped to his feet and dashed frantically for the cliffside. He ran along the flooded ravine, bullets whizzing by his head.

She distinctly felt her captain's mind race as he tried to call on his powers. But he was too tired, his halo too depleted, and all he had left in him was to run. The thumping shots of the Slashers filled their ears, and Lucas grunted—Gemini ached from a disembodied pain, *Lucas's* pain, she realized—as a bullet hit him in the arm. His sword fell from his hand, but there was no time to go back for it. He stumbled past the burning remnants of the watchtower, then scrambled through the dunes bordering the coast. Muddled rays of early morning light spattered across the sandy landscape. They heard clanking sounds, and rolling Slashers flanked him on either side, taking turns to streak past him and spin over his head, all in an effort to knock him off his feet. Jumping and dodging, Lucas somehow weaved through them. Killer Fives soared past and flung lightning from its wings. With a great crack, the bolts struck directly in Lucas's path, jutting up sand to form stalks of glass dead ahead; running downhill, there was no way to avoid them.

Screaming incoherently, Lucas twisted and turned his body in between the glass stalks as the Poacher dove after him and threw its head into the veritable cage it had created, and something red and toothy glinted under its hood. Lucas crouched to avoid the Poacher's maw as he tried to pry himself free. But the glass would not give in, and Lucas yelled out in pain as the ore seared and burned his arms. Although Gemini could not see what feelings or memories the red rock instilled in him, she could feel her captain's anguish, even his fear. The Poacher's maw was just a foot over them.

Ignoring his pain, not daring to look up, Lucas clutched a glass stalk and tried to at least bend it, but to no avail. He was trapped. Then the Blood Poacher let out an ugly hiss, and Gemini felt something hot and awful wash over them, and she felt sick as tendrils of smoke started to pour out of Lucas's mouth and chest . . .

Lucas shouted and slammed a fist into the ground. His halo gave a sputtering flash. Sand cascaded. Glass shattered, and he rolled down the dune. A broken rod tumbled into his arms. A War Daddy unfurled and sprung into the air, claws and jaws open as it prepared to pounce upon him. But Lucas jabbed the glass rod right into the Slasher's gut and heaved the broken stalk and the beast he had impaled over his head. The Slasher went sailing past him. Screeching in anger, the Blood Poacher dived towards him, tails tearing through the dunes, and Lucas threw himself down another slope.

He landed hard atop a crown of reeds and rock, but he had no choice but to spring back up, ignore the spinning in his head, and keep moving. Gemini could hear the roaring of the waves; they were close to the shore. There was a smoldering skiff nearby, and she dully wondered if it was the same airboat that Peppy and Griffin had crashed earlier. Three Slasher Kappos unfurled around Lucas, and the Blood Poacher hovered over them. All around the beach, dozens of leatherheads were ambling over dunes, eager to watch the Durationist die.

Lucas lifted his grudge shot. The War Daddies hissed at him and raised their rifles, thinking the chase had come to an end. Lucas pointed the weapon repeatedly at all three of them, until it occurred to him that the crashed airboat might still have fuel in it . . .

The Poacher's tails jutted down at him like a blizzard of maces, but Lucas dodged the whips and raised his rifle as the Slashers closed in. He pulled the trigger, firing right at the crashed skiff.

He had already resumed his sprint when the blast sent all three Slashers to the ground. Now it was just him dashing across the scrolling sand, Killer Fives gliding after him, a whole host of leatherheads and War Daddies charging behind their commander. Gemini knew the situation was grim. Lucas was running out of luck, and he was far past exhaustion. It was hard to see how he would not be killed when there was nothing left ahead of him but the coast. The Jamaica Sound was sprawled out in front of him, and they saw Grant's Lighthouse escaping the gloom at last, its beam rising over the dunes, green mist coalescing around its lantern. There was a beacon there, and Gemini knew that had been her captain's plan—to somehow turn it on—but there was no way to get to it with miles of water between them . . .

Lucas heard the warped screeches behind him, the rushing of wings, and then lightning again cast twisted glass around him. He somehow dodged his way through it all, just as the jagged tail appeared in his way on a course to rip open his chest. Lucas slid onto his back, the tail missing his head by inches.

But, at the expense of avoiding dismemberment, he began to tumble out of control down the side of a steep dune. The Poacher swept past, claws grating into his back. Lucas tried to raise his rifle, but a scythe batted it out of his grip and out of sight. He went careening downward, and Gemini was dizzy from all the spinning and had no idea what the hell was happening, for all the pain was finally catching up with both of them as her captain hurtled through a void, occasionally crashing against rough sand, occasionally seeing the White Eyes above—

Crash.

Gemini felt fear as Lucas tasted blood. He staggered to his feet as Kappos slid down the large dune. Killer Fives circled past. He took a lame step forward before collapsing on one knee. He had made it to the beach. Water periodically lapped his legs, and the sea breeze smelled as strong as ever. The beacon from the lighthouse rotated past once or twice, but the light didn't seem to touch the Poacher or the Kappos as they descended around him. A crimson tint fell upon the shore.

"Let me kill him."

Lucas and Gemini looked up. A tall, broad man in a black sweater walked up the beach. He carried a broadsword in his gauntlet hand, which encased a blackened halo. A necklace of red rocks hung from his neck. His face was covered in duress lines; his eyes were smoldering holes.

"Let me kill him," the thing that was once Ahmed from Pilgrim's Bay, Captain of Tremont United, asked of its master. *"Let me prove my worth to the Fathom."*

Killer Fives simply hovered above them, hissing what must have been its assent.

It faintly occurred to Gemini and Lucas that Red Tide had just entered the Metro Reef, and that somewhere on the codex the Courier was trying to tell them that the Red Tide airship was already engaging the Echomar's Doom Ship. But what did it matter? By the time the fleet got here, it would be too late. Again, with what little sense of herself Gemini still had left, she wished Lucas would just let her go; there was no way he would stand a chance while tethered to her soul.

Yet, at the appearance of the traitor, Lucas's attitude had changed. His breathing had calmed, and he was staring the Thrall down with a resolute glare. There was a swooshing sound, and then showers of sparks and flames from a Kappo who couldn't get out of the way as the zeitblatt hurtled all the way across the beach to land in Lucas's raised gauntlet. The blade thrummed in sync with his halo, and while Gemini saw that its glow was still weak, it was again brimming with the red and blue patterns from when he and Liz had stopped the flood. Lucas's left arm hung awkwardly from the bullet wound, but he raised the sword confidently in his other hand and pointed it at the Thrall.

The beam from the lighthouse blinked past, and in the next instant the Thrall was on him, taking wild swings with his hulking sword. Lucas barely blocked the blows, his arms quivering as he was driven off his heels, his wounds searing from pain. Ahmed from Pilgrim's Bay had been a practitioner of the Icon of *Blood*, using it to engorge his muscles during battle, and the Bounder fighting Lucas did the same, the inroad lines up its arms practically scorching off its rotten skin as it shoved Lucas back with thunderous swings. Had Gemini still had a body, she would have cringed at each blow that her captain barely parried. Somehow, Lucas had just enough anticipation to keep Ahmed's broadsword at bay. But he could not mask the fact that he was fighting with just one arm, or that his body was very weak; after a particularly vicious shove, he stumbled and fell onto his back.

The Kappos were all barking and yelping; the White Eyes were watching. Gemini gave a muted scream and desperately wished she could writhe out of nonexistence to help her captain as he scuttled backwards. The Thrall raised its broadsword . . .

Then the crimson tint was swept away, and Lucas had to raise his wrist to shade his eyes as everything was drowned out in blinding white light. Kappos began to stagger sightlessly, squealing as they collided with one another. The Thrall growled and covered its eyes. The rotating clouds overhead seemed to taper and wither in the scorching exposure. Squinting, Lucas looked around to try to locate the source of the light, but it came from all across the eastern horizon, as if dawn was blasting away the night's storm. Many Kappos simply flopped onto their backs, shaking with spasms until they lay in sizzling heaps, unable to defend themselves from the awful light.

Killer Fives gave a bloodcurdling hiss and shielded itself with its wings. The luminescence seemed to shrink into a single dot on the horizon, and everything else went pitch black. As leatherheads continued to flail around him, Lucas dared to look out to the sound, where the lone star hovered over Grant's Lighthouse. It pulsed once, then began to zigzag across the sky, leaving a brilliant trail of emerald in its wake. The orb punched into the thunderclouds surrounding the Blood Poacher. Lightning lashed out but never reached the ground, and the storm shrieked with thunder and howled with wind as the ball of white energy shot in and out of its sundered base, and a wispy tornado over Lucas's head roped out and died with an undignified sigh. An updraft rushed into the imploding thunderhead, and like a balloon it literally shrunk before Lucas's eyes. Then the sky filled with popping bursts of colors as the Kappos scurried south, where skiffs were hastily landing to pick up as many troops as they could.

The Thrall turned back to him, but Lucas had already sprung back to his feet and was hacking away, his halo as lambent as the murky sunrise. The Thrall tried to push back, its arms swelling with rippling, pulsing bonds of dark thought; but Lucas would not be deterred, parrying every blow, turning every bone-shaking swing his enemy took into a riposte humming with blue light. Lucas stabbed at the Thrall's chest, but the Bounder caught the blow in time and their blades locked. With its surging strength, it pushed Lucas backwards, bending his spine, and it grinned as it tried to snap him in half.

Lucas's halo shone between them. His sword pulsed with rainbow light. With a shout, he shoved the broadsword aside and spun around in a violent whirl of multicolored light.

The red necklace snapped in half. The Thrall's body crumpled at his feet. Its head landed in the waves.

At this point Gemini knew or sensed no more than what Lucas saw. They watched the skiffs crammed with blighters take off, many of them shot down by Red Tide airships as they zipped past the coast. Other Kappos were gunned down as the ships strafed the shore line. The mighty Doom Ship retreated out into the sound, smoke rising from its stern as the blimp-shaped Red Tide flagship gave chase. Somewhere above, a crescent shadow flew over Lucas and followed the storm cruiser out to sea. As the Blood Poacher vanished in a folding curtain of fog, a final message jutted itself into Lucas's head.

—*Mind the Void,* Lucas from Slag Falls. Mind the Void, or the Void will mind *you.*

Then silence. Morning mists and a hazy sky of yellow and pink. The storm had broken up over Metro Reef. The Blood Poacher had left the field. The orb of light nestled itself just over the lighthouse, and then the rays of the morning sun cast out over the Jamaica Sound, and sea and sky flourished with the colors of dawn.

Lucas collapsed to his knees, gasping for air, and a moment later Gemini was next to him, dark shadows still spewing from her chest, her fragment of awareness somewhere between her body and her captain. He grabbed her hand and scooped her a jolt of cogs, but his own halo was very weak, and he had nothing left to give her, certainly not enough to stave off her wounds.

A spitting hiss echoed across the beach. Emerald light washed over the shore, and Lucas sat up straight. He and Gemini were not alone.

"You look lost," a low, purring voice noted.

At first all he could see was the spinning, blinding green flame that floated off the ground. Then the fire shrunk a little, and he saw the palm beneath it, encased in a silver-and-black glove. His eyes ran up the woman's deep sleeve, all the way to a slim, lithe figure dressed in a long, dark sweater. She walked smoothly towards them, like a big game cat stalking its prey. A thick shawl the color of dead autumn leaves covered her head, draped over her right shoulder, and fell to the small of her back. Her face was hidden so that all Lucas could see was a pair of violent points flecked with gray.

The fire danced in the palm of her outstretched gauntlet hand. It was the same trick they said she could do with the sun.

She stopped next to them.

"Need a hand?"

Lucas could see her face more clearly now: soft but unmoving, the lazy semicircles of gray and lavender obscured by a shade of burnt-orange hair. She was staring into the lick of fire. The emerald swirls running through her halo-hand seemed to shine in concert with the flame.

He ignored her. He turned back to Gemini and resumed tracing a finger over her halo.

"So," he said after a few seconds. "How long were you waiting up there?"

Sophia looked into the spitting flame, a faint scowl drawn upon her slender face.

"The beacon isn't a simple thing to turn on, Captain. Not that you were going to find out. Just what was your plan, anyway?"

"To stay alive until help came. Had it come sooner, perhaps fewer people would have died."

Cannons reverberated in the distance. Sophia's lip curled.

"I saved people you left to die in the slums, in case you didn't notice."

"Who all would have died anyways, since the dam blew up. But I guess you decided that wasn't worth the trouble."

"I'm a closer. I enter a fight when I want to."

"Yes, when it suits you."

There were faint cheers and cries of joy from further inland. Gemini's halo remained dim.

"If you have something to say, say it," Sophia snapped.

"You stole our win."

"Ha! You call this a win? Look around, Captain. Your whole team's dead. You should be thanking me for saving you. This is *my* victory . . . and somehow, I don't think I'll have a hard time convincing anyone of that."

Neither spoke for a few moments. Waves crashed close by. Spindrift splattered over them.

Lucas continued to hold Gemini's hand, and he muttered an endless parade of incantations, but it was no use. The inky smoke kept rising in the air.

"You sure you know what you're doing?" Sophia asked.

He didn't reply. Gemini saw what was happening as if she were in a passing dream, but in the infinitesimal awareness that she still possessed, she was certain that Lucas was determined to ignore Sophia's presence, to not even give her the satisfaction of a response. A seagull squawked as it flew by. Gemini heard her body give a rattling cough.

"Let me do it," Sophia insisted.

Lucas laughed coldly at her. Sophia still did not look at him, but her eyebrows rose, and she risked throwing him a side glance. The flame was spinning furiously.

"I figured that's why you bothered to say hello," he said, his voice full of contempt. "No. I will *never* give up the expansion claim. Go back and tell whoever in Londinium is propping you up that you're wasting your time. Or try finding your own token. They're hard to come by, but if you're worthy of wearing one, it shouldn't be impossible. Worthy being the operative word, of course—"

"I wasn't talking about the damn expansion," Sophia said coldly. "I meant *her*. Do you want my help or not?"

Waves crashed. Foam lapped at their feet. Gemini groaned.

"What . . . what can you do?" Lucas said at last, an edge still to his voice. But his anger was rapidly collapsing beneath his own worry, and he sighed as he muttered another useless chant. "I can't—I can't do it. I'm too weak. I need to get—"

There was another hissing noise. Sophia had closed her palm, and the flame suddenly vanished. An ivy-colored fire now hovered over Gemini's heart, and Gemini felt her body stir, heard her voice groan.

Lucas tried to stagger to his feet, but instead he fell to one knee.

"What are you doing?" he rasped.

Sophia didn't respond. Her expression was inscrutable. Then the wisps of shadow started to dissipate and collapse back into Gemini's chest. The fire sunk into her, and the wound beneath her breast began to sear and close. After a moment, the smoke disappeared, and suddenly Gemini was back in her body, coughing uncontrollably, her breath rattled, labored; but nevertheless, she was alive.

"She'll be all right," Sophia said. She finally turned to Lucas. Her charcoal sweater was unmarked save for a violet emblem on the front, an egg with a serpent wrapped around it. The logo stirred something in Lucas's mind, but what he could not say.

Sophia's eyes were fully visible, lavender beacons dappled with heathery ash. She glared at him.

"And for your information, Captain, I *am* worthy to wear my own damn token, and I'll be taking your expansion claim whether you like it or . . ."

She trailed off. Gemini, though barely again conscious, even though her restored senses were already fading fast, swore she saw Sophia's eyes widen ever so slightly, as if she was surprised by something. Almost imperceptibly, she shook her head. Gemini couldn't see Lucas's reaction, as his face was obscured by his hood, but he went very still, and she had the impression that he too was taken aback.

Sophia worked quickly to regain her composure, as if it had never happened. She made a move to hastily cover her gauntlet hand, and

Gemini was certain her captain noticed. Then she turned back into the fog and was gone.

Lucas stared intently at the spot where their peer had vanished. Gemini didn't get it. She was too tired to get much of anything just then.

"Lucas . . . ?" she mumbled weakly. "What . . . what just happened?"

Chants of *"SOPHIA! SOPHIA! SOPHIA!"* rang from the city.

She melded her power with the lighthouse! a thought-talkie had already scooped. *Incredible!*

"SOPHIA!" The chants continued, both on the streets and on the codex. *"SOPHIA! ROSLYN'S HERO!"*

"I'm not sure," Lucas said finally. He squeezed her hand. "But we're going to find out."

EPILOGUE

IT WAS MIDMORNING. THE rising sun and thinning skies did not make the city look any better. Smoke still rose from the skyline. An endless chorus of sirens sang out of harmony. Triages and hospitals were packed with the maimed and the insane, while the codex was flooded with the worried thoughts of people searching for loved ones, as well as the angry, paranoid scoops of citizens demanding answers. The recovery of Metro Reef would be a long, grueling process. But Roslyn as a whole would have to be on the alert for the next attack.

Fernando from South Tempest sat inside the command center that had been set up at a gym across the bay from the city. From downstairs, he heard the frantic footsteps of red- and whitecoats, the clamoring of rabble, and the parade of fans walking home. Somewhere down there, Thom was keeping watch over Ajay while he recovered. Fernando supposed he ought to be down there with them, but escorting the ambassadors out of the city had proved to be a challenging task. A blighter horde ambushed them right at the Founder's Bridge, and Fernando had drained his halo raw getting them through it. He was damn tired, and he wanted to be alone. He propped his boots up on a desk in front of him and drank a glass of Dixie scotch.

All in all, a shitty night to say the least.

A lot of players in his position would be happy right now, he thought. The team above his own had been wiped out. With Tremont United gone, Old Atlantic was now the leader of the Blood Works Society's Durationist corps. Which potentially meant their future was bright: Premiereship and the lion's choices of assignments were all on the table. Except Fernando doubted any of that was coming, because he was certain that the Blood Works Society was going to take a beating in Londinium, which meant the open Premiereship would go to another affiliate. Not to mention that his team had its own problems right now.

He had seen Sophia's betrayal coming for a while. Ever since she first signed with Old Atlantic, she had proved to be a pain in the ass. She freelanced; she never listened to his orders. She was inherently insubordinate, a character trait that Fernando wished the league cracked down on a hell of a lot more than they did. But the Alumni Circle never took his complaints about Sophia seriously. The league offices loved her, she was their poster girl. Besides, he had been told, she gets results.

Maybe, Fernando conceded. But she didn't do it the right way. Fernando didn't give a damn that she had saved the day. Abandoning her team in the middle of a severe storm was the last straw. He wanted Sophia out, and he didn't care if the Blood Works Society vetoed him on it. He had told Bion and Lionel as much just a few minutes ago. Whether those doddering old-timers would back him or not, he had no idea. But he wasn't hopeful. The Alumni Circle had grown more and more toothless over the years, and it was an unspoken rule among the league captains that if you really wanted to get something done, you did not go through League Command, but to the commissioner's office.

Getting rid of Sophia would almost certainly guarantee that Old Atlantic would not be on the ascent. But Fernando didn't care. Truthfully, he didn't want to be in the Premieres anyways. He was a Duke's League captain, and the tasks he tended to get were reasonable enough that he was always able to accomplish them. Fernando enjoyed that kind of predictability. He would like to say he took pride in being part of the DLR, but honest-to-*Over-Soul* truth, he saw it as nothing but a contract: they expected him to do a job, and in return he got a nice wrist and the perks of being a player. He was content with that. The ridiculous (and, in his mind, undeserving) fame and hype that Sophia had brought to their gym had thrown everything out of wack, as would moving any higher up in the league than he presently was. So he was glad to stay put, just like he was hopeful to be rid of his closer.

He took another drink, staring out at the city. He could not tell whether there were still some clouds in the sky or if it was just smoke from all the rubble. The sun was probably a welcome sight for many. After being up all night, it just hurt his eyes. Or maybe the scotch was stronger than he thought.

Some of the true yahoos in the league, like Lionel or Ahmed—well, perhaps not Ahmed—would tell you that being part of the DLR was a point of national pride; others, the truly insane, like Lucas, depicted as it as some sort of spiritual crusade. But it was all bullshit, Fernando knew. They weren't Roslyn's guardians. Vanquishing the Blood Poachers from the earth was clearly not their fate. *No.* The true purpose of the Durationist League of Roslyn was completely and utterly prosaic, and it was something so obvious to Fernando that it astounded him that so few of his peers were willing to tell it like it was.

What kind of soldier had fans? What kind of army competed with itself? And what kind of crusader was ultimately beholden to the coffers of his corporate sponsor?

He refilled his tumbler, gave a private toast, and drank the whole glass in one swift gulp. No, he thought. Duration was not mysterious, it was not enlightening, and it was not the quest of good against evil. Duration was just a sport. They were *entertainment*, plain and simple.

Dimly, he remembered a long screed given by someone in the post-Roslyn movement, out on the steps of city hall in Tremont. *"It's all a scam!"* the man insisted to unbelieving onlookers. *"Londinium controls Vlaz Gal. The storms appear only where the Barra let them! They use our suffering to make the Owners' halos glow. Expose their lies!"*

Fernando had no idea if any of that was true. But he didn't think it was as farfetched as many of his peers did. They scoffed whenever someone doubted things. But Fernando had long suspected that the Barra only permitted the league to exist to begin with because it was by far and away the biggest source of Roslyn's wealth. It sure seemed like those

True Owners of Roslyn had little love for the Durationists otherwise. Some in the Alumni Circle, like Bion or Simon, and of course righteous old Lucas, thought that the Durationists' place in some ecclesiastical battle in the distant future was all but a forgone conclusion.

Even people who hated the Barra—and few outside the Last Church of Roslyn actually liked them—thought this. All Fernando could think was: what distant future? What end time? Everyone, every pilgrim to Roslyn, had come here expecting that *this* was the end time, that upon stepping on this soil they would find peace in the New Life. But that was not to be. People didn't know who their brothers and sisters were, death still came, and the *Over-Soul* was nowhere to be found. The New Life had delivered on nothing, and so Fernando could hardly blame anyone for doubting the whole damn thing. At any rate, he thought any Durationist who felt holier than thou about their line of work ought to remember that their battlefields had galleries where people came to knock off for the evening.

Entertainment. Pure and simple.

He shrugged and refilled his glass. Meanwhile, he had saved those damned ambassadors. He did not get caught up in competition or any delusion of what was right and wrong. He came in, took his blows, and got out. He did his job, unheralded as always, and despite the ugly scene from his window, a good many people were better for it. Now, that was the kind of pride Fernando could get on board with.

He glanced at a clock. The commissioner was supposed to mind him twenty minutes ago. Fernando was annoyed, but on the other hand, he shouldn't have drunk so much while he was waiting.

With nothing else to do, and still not particularly interested in checking on his teammates, he tapped his gauntlet hand and listened to the news roll by.

— *... toll expected to continue to rise. Search-and-rescue missions are ongoing throughout New Bronx and Harlo Valley. The Red Tide Cathedral Durationist club is personally leading rescue operations. Their captain, Trebolio from Red Tide, refused to comment on our breaking story that all four members of Tremont United, Reigning Premiere team from the Blood Works Society, were killed in action overnight. The league has confirmed to us that Tremont United has not reported in following the battle ...*

Fernando guffawed. He assumed the league was just grateful the press hadn't found out about Ahmed yet. That was going to be a tough one to explain.

—*All of Metro Reef is praising Sophia from Belmont Chapel this morning. Mayor Carter has called for her to receive a key to the city. "Wherever she is this morning," he said, "we are indebted to her."*

Fernando would also love to know where Sophia was at the moment, seeing that she had never reported to him after her little stunt.

—*Rallies for Sophia have gone to extreme lengths. The DLR and RCS are strongly advising that people avoid the valley beaches, as the area is littered with dangerous materials following the battle, and the possibility of rogue Kappos still active cannot be discounted. But we're hearing that hundreds are walking to the beach to pray to the lighthouse, and a rally for Sophia from Belmont Chapel has been going on all morning...*

His halo hummed, and Fernando heard chanting and the roar of ocean waves.

"SOPHIA! SOPHIA! ROSLYN'S HERO! LONG LIVE SOPHIA, ROSLYN'S HERO!"

Another drink, he decided.

—*RCS claims that rumors of follow-up attacks down the east coast are hoaxes and advises people to disregard codex warnings unless they come from Commonwealth Services ... In Tremont, the Blood Works Society refuses to comment on the reported death of their Premiere team. August from Tremont, Owner of Londinium, has said that his machifare's hegemony is not his main priority. "Ensuring Roslyn's security is our main goal moving forward," he said. "We will work tirelessly to bring justice to the perpetrators of this heinous attack."*

A nice statement that said absolutely nothing, Fernando thought. And a blatant lie. August was terrified of losing hegemony. What Owner wouldn't be?

—*Echomar Prime Minister Survec continues to deny Vlaz Gal's involvement in the attacks. "This was the work of radicals with no connection to our government," the prime minister said this morning. "We vow to work with our partners in Londinium to hunt these extremists down..."*

Sounded like bullshit. But so did everything to Fernando.

—*Londinium officials have yet to comment on why the Bellatrist failed to send any teams to Metro Reef...*

That bothered Fernando too. He would much rather have fought alongside Herod's men than Lucas's B team and the riffraff of the Cog Mind.

—No official word yet on whether the DLR will call for the league-wide congress known as the Combine in the aftermath of the attack. But sources in Londinium tell us that the call for Open Season is now imminent . . .

Fernando considered it. Open Season would unfortunately require his involvement: that rare event where teams were re-ranked, players signed elsewhere, and the Durationist corps from each machifare tried to prove which among them deserved to lead Roslyn's fight against the Echomar. The winner of the Open Season affected the position of affiliates as much as it did the league, and so it had become a progressively bigger circus over the centuries. Fernando was not looking forward to it. Still, the outcome of the Open Season would not affect him. After it ended, veterans above him would be beneath him, and amateurs below him would ascend beyond. Fernando didn't care. He'd just stay level as always.

"Do you know what I've enjoyed the most about the news so far?"

He glanced up. The translucent image of a man loomed over his desk, tall and dressed entirely in shades of white. A snowy cloak was draped over his broad shoulders, clasped beneath a wintry cravat that hung over the breast of his ivory suit. He stood before the window, and the sun's glare shone through his head, so that only the long silver hair that framed his face could be seen.

Fernando blinked, startled. Without his damn head, he looked exactly like a Barra. Why anyone would want to dress like one of the Black Eyes was beyond him. Just one of many reasons he didn't like this man, who happened to be the commissioner of the league . . .

Fernando shut off the newsfeed. "What did you enjoy?" he asked in an empty voice. He did not remove his feet from the desk.

"Not one mention of Lucas from Slag Falls. As far as the public is concerned, he might as well have died last night. If only we could have been so lucky . . ."

That calm, cultured voice always got on Fernando's nerves. He swore it was phony, though he couldn't put his finger on why.

"I guess the Meta-School's kaput then, huh?"

The ivory man lazily spread his hands. "For all intents and purposes, yes. His team disobeyed League Command by being out there to begin with. He deserved his humiliation, to say the least . . ."

"So you prying the glove off him or what?"

The ivory man tilted his head. Fernando got the impression he was scowling.

"Since he wears a true Token of Power, by astral law we *cannot* forcibly take it from him. However. My ringleaders will meet with him first thing Monday, and I am confident their gaze will compel him to . . . voluntarily give it up."

"We can only hope," Fernando said.

The idea of Lucas from Slag Falls running his own machifare was like asking a leatherhead to be your butler. It was a disaster waiting to happen, and Fernando was very glad to see the Cowl's crazy bid for power die. With the death of Liz, Lucas had very few friends left with any real influence in the league. His buddy Zeno from Radio Row was a Steward only in the most nominal sense of the title; the rest of the alum were fed up with him. Lucas was also close to the Courier, that phantom of the codex whom several players kept counsel with. But the Barra had never particularly cared for him, which made him a dismal ally to rely on at a time like this. Lucas, it seemed, was toast.

Fernando raised his glass to the commissioner, then drank. "Good riddance."

"Which of course brings us to the question of who will take his expansion claim," the commissioner said.

Fernando stared at that absent face. Surely he didn't think *he* was interested? When he had challenged Lucas to that duel seven years ago, it was only at the commissioner's behest; Fernando had no interest in wearing a Token of Power. "That's not why I asked to talk to—"

"I know," the commissioner said, and a hint of a chill entered that regal voice, enough to make Fernando stiffen. He did not like this man, nor half the things they said about him. Both his hands were naked, yet that gold-and-silver halo on his wrist—the only part of him with any real color—ebbed and flowed with a hue that did not look completely normal to Fernando's admittedly bleary eyes.

"This is about your closer. Bion and Lionel already informed me of your request. I am happy to tell you that I will oblige."

Fernando blinked. "You will?"

"Yes. You see, Roslyn's next affiliate will be led by Sophia from Belmont Chapel."

Somewhere downstairs, he heard fans chanting her name.

"Doesn't she need a Token of Power?" he asked aloud.

"That will soon be taken care of," the commissioner said with a dismissive wave. "The deal is all but done. The league office will back her claim in return for her reliance on our, ah, guidance. After last night, it's clear Sophia is our future. I am certain poor August won't get in the way. So fear not, Captain; your star player will be off your hands."

Fernando put his drink down. He rubbed his hands together and stared off into space.

"Well," he said slowly. "Thank you for your, uh, help."

"I do, of course, require one thing from you in return."

Fernando shifted in his seat. "Yes?"

"You've been Sophia's captain for seven years. Is there anything I ought to know about her?"

"*SOPHIA! SOPHIA!*" The chants shook the building.

Fernando rubbed his eyes. How much was he supposed to say? "Well," he said slowly, "you know I think she could learn a thing or two about league protocol."

A haughty laugh escaped that missing face. "Her rogue behavior is no concern of mine. The DLR has handled defiant stars before; we can handle them again. No, I am not asking for your evaluation of her character, Captain; with all due respect, your opinion on that means, ah . . . very little to me. I am talking more about matters of . . . security."

"Security?"

"Yes. Security." The ivory man placed his hands on the desk. The image tilted slightly through the wood, so that the top half of the commissioner floated over the tabletop. He leaned forward and stony gray eyes emerged from the sunlight. "The Barra have vetted her thoroughly, of course, and rarely are my ringleaders wrong about anything. However. We have to be certain. Do you feel certain that Sophia will serve her nation well?"

Fernando rocked in his chair slightly, his hands on the armrest. He pursed his lips. Applause rang from somewhere downstairs.

"I . . . never cared for her Rishi heritage," he said. "I'm not a prejudiced man, commissioner, but their ways influenced her more than I think she publicly admits."

"Ah, fear not. I'm well aware that her relationship with the Rishi

Rojah is more complicated than people know. That's no concern. If anything, her standing among the Wild Nation gives us a great opportunity to bring the Rishi back under our sphere of influence."

Fernando nodded slowly. That was all well and good. But did it excuse the fact that he was convinced Sophia knew some of the Rishi's witchcraft too? There was that time they were scouting in the woodlands of Wanasotah, and she had somehow known where a band of criminal Thrall had been hiding. She'd chalked it up to Now-Sense, but Fernando had seen her talking to those wolves. He was sure of it! Such strange powers had been taught only by the most powerful of the Rishi. Why would she keep that a secret?

"Anything else?" the ivory man asked.

What else? Was he really the only person who thought it was weird that a First Wave pilgrim, a Rishi who had been in Roslyn for almost seven hundred years, just decided to start playing Duration ten seasons ago? Oh sure, he could chalk up all his suspicions to the fact that he disliked Sophia. And he did—deeply! But that did not explain everything. You did not battle with someone on a Durationist team without entering some kind of psychic kinship, no matter how frayed the relationships might otherwise be. Fernando was certain that Sophia's cold, play-for-pay exterior was bogus. He just knew it. He had seen that cool, couldn't-give-a-shit face she loved to affect crack only once. But it was a moment he would never forget.

They had been tracking down a Thrall cell right in Tremont. Sophia loved to take down Bounders; in fact, she seemed to enjoy it more than hunting storms. That was something Fernando had always found a little odd, that she fought human blighters with such an animus. Sometimes he got the sense she was . . . *looking* for a particular one, or maybe trying to get any of them to say something. Well, one of them said something all right, that evening in Tremont.

Fernando had arrived late to the scene. He came into the apartment and found that Sophia had already cleaned up house. Four Thrall lay shot on the floor; all except one of them were dead. Fernando had been about to reprimand her for charging in without him as always when the dying Thrall did something very, very strange. Fernando remembered it like it was yesterday. It raised its rotten hand and yelled *"I KNOW!"* Then it pointed at Sophia's gauntlet hand and screamed—

"Captain? You're wasting my time."

They had never spoken about it. All he remembered was that her perpetual scowl had finally been shattered, however briefly, and that Sophia left the scene with a look of absolute alarm on her face. Fernando had certainly found the whole thing disturbing, but not enough to make a big fuss about it. After all, Thrall often said inexplicable things in their death throes; they were, of course, puppets of the Echomar. And who could doubt Sophia's record against their enemy? Yet . . .

". . . freelancing," he was saying. "I don't care for her freelancing."

The commissioner laughed. "Once again, style of play is hardly a worry for me. Had the rest of your team played more aggressively, perhaps you would not have taken the beating you did! At any rate, I had to do this by the book. Rest assured, Captain, she will be off your team by Monday. Combine will be next weekend. Your presence is of course required. Until then."

The ivory man vanished.

The sky was clearing. The sun was bright. Fernando studied the empty glass on the desk. No, he did not like the idea of Sophia from Belmont Chapel running her own machifare, not any more than he liked the idea of Lucas's Meta-School. But what was he supposed to do? It was not his job to care. Sophia would be off his team. That was all that mattered.

The chanting downstairs was muffled, wordless. But Fernando could still hear the word that rang through that apartment.

"*F-FAKE!!*" the Thrall had screamed, pointing at Sophia's halo-hand, right before she put a beam of light between its eyes.

He stood up, sighed. Now seemed like a good time to check on his teammates.

You've reached the end of *The Icons of Man: Book One*. But the story has just begun.

If you enjoyed this book, please go to Amazon and leave a review!

Check out www.iconsofman.com to join our mailing list, learn more about *The Icons of Man*, and to read the author's blog!

Can't wait for the next installment? Scan the QR code below and go to our secret web page to check out **bonus features, behind-the-page info, and more!**

Thanks

One of the best things I did working on this book was to get in touch with professionals who are far more competent than me, and who forced me to up my own game. Special thanks to my editor, Sarah Kolb-Williams (http://www.kolbwilliams.com/), who breathed a desperately needed clarity and professionalism into my work. Many thanks also to my cover artist, Chris Puglise (https://www.instagram.com/cpuglise9/), who was able to take my ideas in express them in a vivid way that my words alone could not do justice to. Thanks too to the venerable Hector Garcia for his work on the Spanish Translation; and to Ilse Garcia and Jeff Bernstein for their test reading.

Writing is a product of one's own life experiences, and in many ways I am just a product of the people I know. Fortunately, I have managed to keep good company, and I think the end result reflects their influence.

Thank you Christian McMillian, whose intellectual influence on me was and continues to be profound, and who singlehandedly set my mind on paths hitherto unexplored—you are not only a friend, but a teacher to me. More importantly, thanks for telling me to never let the bastards get me down, and for reminding me that none of this is supposed to be easy.

Thank you Mike Littrell, both for his stellar job with formatting this book and helping me get everything ready in the eleventh hour—you are a consumate producer of all arts. More importantly, thanks for encouraging me to stay on this path, starting with that printed version of my bad fan-fiction you handed me years ago. I can promise you that it will sit on my desk until the day I die.

Thank you Tom Murray, for being my de facto sounding board, developmental editor, and writing commiserator on this project and countless aborted others, dating back to our adolescence—you are a better writer and stylist than I could ever hope to be, and your instincts and judgment are an absolute compass that I shall continue to rely on. Thank you for keeping me honest.

Thank you Henry C., who I am indebted to in too many ways to really list here, but who more than anyone else gave me the guts to make the many life choices that led me to this point, and whose own conviction, integrity and creative genius I can only dare to even poorly imitate. I may have left the room first, but you are the better man. Special thanks too to Dianne and Amy for their wisdom, generousity and support.

Finally, thank to my family for all their patience and support over the years, for instilling in me the right values while also giving me the latitude to figure things out for myself. Thanks to Carolyn Kiczek for the amazing leap of faith she readily took to help me see this through. Thanks to my brother for showing me the way to freedom long before I knew the true meaning of the word. Thanks to my father, for pushing me to be great and to always chase my dreams; and to my mother, for her unconditional love and her own love of the written word. I am forever indebted to you all.

About the Author

Robert H. Langan is a PhD Dropout and a white box philosopher; currently he is almost a personal trainer and an aspiring uber driver; he upcycles furniture but doesn't know how to swim; he was fired from one grocery store for plotting a coup, but incidentally he quit another out of contempt. He lives in the New Jersey Pine Barrens, in a self-imposed but mutually beneficial exile.

www.iconsofman.com

Made in the USA
Middletown, DE
03 January 2018